Kill and Tell

Adam Creed was born in Salford and read PPE at Balliol College, Oxford before working in the City. He abandoned his career to study writing at Sheffield Hallam University, following which he worked with writers in prison. He is now Head of Writing at Liverpool John Moores University and Project Leader of Free to Write.

Kill and Tell is the fifth novel in the DI Staffe series, which also includes *Suffer the Children*, *Willing Flesh*, *Pain of Death* and *Death in the Sun*.

Follow him on Twitter @DamCreed and visit adamcreed.co.uk

Kill and Tell

A DI STAFFE INVESTIGATION

ADAM CREED

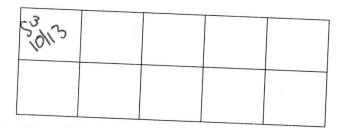

ff

faber and faber

First published in this edition in 2013
by Faber and Faber Limited
Bloomsbury House
74–77 Great Russell Street
London WC1B 3DA

Typeset by Faber and Faber Ltd.
Printed and bound by CPI Group (UK) Ltd, Croydon CR0 4YY

A CIP record for this book
is available from the British Library

ISBN 978–0–571–27500–7

FSC
www.fsc.org
MIX
Paper from
responsible sources
FSC® C101712

2 4 6 8 10 9 7 5 3 1

For
Mary Ruth Creer
1930–2012

One

Carmelo looks at the gap his missing finger has left between his wrinkled wedding and index fingers. The finger has been missing since he was a very young man and its absence reminds him of his shame.

He holds the child tight and the baby nestles its warm head in the folds of Carmelo's old neck, and he strokes the back of the child's downy skull with his three fingers.

Carmelo has learned to live without the things he lacks, and in moments like these he thanks God for the life he has been gifted. He says 'Sorry' for his part in not being able to love his own son. He could have been around more, but those were the busiest years: London and Brighton, sometimes Sicily. In fact, when his only son Attilio was six months old, the same age as baby Gustav here, Carmelo left poor Attilio with his manservant, Jacobo, for three whole months. Jacobo suffered the infant screaming the night sky to shreds. The baby had killed his mother, as his first act in the world. Maybe that has something to do with it.

Baby Gustav coos and shifts himself deeper into Carmelo's neck. Carmelo comes once a week and the baby's mother, Vanya, always marvels at how Carmelo can lull the child into sleep. 'You're a marvel, Carmelo,' says Vanya, coming across and passing her arm through his, wishing she had a father like Carmelo.

But all Carmelo can think is, 'Today will be the day they come. This is the day when it is all reckoned. I have to act.' He has felt this before, but never with such gravity. His breath shortens and he coughs, dry. He hands the baby to Vanya and coughs again and again into his handkerchief.

Vanya lays baby Gustav down in the cot Carmelo bought, in the corner of the three-room apartment that Carmelo pays for. And the husband, Bogdan, watches all this with a sour look on his face. He swallows the last morsel of his pride as he says nothing when Carmelo presses a roll of twenties into Vanya's hand; nor as she kisses Carmelo and thanks him, saying shouldn't he see a doctor?

Bogdan puts half the money in the jar for Poland. Later, he will sleep unsoundly and in the dead of night he will rise to work the night shift that Carmelo found for him. Carmelo says he knows what it is like for immigrants. He was one once.

Carmelo had seen Vanya cleaning in the casino of one of his friends when she was six months pregnant. He had slipped her a hundred and told her to go straight home and rest, and that he would call on her at home and fix up her husband with a decent job. A mother should be a mother, he had said.

A week after he first found her, Carmelo called on Vanya. She was coiled on the sofa, her tears all run dry. She had just been to the hospital for the final scan and her voice croaked as she told Carmelo that the doctor said the baby had a bad heart and he really needed ultrasound to have any chance of survival but they couldn't have it on the National Health. The doctor said the baby's heart weighed the same as a twenty-pound note, as opposed to hers which was the weight of a pound of pork. 'A pound of anything,' Carmelo had said, comforting her, saying he would make everything all right, sending the baby, inside its mother, to Milan, where they scanned him some more and opened his valves.

When baby Gustav was born, his heart worked just fine, and now it seems he will have a mainly healthy life. Carmelo knows the value of good medicine, and timely interventions.

He dons his hat and Vanya helps him on with his coat. Carmelo wears a winter Crombie all year long. He likes the weight of it, can't bear to be cold. She pats his shoulders and straightens the sleeves as Carmelo and Bogdan exchange a look. Carmelo wishes Bogdan wouldn't regard him so. He once told Bogdan, 'It is a gift, to accept kindness without flinching.' Bogdan had shrugged, said nothing, but wondered if one day or night he might have to do something for Carmelo: proof that these favours are not kindnesses, but prepayments.

Today, Bogdan rises from his chair and tells his wife he is going to get black bread and some stamps for Poland. He leaves the flat at the same time as Carmelo and as the old man gets his keys out for the Daimler, Bogdan says, 'I just want to say thank you, Mister Trapani. Thank you for everything you do for my wife and the baby. I hope I can be more like you some day.'

'You wouldn't want that, my friend. You're better the way you are.'

'That's easy for you to say.'

The men look at each other. Eventually, Carmelo says, 'We'll be even, when all is done. Have no doubt.'

'Is there something I will have to do for you? If so, I would like to know. It makes me afraid.'

'What makes you think like that?' Carmelo bites his bottom lip, as if he was in pain. 'Fear can be our friend. In Sicily, my grandfather was a fisherman and he used to tell me, "Carmelo, you must be afraid of the sea. It will kill you if you are not afraid." But that sea gave my grandfather a livelihood. It brought him joy and food

3

and friendships. Without the sea, he would have been dead.'

'Did it kill him in the end?'

'Oh no. He made an enemy. He was a proud man, my grandfather, and that killed him, not the simple matter of going to sea.' Carmelo watches Bogdan put his helmet on, kick the moped off its stand. He says, 'You must do whatever it takes to make your baby's life complete, even if one day you will have to harm him.'

Bogdan sits astride his moped, puzzled. He watches Carmelo get into his Daimler, manoeuvring into the traffic on Cambridge Heath Road.

Carmelo sits at the lights and looks back at Bogdan, who raises a thumb at him, as if he might have got the point. The lights go green and Carmelo moves away, Bogdan still on his moped outside his flat. Carmelo likes to drive. He does it slowly and cautiously with Radio Three murmuring just above the sound of the engine, like sea and breeze.

Today – though there is nothing in his rear-view mirror or his side mirrors to prove it – Carmelo is sure he is being watched and as the traffic peters away on the short drive to his house, he constantly checks his mirrors. Eyes are on him, and his time is come. He wonders if there might possibly be no such thing as hell.

When he gets to the gates of his mansion, which he remodelled after the war, here in the loveliest secret corner of the City, Carmelo presses the button on his remote control. The gates glide inward, to his private world. He takes time to smile up at the CCTV camera then looks in his mirrors a last time, before going through. He can see nobody and he drives the car cautiously into the garage, belatedly pressing for the gates to close. Sometimes he forgets.

He lets himself in the front door and calls 'Jacobo!' but there is no reply, so he telephones Goldman himself. The preparations are complete. He is almost there. He breathes in as deep as he can, feels his heart flutter. He calls the policeman and waits, is told that the Chief Inspector is in an important meeting. 'Do you want to leave a message?' the man says.

'No. This also is important. Of the very highest importance.'

*

Staffe heaves the parcel onto the scales and the anxious postmistress tells him it will be fifty-six pounds. She has big eyes and almost no lips at all. The way she looks at him, he thinks she can't tell that he's actually worth a few bob. 'Is it of value?' she says.

'It cost less than the stamps!' he laughs. 'It's only piccalilli I made myself. Is that allowed? To post abroad, I mean.'

'You shouldn't have said.'

'My sister lives in the middle of nowhere. In the Spanish middle of nowhere. She misses home.'

'Who taught you to make the piccalilli?'

Staffe feels sad for an instant, then glowingly happy. 'My mother.'

'And she didn't teach your sister?'

'We're very different.'

'You must love her very much.'

Staffe wonders whether the postmistress refers to his mother or his sister. He gives her three twenties and looks at his watch, sees he is already late and says, 'Put the change in the charity box.'

He walks up the Caledonian Road, which disappears at the cusp of a small rise, just the blue of sky beyond, between the low rows of shops and flats and the occasional office block – and the prison, skulking like an angry Victorian giant.

Later, he will go into Leadengate, to trawl through all the interviews his sergeant, DS Pulford, ever conducted with any member of the e.gang, and to document all the calls his sergeant made, from home, mobile and the office, going back through all the months between when Staffe was shot and his shooter, Jadus Golding, was murdered. That was just three weeks ago and his sergeant is remanded on bail for it. Suspect number one.

A part of him wishes he could amble on, towards the sky at the end of the street, but he knows what he must do and he churns the questions he must ask Pulford. As he does it – as if he is being whispered to, from across a Spanish desert – he touches his chest, where his scars are almost healed.

The meat wagons queue outside the electronic gates of the jail, bringing fresh. Twenty yards away, the loved ones wait for their visits. The women are young, but their faces are already hard and their children cling on, perching on hips, or tugging at the shortest imaginable skirts. Staffe goes up to the window, past the queue and shows the officer his warrant card, telling him the purpose of his visit.

'You've just walked past the queue, now get to the back,' says the PO, smirking, swivelling on his seat and saying something to his colleague behind the grille that makes them both laugh – at Staffe's expense.

*

DS Pulford is led into the visitor centre by a sneering PO who takes delight in confiscating the sergeant's clutch of books and folders. 'Bit fuckin' old for school, aren't you?' he says.

Pulford puts a brave face on it, sits opposite Staffe and says, 'I came straight from the library. I only get to go once a week. Today, they had what I was after, but the choice isn't good.'

'What are you up to, David?' says Staffe.

'I'm studying for an MA.'

'I mean with these damned charges. There's talk of this having to go to trial if we don't come up with some evidence soon.'

'I've got a supervisor at UCL – one of the most eminent criminologists—'

'For God's sake! You need to focus.'

'That's precisely what I'm doing.'

'You didn't kill Jadus Golding,' says Staffe.

'Is that a question?' says Pulford.

'It would be good to hear you say it.'

'Do I need to?'

'Unless we can come up with some evidence, you will have to say it to a jury.'

'You're not a jury.'

'Say it.'

'I didn't do it.' Pulford says it the way a teenage boy might goad a parent.

'Christ, Pulford! This isn't a game.' Staffe sees that his sergeant's mouth is weak. Pulford breathes deep, shakes his head as if he is shivering. 'Are they looking after you?'

'Some of the POs are all right, but I'm a copper.' He nods at the PO who brought him in. 'That's Crawshaw. He's a bit of a twat.'

'Have they got you in isolation?'

'When I first came in, but I don't want that. It makes them think you've something to be afraid of.'

'And have you? There's two members of the e.gang in here. Did you know?'

Pulford gives Staffe a withering look. 'I know all right.' Jadus Golding, of whose murder the DS stands accused, was a member of the e.gang.

'Christ, Pulford. Is there *anything* you've not told us?'

Pulford looks away.

'There is! It could get you out of here.'

'I've told you everything I can, sir. And that's the truth.'

'How can the truth hurt you – if you're innocent?'

'Sometimes, on the Force, you only see half the story. It's the perspective we have. Do you see that?'

'Tell me what you're afraid of, Pulford.'

Pulford says nothing. His eyes say, 'Plenty.'

'There's a number you kept calling from your mobile. It's unidentifiable, but I called it the other day and we got a trig on it before they could turn it off. It was somewhere on the Attlee.'

'Sylvie wrote to me.'

'She always liked you.'

'Is there a chance the two of you might . . . you know?'

'We're through,' says Staffe, feeling peculiar at hearing Sylvie's name. The first time in a long time. 'Now, who were you phoning on the Attlee? These calls were all made at times you weren't on duty.'

'She wrote some kind things, but I think she found it upsetting. Maybe you could tell her not to write again.'

'I told you, that's all over. Stop changing the subject.'

'Maybe you should call her.'

'Just tell me who the fuck you were calling!'

'If I could, I would.'

'At least explain why you can't tell me.'

'There is something you can do.'

'Tell me.'

Pulford hands him a piece of paper. 'Can you download me this article? They don't let us access the Internet.'

'My God! How long are you planning on being in here?'

Two

The knock at the door makes Carmelo's withering heart judder. He has expected it but now it is come, he fears he might not be able to prevail. Just one final effort and he will be saved. One more day. Half a day, even.

From the shape of the man's head and shoulders in the frosted pane to the large front door, he thinks it might not be quite who he was expecting. And he silently berates himself for not being prepared.

As he opens the door, he sees that he is right, but he opens the door nonetheless. It is too late and the future is too uncertain, the end far too nigh, to do anything else. The time is come and Carmelo is utterly fearful of all the things he has to do. He turns away from his visitor and out of habit, calls for Jacobo to make drinks. 'Jacobo!' he calls with a trembling voice that cracks. But perhaps Jacobo isn't here. Carmelo had a nap after he telephoned Goldman and isn't sure how long ago that was. He clears his throat and shouts again, this time at the top of his voice. 'Jacobo! Come!'

Carmelo waits, listens, hears nothing and shuffles slowly across the marble floor in his carpet slippers, taking pause to look up at the ceiling. He commissioned it sixty years ago – and now, in this instant, it brings him rare pleasure. It is good to bring beauty into the world.

He listens for Jacobo coming, but the old house clicks with a frail silence. Jacobo is not coming, and he feels the breath of his visitor on his neck. Carmelo steps to one side and shows him into the drawing room.

Carmelo wishes he had cleaned his gun. He hasn't used it in God knows how long. It is an ugly gun – a Beretta 34 – and it pulls heavy. He wonders if his finger will be up to it. He can see in his visitor's eyes that he is intent, but Carmelo can't allow himself to be taken yet. He has unfinished business of the very highest order. If only that damned policeman could have seen him today – now everything is in place. Just one more day is all Carmelo requires to prepare for eternity.

He offers his visitor a seat on the sofa by the french window that gives onto the formal, Italianate garden at the rear, and pulls the cord by the fireplace.

'Perhaps you gave him the afternoon off,' he says, smiling eagerly. 'Too generous for your own good,' he laughs. 'Or maybe you forgot yourself.'

'You know where the drinks are kept.'

The visitor looks at the cocktail cabinet. 'The one they stripped from Mussolini's palace in Firenze. How did you lay your hands on it, again? I'm sure you told me once, but I forgot.'

'I never told you that. Did I?' Carmelo is angry but he musters a smile. 'Help yourself to some grappa while I'm gone. I'll just be a minute or so.'

'It's not my cup of tea.'

'It's all I have. It's how I lived so long.'

'Then maybe I should try a little.'

Carmelo turns and excuses himself, muttering, 'Where the hell is Jacobo?', wondering if it is his afternoon off. Is it Wednesday? Maybe he took advantage – after all these years serving his master.

He takes the lift to his bedroom, a ridiculously large, baroque room which he made by knocking down a wall before the place was listed. It's out of keeping with the house, which is gothic, but the grand proportions lift his heart. It reminds him of his uncle's house in Palermo. Carmelo moves a little faster now he is on his own. It will pay to be one step ahead.

The dressing table is all the way across in the bay window, looking over the garden. The nearest neighbour is way beyond large trees that have always been here. He remembers ruminating, when he came into his first large pool of money, whether to venture to Hampstead, but he found this place – the real thing and right in the heart of his world. The branches of the old oaks and the whole of the newer cypresses sway gently. He opens the drawer, picks up the pistol from alongside his tortoiseshell brushes. It is heavy in his hands and he places it on the dressing table's polished walnut.

Looking at it, he calls the chief inspector again, but this time he gets the answerphone and a series of options. 'Damn you,' he says. If only he could have moved the money earlier; faster. He looks at the gun again, prays it won't come to this, but if it does his aim will be true enough to buy another day. After all these years, it comes to just one day.

Carmelo picks up the gun with his left hand because the middle finger of his right is absent. He thinks how much more Saint Peter might hold him to account, had life gone another way. He pushes out the release catch and pulls the magazine, discharging the bullets from their clip. He replaces the empty magazine and pulls on the trigger. The hammer clunks heavy in the lonely house. As he returns the bullets, he thanks God for the Italian marble that constitutes his floors. There will be blood, but Jacobo can mop up. Together, they will wipe clean this smear of new history.

His blood courses a little faster and to stiffen his ardour, he re-affirms that these days on earth are just a part of our scheme: a mere section for the body, before the soul.

When he sees the chief inspector, Carmelo will confess. He will confess his ancient crime. Nobody can silence him, not all these years on.

Carmelo walks quite briskly to the lift. The blood is really shifting now, across the fibres that line his arteries. The gun is heavy in one hand as Carmelo presses the *G* button in the lift with the index finger of his other, but steps quickly backwards out of the lift as the doors close on the empty chamber. Instead, he takes the broad, oak staircase, peeking to see if his visitor is waiting down below for the lift. But as Carmelo descends, coming level with the chandelier, he sees the whole of the hallway sprawl out below, empty. The door to the drawing room is still closed.

He opens the door slowly, the gun behind his back and his finger on the trigger. The man is standing by the french windows. He half-turns, sips from his grappa, saying, 'I poured you one.'

Carmelo tightens the grip of his right hand on the pistol, wishes his house was not so grand, its rooms not so large. He doubts if he could even hit the french windows with his shot, let alone the man standing in front of them, so he walks to the cock-tail cabinet – just five yards or so from the target. He reaches out with his left, picks up the grappa. Carmelo holds it with his thumb and three fingers, wants to be one pace closer, to make sure. He will try to hit him in the shoulder, then the leg.

He raises the glass, suddenly wanting a taste of the aquavit, its effect; the spirit burns his lips. It stings his mouth. It makes his eyes water. It burns his throat and his guest smiles. It is such a familiar smile and the man comes towards him, reaching out. Carmelo brings the pistol from behind his back and tries to lift it. He tries to point it at his quarry but his hand is suddenly loose. The grappa really burns him now and he hears the pistol crash onto the marble and his legs give way. When his head smashes on the marble, he thinks he might blemish it.

Carmelo brings his knees to his chest and he tries to make himself sick, but he can't.

From above, he looks like a question mark on his fine marble floor. Today, there is a thin vein of red, where Carmelo's blood makes its slow course.

*

Staffe sits alone, just the creaking joints of Leadengate's ghosts and the low whirr of a computer somewhere. It seems years since he watched the sun set beyond Holborn Viaduct, the last tendrils of tail-lights reddening the City gloam. The coral dusks of Andalucía seem far away as he turns away from the window and returns to his whiteboard, makes a few adjustments. Presses 'Print'.

In the fourteen days before Jadus Golding was shot dead by the very gun that discharged two bullets into Staffe's own torso, DS David Pulford was sighted eight times on the Limekiln Estate, stalking Jadus's lover, Jasmine Cash – the mother of Golding's daughter, Millie. On each occasion, Pulford was off duty. On six occasions, within an hour of these sightings, sworn by affidavit, Pulford had called the mobile number they traced to the Attlee Estate, just a few hundred yards from the Limekiln.

According to the council list on his desk, and cross-referencing the latest aggregation of charge sheets for the e.gang, there are indeed just two known gang members living on the Attlee Estate.

Outside his office, the coffee machine begins to chunter. He takes the yellow highlighter pen and passes it along the names of the Limekiln's e.gang residents, Brandon Latymer and Shawne Haddaway. He taps into his computer, entering the search data, and as he waits for the records of Messrs Latymer and Haddaway to print out, the coffee machine expectorates a second time. He spins slowly on his chair, feels his heart gladden as Josie appears in the doorway, holding two plastic cups of hot chocolate. He reaches into his drawer, pulls out the bottle of Havana Anejo rum.

They each slurp, to make more room, and Staffe glugs a helping of rum into each of the cups. They shared the drink on his roof in Andalucía, watching the sun go down.

'Remember Spain?' she says. 'You said you'd take it easy.'

He remembers Spain. He remembers that he was going to stay; remembers, too, how glad he was to see her walking across the square the day they dug up Astrid Cano. 'Every day we don't get closer to finding Jadus Golding's killer, Pulford's chances diminish. You know that. You can't tell the case to take it easy. You can't tell Golding's killer to "take it easy".'

'You went to see him again today?'

'Have you any idea what it is he's not telling us?'

'That's why Pennington sent me to bring you back. Pulford wouldn't say anything *at all* to us. What did he say to you?'

'He told me he knows something. He said he couldn't tell me.'

'You mean he won't.'

'No.' Staffe finishes his cocoa. It doesn't taste the same without cicadas in the walnut tree, the heat of an African breeze coming up from the sea. 'He *can't* tell us.'

'And what do you think it might be that he can't tell us?'

'I don't know, but he's afraid, Josie.'

'Pulford's not like that.'

'That's what I thought. So maybe we should assume he's not afraid for himself.' Staffe picks up the sheets for Haddaway and Latymer, places his hand on Josie's elbow and steers her towards the door, turns off the light – and it is immediately apparent that the night has crept up, unannounced.

Three

He blinks, bleary-eyed and bare-chested. 'How long have you been here?' Staffe rubs his face hard. 'Did I hear the phone?'

'It was me,' she says. Josie can't take her eyes off Staffe's two scars, one between the left pectoral and the crease of his armpit; the other below the heart in the soft flesh above the waistband of his boxer shorts. The scars are bright pink, the rest of him still darkly tanned.

'Why are you here?' He squints at the clock. It says it is nine-twenty.

'I was phoning you for ages. Too much cocoa, maybe. Or too much Havana Club. Since when did you sleep twelve hours a night?' Josie's eyes are plump, from lack of sleep. 'I told Pennington to let you be, but he insisted I come round. I have a key, remember? I watered your plants while you were in Spain.'

'What does Pennington want?'

'I told him you were supposed to be taking it easy, sir.' She bites her lip and for a long moment they exchange a look.

'Never mind.' He pulls on a blue checked shirt, frayed at the collar. 'So what the hell is it?'

'Someone called Carmelo. He said it'd ring a bell with you.'

'Carmelo?' Staffe's eyes open wide and he steps into his trousers – a scrunched-up pair of Dockers. 'Carmelo Trapani?'

'That's the one.'

Staffe rubs his face again, this time the way you would T-cut a car. 'He must be getting on by now. What's happened?'

'We're not sure. A neighbour called to say his gates were open and a couple of uniforms went round, found the garage open and blood on his floor, but no sign of anyone. Apparently, he's worth millions. How do you know him?'

'I don't. Not really, but Jessop had a bit of an obsession. It goes back to Calvi.'

'God's banker?' says Josie. 'Hanged from Blackfriars Bridge?'

'Yes, but Carmelo was clean as a whistle. You ask me, he's a good man. A kind man.' Staffe drifts away. Since he came back from Spain, he finds it difficult to maintain his concentration. He remembers that Carmelo Trapani was once kind to his friend Rosa. Carmelo had taken one of his associates to one side when he had wanted to stake a claim on her. Rosa, on the game and vulnerable to such affairs of the heart.

'Pennington is worried, sir. He says this could flare up in our faces.'

'We should be focusing on Pulford, not missing persons. We've got to find who killed Jadus Golding.'

'We have no choice,' says Josie.

*

Attilio Trapani cuts a fine figure. He is wearing a splendidly tailored shooting jacket and perfectly sculpted tweed breeches with a moleskin waistcoat to boot. He seems the archetype of an English country gentleman. But something is amiss. His nose is Roman and his skin the colour of walnut husks. His hair is waxed: combed back and blue-black. He is roasting his bespoke Latin backside in front of a seven-foot medieval fireplace of dressed stone in the hall of Ockingham Manor.

He stands at the centre of a coterie of large-jawed English playboys and an Arab gentleman in his thobe, lounging in club chairs in a shooting den. The heads of kills adorn the room, as does a sixty-inch plasma screen fed by the Racing Channel.

As Staffe and Josie are shown in by a straight-backed butler, the coterie breaks into a guffawing outburst of laughter. This, Staffe assumes, cannot be the man whose beloved father has just disappeared, leaving a trail of blood. This, Carmelo's only son, seemingly preoccupied with a shooting party.

When the laughter subsides, Attilio says, 'Ahaa. My visitors. You must excuse me a moment or two, gentlemen.'

To which the gathering solemnly nods, heads bowed, as if they might suspect something. Attilio leads Staffe and Josie through an ante-room into the original, Jacobean part of the manor. In a dark library, the curtains are half-drawn and a beautiful woman sits on a settle beneath a mullioned window. She is forty-something and dressed in low-waisted jeans and a tailored designer lumberjack blouse. Her mouth is grimly pursed and she has a handkerchief scrunched in a tight fist. Closer inspection shows that her dark eyes are red, her mascara in distress. Attilio says, 'My wife, Helena,' and he erupts into grief.

'My God, Tilio!' Helena stands quickly and rushes to him, loses herself in his big arms as his vast shoulders shake. Slowly, the two of them subside to their knees. Helena calls, 'Help me! Please!'

Staffe and Josie rush towards them, reaching down under Attilio's dead weight, trying to lift him off Helena. He has passed out but they manage to roll him onto his side.

Helena unbuttons her husband's waistcoat and shirt, explaining to Staffe that she had wanted to cancel the shoot, but Attilio insisted it go ahead because these men are important connections and his father – God bless his soul – would turn in his . . .

Staffe puts a hand on her shoulder. 'It's OK, there's nothing to say that he is dead.'

'. . . he'd have turned in his grave. That's what Attilio said. He had tears in his eyes when he said it. These bloody Trapanis. They're impossible!'

'Where were you when you heard?'

'I was having breakfast when the Beauvoir gardener rang and told us Carmelo was gone. Poor Attilio, he was out on the shoot.'

Helena looks Staffe hard in the eye. Her features are pale and brittle. In her eyes she is hard and cold. She says, 'Carmelo was the gentlest soul, the loveliest man.'

Staffe's BlackBerry beeps. 'I'm sure he still is. And perhaps he wouldn't have wanted you to disappoint your connections.' He glances at the message and Attilio begins to stir, sitting up, leaning forward and taking great mouthfuls of air. 'But maybe not everyone thought Carmelo a lovely man.'

Helena watches her husband, a look of disappointment in her eyes, as if regarding a less favoured son.

'We know your father had property interests,' says Staffe. 'But do you mind me asking, were you involved in the family business, Mister Trapani?'

Attilio says, 'No. We breed. And train.'

'He's brilliant,' says Helena, a brightness returning to her eyes. Her chin rises a couple of notches as she says it. 'The training is quite new, but it's all we've ever wanted. It's how we met – through our horses.'

'But you must help run your father's portfolio,' says Staffe. 'I understand you're his only son. His only child.'

'Never touched it.'

'You will,' says Staffe. 'If your father really is gone.'

'We will have to do this later. I must get back to my guests. They will be leaving soon.'

Standing, Helena says, 'You can wait, if you must. And in response to your insinuations, we were shooting all day and had a dinner until the early hours. There are eight in the shooting party and we have five staff. You can talk to the staff, of course – that will be alibi enough.'

'Alibi?' murmurs Attilio, quite incredulous. 'You can't talk to the guests. Not here; not now.' He walks unsteadily to a large, intricately carved Jacobean chest and sits heavily on its lid, begins to whimper, his shoulders shaking. Helena stands over him, says, 'What on earth is the matter with you, man?'

*

An hour later, when Staffe and Josie have taken preliminary statements from all the staff at Ockingham Manor – ascertaining that Attilio and Helena had indeed been entertaining all day and night, until one-thirty in the morning – they are shown out of the house to the rear courtyard and stables. The beaters stand in an open barn at the far end of the garage block, hanging the day's kill. Attilio is in the latter stages of bidding his guests farewell. The English load their guns into the boots of Range Rovers. When they are all gone, just the Saudi gentleman remains. He hangs his head in sympathy as Attilio confides a little of his stiff-lipped suffering.

Staffe and Josie look on, not wanting to interrupt an intensely private moment. Helena comes round from the front, joins Attilio and the Saudi, who has dark, glinting eyes and a sculpted jaw.

As they wait, Staffe considers how London seems a whole world away from here. But in light traffic and with your foot down, you could make it from here to Beauvoir Place in just over an hour.

The Saudi gentleman raises a hand and a modest Land Rover trucks across the gravel, pulls alongside the three of them. He shakes Attilio's hand, kisses Helena: striking, sultry Helena. Staffe says to Josie, 'She's not exactly what you expect of a dowager.'

'A dowager?'

'A wife who survives her husband – if he's a duke.'

'Ahaa. I've checked up on our Helena and she'd only been married to the last husband for five years. He was a mere lord, actually. Died in a riding accident.'

'When was that?'

'It was since the hunting ban. There was a bit of a cover-up over the circumstances, they reckon – an illegal hunt, you know.' Josie refers to her notes. 'Three years ago.'

'Well, Attilio didn't hang about. I wonder if he and the lovely Helena knew each other already?'

'I suppose that's just found its way into my inbox. But you know how well connected Lady Helena is. She's well above the common business of kidnapping and murder.'

'No, she's not,' says Staffe. 'She's a distant cousin of the heir to the throne. Perfectly equipped!'

They both stifle their laughter, caught watching by the Saudi as he drives off. It seems there is something different in his eyes now. Guilt, perhaps, and he looks quickly away.

Josie says, 'But she was cast out years ago. Not quite cut out for royal life.'

As soon as the Land Rover disappears, Attilio's face turns to thunder and Helena jabs a finger into his chest, begins to berate him. After a minute or so, she storms off around the front of the house, and Attilio is left looking at the gravel beneath his feet. He looks afraid and out of place. But mostly afraid.

Four

Staffe can remember when Beauvoir Place was a down-at-heel East End square, but now it's the home to investment bankers and media hounds – just a hop, skip and a tango lunge to Hoxton's fleshpots and artisan bakeries.

He parks up on the far side of the square, walks slowly round, taking in the gothic splendour, and pauses outside Carmelo's house. The major part of him wants to hotfoot across to the Attlee Estate and chase down Latymer and Haddaway – to find the gun that killed Jadus Golding; the very same weapon that Jadus had used on him; the evidence that might free Pulford. But Pennington is insistent he finds Carmelo Trapani. He looks up at Carmelo's place, thinks surely a ransom note will appear soon; or a body.

Walking up the path through the open, large electronic gates, Staffe is gratified to see the house seems in perfect keeping with the intentions of its architect with its Dutch gables, but when he looks carefully, Staffe spies the occasional Italianate detailing on the window masonry which would be more at home on the shores of Lake Como. By and large, though, it seems Carmelo Trapani was a man of both wealth and taste. Was? He still might be.

Staffe has read up all Carmelo's files, smiling to himself at one point when he saw Jessop's signature at the bottom of an interview in the wake of the Calvi hanging. There was no link between Calvi and Carmelo, but Staffe had enjoyed seeing the infantile scrawl of Jessop in those margins. Guilty Jessop, his first ever boss. On the run now, unlike innocent Pulford.

Carmelo stayed in Stepney throughout the war, one step ahead of the interners, and perhaps left alone because of his disability – or not. Later, he acquired a significant property empire in west London, renting out rooms to immigrants from Empire.

When Staffe reaches the front door, he sees a humble sign, carved crudely in wood and hanging unceremoniously on two lengths of chain. It says 'Palazzo Adriano'. He takes the sign between thumb and finger, lets it swing. It is out of keeping.

SOCOs are hard at it in the hallway. The frescoed ceiling depicts Jesus rising up to heaven: Mary waiting with cherubim and angels – all rendered in a sickly palette borrowed from sweet-shops. The ceiling is bordered with renditions of Italian hills.

Stepping into the drawing room, Staffe feels a glow in his belly, like the first open fire of winter. He sniffs. 'Disinfectant.' He sniffs again, deeper. 'Did you get that?' he says to the SOCO crouching by the french window, dusting away with a tiny brush.

DI Frank Rimmer sidles up to Staffe, light on his feet. He is a slight man, immaculately suited and with the weight of the world pressing down on his brow. He says, 'We got it. The place has been wiped clean, Staffe.'

'But they left the blood. Why clean the place and leave the blood?' Both men look at the dried trail of blood on the marble floor.

Rimmer is the same rank as Staffe and in his father's footsteps, but struggling to fill them; it strikes Staffe as odd that Pennington wants the two of them on this case.

'Is there a housekeeper? Does the disinfectant match the ones in the house, or is it foreign?'

'We haven't tracked the housekeeper down yet.'

'Well, get her! We need to know when she last cleaned the place and when she last saw Carmelo.' Staffe turns his back on Rimmer, approaches the SOCO. 'Is the disinfectant evenly distributed?'

'It seems to be everywhere. We can't tell if there is a greater concentration, but there is—' He stands up, takes three paces and crouches again, just six feet from the cocktail cabinet. '—if you look closely, some slight degradation to the surface of the marble around the blood.'

'So they cleaned around the blood.' Staffe opens the cocktail cabinet. Inside, a row of four delicate, tulip-shaped shot glasses. He picks one up, inspects and replaces it. The glass is Murano, the dust is north London and he sees two circular feints in the light film of dust. 'There would have been two more glasses. Like this.' He holds up a glass.

'Not here, sir.'

'Any sign of broken glass?'

'No.'

'Dishwasher?'

'Empty, sir.'

The first whiff of a ghost. And on the shelf below the glasses, a row of four Nardini bottles of grappa. One has its seal broken and is empty down to just below the neck. Maybe a couple of measures. He tells the SOCO to have the contents tested and goes across to the french windows.

The garden is perfectly manicured. 'There'll be a gardener. Find the gardener, and the bloody housekeeper.'

Rimmer leaves, saying nothing, and passes Josie on the way in, carrying a pile of papers. She wears disposable gloves and asks the SOCO if she can use the table. He nods and she sets out the papers in a line. 'Carmelo employed three staff, sir. A cleaner and a gardener. He's the one who phoned in.'

Staffe looks at an oil painting on the chimney breast. It has a beguiling, coral light, depicts down-at-heel folk fishing off a promenade. In the background, an exotic city. 'Go on.'

'And someone called Jacobo Sartori who gets paid the most. Four grand a month.'

'That's too much for a housekeeper; too much for any domestic servant, surely. Get hold of him.'

'He's not at home. His wife, Appolina, says he often stayed here – especially weekends. She's worried, sir. In pieces, actually.'

'Then you can chalk up Jacobo Sartori and put him down as a suspect.'

'Alongside the son,' says Rimmer. 'I've spoken to the neighbours. Apparently, Carmelo and the son don't get on.'

'It wasn't the son,' says Staffe, catching himself unawares and not sure why he feels so strongly.

*

Appolina Sartori is spaghetti thin and wears a cream trouser suit with a green tabard over it. She has a fine head of grey hair scraped into a bun and moves warily. Her voice is tender and breaks at the end of each short sentence.

Staffe sits opposite Appolina on an expensive and newly re-upholstered Georgian settee. He places his hands on his knees in deference to her years and to her anxiety. 'You have heard about Signor Trapani?'

Appolina puts her hands together, in prayer. She closes her eyes and nods her head slowly. 'Attilio told me what happened. They are beasts.'

'Who are beasts?'

'Whoever did it.'

The way Appolina said, 'They are beasts' implies particular beasts. 'Who do you think did it?'

'I barely saw Carmelo. It was Jacobo who spent the time.'

'Jacobo will be very upset,' says Staffe.

'All his life he devoted.'

'And have you heard from Jacobo since?'

'No.' She shakes her head solemnly. 'He went there to prepare dinner. Carmelo adored Jacobo's *puttanesca*. He took his suitcase with him.'

'Would he normally take a suitcase to work?'

'He has a room there. Carmelo kept asking Jacobo to go to Beauvoir Place. To live.'

'You have a beautiful home here.' Staffe looks around the sitting room of the double-fronted Victorian villa. They are in Cranley Gardens, briefly famous for Dennis Nilsen having killed three of his many just up the road at number twenty-three. Staffe resists the urge to ask Appolina if she was one of the neighbours who reported the smell to the police, or found body parts in her plumbing.

'It is *our* home. Our life. Not Carmelo's.' Her eyes glisten and they each look at the photographs on top of her cocktail cabinet, which has cabriole legs – just like the one in Carmelo's drawing room. The photographs chronicle Jacobo's life, from young man in a baggy suit and fedora to an old man in baggy suit and fedora. He cuts a slight figure with soft eyes and a bobble on the end of his nose. Staffe picks up an early photo of Jacobo with an ice-cream, a sandstone cliff towering behind him. 'He is a handsome man.'

'It was taken in Cefalù.'

'In Sicily?'

She nods, smiles briefly but it goes out, like a snuffed candle. 'That was a long time ago but every year I love him more. When you get close, when there is less time to come, life is more precious. Some people say life is less when you are old, but it is more. So we must be together, you see. I can't bear it – for Jacobo to leave me alone.' She fixes her sights on Staffe, imploring. 'You *will* find him?'

'Of course. We need to ask to him about Carmelo.' He picks up a photograph of Jacobo beside a bandstand with a pier and seams of pebble beach and milky sea in the background. He recognises it as Brighton. 'Can I take this? I will get a copy made and return the original.'

'If it helps,' says Appolina, resigned.

Staffe knows Jacobo is Carmelo's housekeeper. He knows Jacobo gets four thousand a month from Carmelo's account, and he knows this is clearly too much. He knows, also, that Jacobo and Appolina's house, were it to be sold tomorrow, would fetch well over a million. In crime, as in life, everything has to add up.

And he remembers what Jessop said – dear, deluded Jessop. 'Follow the money, William. Follow the money and you'll find the shit.'

He hates himself for saying it, but he asks Appolina nonetheless: 'If Jacobo had to run, where would he run?'

A tear from each eye runs down her cheeks. Staffe goes to her, wrapping her in his big arms – careful not to crush the frail thing.

Feeling the soft skin of her forehead cold against his neck and looking over her head, Staffe sees a little of Appolina on display. On shelves, there is Dante and Vasari's *Lives of the Artists*, as well as Danielle Steel and Esther Samuels. And there are opera scores, too. On the sideboard, a copy of today's *La Stampa*. 'Jacobo knows something, doesn't he? You must tell me, if you want us to save him.'

'Save?' she whispers, hardly daring to utter.

'We must save him. What does he know?'

'There was—'

'Tell me,' implores Staffe.

'Nothing. I'm being silly.'

'Tell me. His life could be in your hands, *signora* Sartori.'

Appolina shivers, as if she dislikes her own name. 'It's nothing.'

He un-holds Appolina, leans away and tries to fathom what it is that can keep a person – an intelligent, strong woman such as Appolina – *so* betrothed to a man so humble in aspiration. 'You must tell me this thing that burdens you.'

'I bear no burden. My life has been a gift.'

'Where would he go? You must tell me.'

'He was always with Carmelo, or here.'

Staffe thinks: *That's what he told you.*

'We always planned to live by the sea. One day, we will, is what I always thought, but now the one day is here, and maybe it is gone. How did we get to be so old, and still tied to Carmelo?' Appolina doesn't look at Staffe when she says this. She is addressing somebody not here.

'You're from Sicily, too?'

Appolina shakes her head. 'I am a Roman. My mother warned me. Perhaps she was right.'

'You met Jacobo over here? In England?'

She smiles. 'Carmelo introduced us. I was one of his seam-stresses on the Mile End Road. They were hard times. So hard, to survive then.'

*

Pulford's eyes are dark and he seems a little bloated in the face. There is something less alive about him.

Staffe hands him the book he requested, and the photocopied article by a chap called Hutchison. He had skimmed through and it looked interesting. He wishes he had more time to dwell on the wider world; the world gone by and all its stories.

'You've got two minutes, that's all. You want to see him, you should book a visit like everyone else.' The PO looks at Pulford as if he is everyday scum. 'He's no special case.'

'He is,' says Staffe.

'No, I'm not!' says Pulford. He seems afraid.

Staffe watches the PO retreat to his position by the alarm bell. 'Is that Crawshaw?'

Pulford looks at the article and his frown softens, becoming a smile as he turns the pages.

'You're enjoying your studies?'

'It makes sense of what we do, sir.'

Staffe watches Pulford open a clear, plastic file. In the file is a printout of Google Earth, with the http: strapline at the top – clearly taken from the Internet. Pulford slides in the article. As he does, Staffe tries to see the subject of the Google Earth printout, but the Hutchison article covers it up.

Pulford holds up the book, wiggles it and says, 'You know,

there's nothing new in any of what we do. Crime is repeating itself, the way it always did. It used to be Caribbeans and Italians, and even the Jewish communities, who formed alliances. Now, it's Turks and Serbs, and the old Soviet nations who come here to ply their trades. We've always been a melting pot, here in London.'

'A land of opportunity,' says Staffe and they both laugh.

Crawshaw shoots a disapproving look and talks into his radio. Within a minute, a new PO appears in the visitor centre, to pat Pulford down and take him back to twenty-three-hour lock-down and the virtual world of learning; his only escape.

When Pulford is gone, Staffe says to Crawshaw, 'They're not allowed the Internet in here?'

'No fuckin' way. Information is our enemy. It's a fuckin' killer,' he laughs.

At the gate, Staffe is processed back onto what Pulford is already calling 'Road'. His mobile phone is returned and he thinks about how he should cherish every drop from every day. He makes himself call her.

On the Pentonville Road, he finds Sylvie in his menu and he listens to her voice apologising that she isn't around but inviting him to leave a message. She enthuses that she will call back as soon as possible. But she could be talking to anybody, so he rings off without leaving a message, walking as fast as he can down the Caledonian Road to Clerkenwell and then Leadengate, happy to feel the earth under his feet.

Five

Staffe writes his jottings up into lists on a piece of A3. He tries to find some order amongst his own thoughts as Leadengate's old arteries crackle.

The door creaks open and Jombaugh comes in, carrying a plate and two pieces of the baked cheesecake his wife makes. 'What's all this?' he says, looking at Staffe's lists. He peers over his pince-nez glasses. 'Aah.' Jombaugh doesn't have a face for spectacles. His face is big and pitted and his hair is like steel wool. His uniform always looks a size too small for him. 'You're following the money. Bound to end up in shit,' he laughs.

'Carmelo Trapani's house is worth three, maybe four million. No mortgage. He's a director of dozens of companies in the UK and from the look of things, dozens more in Monaco and Guernsey, including some new trusts set up in the last week.'

'Shuffling the pack?'

'I'm waiting for his lawyer to call me, but he's got to be worth at least ten million, probably more, and even his butler lives in a big old gaff in Muswell Hill.'

'And it's all going to the one son.'

'You'd think so,' says Staffe, picking up the phone, dialling Carmelo Trapani's solicitor.

Martin Goldman answers immediately and in a meek voice explains he is not in a position to discuss Carmelo Trapani's last will and testament. He pauses. 'In fact, it may be nothing at all to do with us.'

'But you are Carmelo's lawyer, are you not?'

'I asked Carmelo on several occasions if there was anything he wanted to tend, in that regard, and he was quite cagey. That may be more than I should divulge.'

'Surely you can offer an estimate of Mister Trapani's wealth?'

'It is only an estimate, but it wouldn't be less than twenty million. I am not his accountant.'

'But you are supposed to represent his best interests. If anything happens to Carmelo, and it transpires that you had information that could have helped us, or if you knew something that might have prevented us from going down a blind alley—'

'I know!' Goldman is breathing heavily now. 'But I have said all I can say.'

'I can tell you know something. Don't take me for a fool, Mister Goldman.'

The phone lapses to silence again.

'Would you describe his recent behaviour as unusual in any way?'

'He brought me a letter last week and said if anything untoward happened, I was to open it.'

'And what does it say?'

'I don't know.'

'Wouldn't you say that Carmelo's disappearance from the face of the earth is untoward? Now, Mister Goldman, will you please open that letter and tell me what is in it.'

'There are conditions.'

'What conditions?'

'I'll call you back.'

The phone clicks dead.

Jombaugh blows out his cheeks. 'What about the son? Does he need the money?'

Staffe jabs his finger at the sheet of jottings. 'Attilio Trapani, a bloodstock agent and horse breeder, but there's barely a mention of him in Tattersalls' sales.'

'He could be acting as agent.'

'Attilio has no registered companies in the UK, even though he's supposed to be a racehorse trainer, and apart from a one-bedder in Ladbroke Grove, he's got no other property in the UK. There doesn't seem to be any regular payment from Carmelo to Attilio.'

'But he's got a fancy wife by all accounts.'

'Helena Ballantyne owns Ockingham Manor. It's worth a few million, but she's got a mortgage of two million against it and that must be racking up at six thousand a month. Plus, she's got a million-quid flat in Ebury Street with a half-million mortgage taken out only three years ago.'

'I know she's posh, but is she minted?'

'Her social activity is pretty extravagant: Chinawhites, Gstaad, Taormina.' Staffe puts a ring around 'Taormina' and draws a line across to his Attilio list.

'Taormina?' says Josie, coming in and smiling to herself. Staffe thinks she must have seen her new bloke, Conor. She holds out a cardboard cup of designer coffee between Staffe and Jombaugh, and says, 'You'll have to fight over it.'

Staffe says, 'Taormina?'

'It's a fancy resort in Sicily. Brad and Madonna like it, so they say.'

'I know what it is. In fact, it's where Attilio and Helena Ballantyne first met.'

'Dominic Ballantyne was still in the saddle at the time.' Josie reaches down into her bag, pulls out a copy of *Hello!* magazine and tosses it across to Staffe.

In the back pages of social round-up, Attilio Trapani is pictured between Helena and Dominic Ballantyne, his large, bronze arms draped over the English couple's shoulders at a charity gala. Eighteen months later, Dominic Ballantyne would snap his neck in two, falling sixteen hands from a horse on his own Ockingham estate.

'Did you look into Dominic Ballantyne's death?'

'I was hoping to get some sleep tonight – for a change!' Josie's eyes are heavy.

Jombaugh's bleeper goes off and he gets out of his chair, pretending to be an old man. As he leaves he takes the coffee and beckons Staffe across, whispers, 'Go easy on her, Will. So she's got a boyfriend . . . You should be pleased for her.' He winks, slaps Staffe on the shoulder and raises his cup, as if he were toasting. 'Very tasty.'

Staffe says to Josie, 'Just do it as quick as you can.'

Josie pulls out a stapled stack of photocopied paper from her shoulder bag. 'Ta-dah! See, I don't have to sleep. There wasn't an inquiry and the police were satisfied there was nothing untoward. Disappointed?'

'That's not the right word.'

'Well, I do have *something* else for you.' Josie goes into her bag a third time, hands him a copy of *Horse and Hound* with a photograph of Attilio Trapani above a strapline that says, 'Amateur breeder Attilio Trapani plans to expand.' The article mentions the tremendous support he received from Helena Ballantyne, the widow of Attilio's great friend Dominic Ballantyne. 'Trapani acquired for the Ballantynes the very horse from which Dominic fell to his death.'

'Blimey,' says Staffe. 'This was just a month after Ballantyne died.' He drags his fingers through his hair and smiles at Josie, wants to say how proud he is.

'What?' she says, tilting her head. 'What is it?' The soft flesh between her eyebrows crinkles.

'This Conor. He's a lucky bloke. I hope he's treating you—'

The door creaks open and Staffe and Josie both look round, surprised to see Pennington. Instinctively, they both look up at the clock.

'I've got a bad feeling about this Carmelo business,' says Pennington.

'Chancellor has been hard at it, sir. We're building the links to Attilio Trapani.'

'And what about Pulford?'

'He's not telling me any more than he told you.'

'Christ! I'm sorry about this Trapani thing.' Pennington never apologises.

The DCI sits down heavily in a chair by the window. His eyes are dark and heavy in his jaundiced face. With a gaunt gaze, he looks out across the rooftops, down Cloth Fair to the meat market, and sighs, 'Internal Investigations aren't pulling up any trees. What a bloody mess. I hoped he would open up to you.'

'I have a lead. I can't say it's anything yet, sir, but there's some e.gang members on the Attlee.'

'We know that, for God's sake.'

'And there's a Google Earth search.'

'A what?'

'In prison, they're not supposed—'

'Don't step on any toes – especially Internal Investigations.'

'Great. Go where the angels are frightened of treading, but

make sure you don't ruffle Professional Standards' feathers.'

'Keep your head below the bastard parapet, is all. I'm not sure how long we've got before the CPS really push for a trial date.'

'It can't go to trial!'

'It will – if we don't get some evidence soon. Make sure you work closely with Rimmer on the Trapani case, but make it look as though it's taking all your time. Now, Rimmer tells me Trapani drove a Daimler. It was a jalopy, but his pride and joy. And it's gone.'

'We'll track it on the cameras, sir,' says Josie.

Pennington nods to her, suggesting that she does it straight-away, and elsewhere. When she is gone he hisses under his breath, 'You know what I'm saying, Will?'

'Cut myself in two and hide one half.'

'And take it easy with the e.gang. I don't want us accused.'

'Accused?'

'You know what the press are like. Pulford is charged with shooting a black man. It could kick off at any time.' Pennington taps *The News.* 'Keep the wolves from our door, Staffe. Be sure you do, but bloody well find what Pulford is afraid of. Now, do you have any of that rum you keep stashed away?'

Staffe pours them each a cup and Pennington necks his in one, holds out his cup for more. Staffe says, 'There's something else, isn't there, sir?'

Pennington nods. 'Keep it to yourself.'

'Absolutely.'

Pennington sighs. 'He wanted me to meet him. He called me.'

'Who?'

'Trapani. The day before he disappeared. I was up to here.' Pennington puts a hand above his head.

'And you didn't tell anyone?'

'I have now, but it looks bad. Christ, we've got to get to the bottom of this, Will. You wouldn't believe what shit's going off at the moment.' Pennington looks at him hard. 'Watch yourself, Will, is all I can say.'

Staffe watches him leave and tries to work out how the hell Pulford had got hold of a Google Earth printout in prison. Soon, his thoughts turn to Jessop, another colleague who ended up on the wrong side of the law – and now Pennington's behaving oddly.

The phone rings and it is Finbar Hare saying he has asked around about Carmelo Trapani and does Staffe want to meet up? It is music to Staffe's ears – the chance to listen to the voice of a different kind of reason.

*

The George and Vulture was Jessop's favourite place, with its dark panelling and linen and silver; its calves' liver and chops and decrepit waiters.

'I asked around about Carmelo,' says Finbar, talking low and smearing his potted shrimp onto his toast. Staffe and Finbar didn't find each other until relatively late in life, but looking at Finbar Hare now, Staffe muses upon how alike they are; and so very different. Finbar has clearly had a couple of sharpeners already and seems not to have a care in the world, even though he is responsible for two billion pounds of shareholder funds.

'What have you come up with?'

'How come he's on your radar? He's an old fella. Can't you let him die in peace?'

'Too late for that. I've got his corporate profile.' Staffe hands a printout across.

The waiter brings a large turbot to the table, begins to carve, and Fin says, 'He also had his finger in an investment trust a few years ago. We've just poached one of the top banking analysts in Europe from Hispania. Carmelo was in with a fellow called Abie Myers, but he ditched the stock a month or so ago.'

'You'll keep this to yourself, Fin.'

Finbar puts a finger to his lips, whispers, 'You're in the club, Will. You're an honorary member. We both keep schtum, right?' He begins to set about his turbot, says, 'Now, tell me about that beautiful girl of yours.'

'I haven't got one.'

'Sylvie, you fool. You don't let fish like her through the net, my man. I've told you before, you should—'

'Leave it, Fin. Please.' Staffe picks at his fish, listens to the low rumble of secret deals, the chink of silver on china. His thoughts drift.

'Will?'

He looks up, sees Finbar looking at him quizzically.

'Are you all right?'

'I'm fine.'

'You don't look it.'

'I've been getting tired, just lately.'

'Christ, man, you need to loosen up. Here.' He reaches across with the bottle and Staffe shakes his head, wonders what life would have been like spent in a suit and on expenses – had he not chosen the Force.

Fin smiles, raises his glass, as if he hasn't a care in the world. But Staffe knows that isn't the case.

Six

Josie pauses the CCTV footage again, scrutinises the man on the screen and she saves him as a still image, dragging him to her folder marked 'Carmelo's House Day of Disappearance'.

The image is foreshortened and taken from above, but Josie can see that he wears an overcoat with the collar turned up and a hat. His face is obscured and he moves slowly. He doesn't look around, simply goes straight to the entry pad at the side of the main gates and taps in a code, gains access immediately through the iron gate in the high wall. The time was four seventeen. Carmelo's Daimler had left through the gates twice on the day of his abduction, and arrived once, but that was the only other traffic. Josie clicks another saved file and watches the Daimler leave for its second time, at six thirty-two.

Staffe comes across to her desk, says, 'Is this the CCTV footage from Beauvoir Place?'

'There's just one man going in, all day.'

'And the car?'

'It's Carmelo's. It left at half six in the evening, but he wasn't driving.'

'How do you know?'

'The man who went in didn't come out again. Unless he's still in the house—'

Josie clicks the icon for the still of the man.

'It's not much to go on,' says Staffe, looking at the grainy enlargement of the elevated and rear view of the man in the hat. 'Is that the best we've got?'

'Afraid so, sir, except that he must have known Carmelo. He had the code for the gate.' Josie's phone beeps and she looks at the screen, walks to the window. 'I can't really talk now – work.' She looks out of the window and wraps her free arm across her body, clasps her own shoulder. She laughs softly into the phone – a private joke. 'Maybe later.' She looks over the shoulder, towards Staffe, who is watching her. He looks away and she says, 'I'll call you. OK. Right.' She laughs again, says, 'Don't!' in a joking way and clicks off. Returning to her desk, she says, 'Sorry about that.'

He makes a tight smile. 'If you can spare a minute, Attilio Trapani is coming across to give his statement.'

'You don't want me there, do you? I was going to call on Carmelo's accountant.'

'I'll do that when we're done.'

'So what's in store for me?'

'That depends.'

Staffe goes to the window. Outside, it is suddenly darker than dusk and a jag of lightning darts across the narrow strip of sky. 'When Attilio leaves here, follow him. Everywhere he goes.'

'For how long?'

'As long as it takes.' Staffe points down below, to Cloth Fair, where a motorcycle appears, gliding quietly along the street. It is unmarked and the rider has a spare helmet strapped to the rear seat. 'Use him, if you need to. He's one of ours.'

The rider lifts his visor, looks up and salutes.

'I'm wearing a skirt. I—'

But Staffe is gone.

Attilio's face is red and he chews his lip. Staffe notices that just to the right of his Adam's apple, he has a small cut. He can't remember if Attilio had it when they interviewed him down at Ockingham Manor. 'What's that?'

Attilio's gaze is unfocused, his mind elsewhere.

'The mark on your neck. Where did it come from?'

Attilio puts a finger to his throat, feels where the skin is broken. 'Must have been shaving.'

Staffe leans forward, peering. 'Funny-shaped razor you use.' *Like the tip of a knife*, he thinks. 'Tell me about your father.'

'My father and I were never close. And of course, I never knew my mother. He was all I had and, you know—' He looks up at Staffe again. 'That was never enough. Not for either of us.'

He looks at his statement, begins to read it and glazes over. 'He never held me. Did I say that already?' He signs the statement, says, 'My wife and the servants will verify it.'

'And your guests, of course.'

'I'd rather you didn't trouble them. It's not done.'

'Done?' Staffe wonders who the hell Lady Ballantyne's latest husband thinks he is. 'What about Fahd Jahmood?'

'How do you know him?'

'It's my business to know everything about Carmelo.'

'Jahmood doesn't know my father.'

'How can I be sure?'

'I'd like to go now.'

'When this is all dusted and done, you will thank us, for finding the man who stole into your father's house and slipped that mickey into his grappa and watched him pass out and crack his head on the floor, then drove him away in his own car. It was someone he knows, of course, and they even disposed of those two Murano tulip glasses. I bet your father loved those glasses. I bet he savoured every sip of grappa he took from them. They're forty, maybe fifty years old. And now there's only four.'

'Shut up! They were a present – for my mother.'

'What happened to her?'

'I killed her.'

'What!'

'And then I was born. That's what killed her.' Attilio stands up. 'So how could he love me?'

'We have to find him, Attilio. He is old, and if he is alive, he may well be suffering.'

'How can I help? I don't know where he is and that's the God's honest truth.'

'They put him in the boot of his own car. He shouldn't have left home for the last time in the boot of his car.'

Slowly, Attilio bends further and further over, his head in his hands. 'For God's sake,' he mumbles. 'You don't think I had anything to do with this, do you?'

'Where's Jacobo?' Staffe puts his hand gently on Attilio's shoulder. 'Jacobo and your father have a secret. I know.'

Attilio stiffens. 'How do you know?'

It is strange, muses Staffe, that Attilio asks this, rather than 'What secret?'

'Appolina as good as told me, but she's afraid. It seems that everybody's afraid.'

Attilio clams up and Staffe leads the way into reception, says he is sorry if Attilio suffered any distress and he knows what it is like to lose your parents.

44

'No, you don't,' says Attilio.

The memory of his mother, laid out in Bilbao, repeats on Staffe. She was covered up by a thin cream sheet and from the shape she made, he could tell she was not all there. He has nightmares about what the remains of her would have looked like, beneath the shroud. He looks at Carmelo's son and all he can see is what is absent.

Outside, the rain is pelting down now and thunder rumbles over the meat market.

Staffe offers Attilio his hand and they shake, uncertainly. He watches him go, looks across to the other side of the road, sees Josie taking shelter and looking daggers at him, her hair in thick, drenched strands. Up the road, the motorcycle revs – ready to go. Attilio hails a cab. Josie scurries to the rider and Staffe goes back in, makes his call.

Seven

The sign 'Goldman and Son, Accountants' is a narrow brass plaque on a blue door next door to a Lebanese restaurant called Shawiba on Hackney High Street. Sbaring a little Middle-Eastern rapprochement, a fellow in a *yarmulke* sits with a young man in a *burnous*, exchanging sucks on a hookah pipe beneath Shawiba's canopy.

A voice rattles in the speaker grille, and Staffe says, 'Mister Goldman? I'm from City Police. DI Wagstaffe.'

The electric lock on the blue door whirrs and Staffe goes through. The hallway is narrow and the steps are ridiculously steep, the bulb insufficient, but the décor is fresh and the carpet new.

Staffe wonders, as he climbs, how Carmelo would have managed with the stairs. Before he reaches the top, a man appears. 'Mister Goldman?' says Staffe.

The man's suit is cut in the style of Jean-Paul Belmondo and his hair is slicked forward at the sides and tufted up at the top.

'The son,' laughs the slicker, 'Anthony,' turning on his heel and walking into a modern, open-plan office, surprisingly spacious and incredibly light. There are only two desks and at one, a beautiful young woman with long, raven hair is busy with her computer – fingers clattering super-fast. There is no paper on her sleek, glass desk. Staffe tries not to look, but her blouse is a half-size too small, a button too undone. She looks up, smiling, but her fingers keep clattering and behind her, on the wall, is a framed certificate. Ms E Thyssen-Wills.

'And your father?' says Staffe. 'Does he still look after Mister Trapani?'

'You speak as if Carmelo is still with us. We feared the worst when Attilio advised what had happened.'

'You represent Attilio Trapani, too?'

'You know I'm not going to divulge that, Inspector Wagstaffe, unless Mister Trapani instructs me so.' He winks and indicates that Staffe should sit in one of the deep-cushioned, cream armchairs.

Smooth fucker, thinks Staffe. He says, '*Does* your father represent Carmelo Trapani?'

'My father is retired.'

'So you handle Carmelo.'

'That's the wrong word, but I administer his investments.' Goldman's eyes are too light. Just then, they blinked too fast.

Staffe suspects contact lenses; his nails are manicured, but his skin is a little loose around the neck – a little too tight around the eyes. 'You seem a little young,' he says.

Staffe hears a stifled snort behind him and Goldman shoots a look at Ms Thyssen-Wills. 'Look, I'm busy, and I won't answer anything about Carmelo until I have an instruction or you have a warrant. If you don't have any meaningful questions I can an-swer—'

'Tell me about Martin, your brother.'

'Martin used to do this, but he wasn't as suited as me. It's a dirty business, inspector.' He laughs. 'Father soon saw it was I who had the knack with money.'

Staffe stands.

'Did Carmelo share his opinion?'

'What's that supposed to mean?'

'He was moving his portfolio around, from what I've heard. Didn't he dissociate himself from Abraham Myers?'

'Like I said—' says Goldman.

'You said you had a knack for money. Did you mean you had a knack for figures?'

'I suspect you have a gift for finding the truth. It's what you'd want in a policeman, but it's not the same as having a gift for the law.'

'Very clever,' says Staffe, leaving.

'Is that it? You're done?'

'Not by a long chalk. Next time, we'll be even closer to the truth and the lies will be there for all to see.'

'You only just got here.'

'You're not going to tell me anything. It's what I came to find out, Mister Goldman.'

*

Josie is in Veneto's, an old-school sandwich shop with a few stools in the window, which is where she perches, alongside two damp, steaming cycle couriers who talk in a metro patois, constantly saying 'dude', 'random', 'awesome'.

The rain comes and goes. When it comes, it is biblical and people rush to the sides of this ornate, Victorian arcade, sloping into the coffee shops and spaghetti houses that line Sicilian Avenue. Just across from Veneto's is Blum's, advertising chicken soup and salt beef on its ancient sign.

Josie can see straight into Blums and Attilio is sitting in the back with a Jewish man slightly older but not nearly so kempt. They have been there an hour now and the waiter has stopped bothering them.

Her phone goes and she looks down, feels a small surge in her tummy. 'Conor calling'. She looks at her watch, sees it is ten to and she is not yet late. 'Hi you,' she says.

'I'm here already. Finished early.'

'I'm tied up.'

'Oh my.'

'I was about to call, but I—'

'You're going to blow me off, aren't you?'

'I'm sorry, Conor.'

'I hope they're paying you well.'

Josie looks to the sky. The rain has stopped and a chasm of blue dares to open up. People in the streets are looking up.

'You still there? Hey, it's sunny. Is it sunny where you are?'

'You're smoking,' she says.

'How d'you know that?'

'You can't see the sky from inside the Polar Bear.'

'Ahaa. My little Miss Marple.'

'I've got my surgical stockings on.'

'Stop it, you're driving me wild!'

Attilio Trapani comes to the door of Blum's. He looks at the sky and says something to his companion in the *yarmulke*. They walk to the end of Sicilian Avenue and a car slows down, on Southampton Row. Attilio and his companion get in.

Josie's rider appears outside Veneto's and she fumbles in her pocket for money, says to Conor, 'I'll call you.'

'What? Is that it?'

She puts a fiver on the counter and hurries out, clicking her phone off and hitching her skirt, getting a few looks as she hooks her leg over the motorbike's seat, feeling the force as the rider speeds off, weaving traffic all the way back round to Holborn and right onto Oxford Street, heading west and spending most of the journey on the wrong side of the road, buses coming at them. The sound of horns is constant all the way to Oxford Circus, when they catch up with Attilio's car, slowing right down and keeping two or three cars between them all the way into and out the other side of Mayfair, pulling up outside Les Ambassadeurs.

Josie knows enough about Les Ambassadeurs to realise this is the end of the line. Herein lies a casino and one of the finest dining rooms in all of London town. For members only. Attilio could be here until two in the morning.

A brace of overly pretty girls in short, shifting cocktail dresses loop arms and smile as they pass Attilio. His companion remains in the car, which moves off. As Attilio disappears into the club, Josie can see he is greeted by the dark-eyed and beautiful Arab who was at Ockingham Manor the other day.

Josie calls Staffe, relates the events of the past two hours, telling him about Attilio's companion in the *yarmulke*.

'Martin Goldman?'

'Who the hell is Martin Goldman?'

'The Trapani family lawyer. Blum's, you say. And now Les Ambass,' says Staffe. 'From one side of the West Bank to the other.'

'What?'

'I'm guessing he hooked up with Fahd Jahmood.'

'There's no way I'll be able to get in there.'

'That's OK. There's someone I know who's a member.'

It's quiet on the line, and she can tell Staffe wants something.

Eventually, she says, 'You only have to ask, sir. Is it to do with Pulford?'

'You know me too well. I was going to go up onto the Attlee, see if I could catch up with Shawne Haddaway. I need to see if our friend Haddaway has been visiting Google Earth recently.'

'That sounds a bit random, sir.'

'I saw a printout in Pulford's papers and I know he's not allowed access to the Internet inside prison. I've got a bad feeling about it.'

'I'll do it, but you know what Pennington said about staying away from the e.gang.'

'It's OK. Leave it to me.'

'No! I want to do it, sir.'

'Be careful, Josie.'

She hangs up, calls Conor and from the sound of things, he is in company. 'I've just finished,' she tells him. 'There's something I have to do later, but I'll come over now.'

'Aaah, damn. We're on our way up north – Belsize Park or something. I'll call you.'

She wants to say, 'We? Who is we? And why aren't you inviting me?' But instead she says, 'OK. Call me,' and clicks off.

The sun goes in again, like someone switching a light off.

*

Pulford presses his face against the cold steel window frame. Through the narrow slots of toughened glass, he looks up at the sky. There's all kinds of madness going off today.

A bang makes him jump and he catches his cheek on the rough junction of the metal window frame where somebody has had a go at dismantling it. The slightest thing seems to get him going lately.

'Pulford!' shouts a PO, through the door. 'Feeding time.'

'Not for me, Mister Crawshaw,' he calls. But the door opens

anyway and a large inmate fills the frame, holding Pulford's tray.

'I said—'

'Yeah? What did you say, you fucking frag? Why you on this wing, Pulford, if you're not a fucking snitch?' The orderly throws the tray on his bed and the mulch of spuds and fish spills onto his sheets. 'Or a fucking fiddler.'

Pulford knows the orderly. This is Beef, one of the hardest men in the jail, on the verge of acquiring don status, as well as being a senior partner in the e.gang.

'Levi,' says Pulford, to Beef.

'Don't call me Levi,' says Levi Salmon. 'Name's Beef, you frag.' Levi Salmon is known as Beef for good reason. He has shoulders like a bull and is over six foot but his waist is narrower than his neck. His trick in the yard is to give a con a free hit. Pulford saw it the other day and Beef didn't even blink when an armed robber from Canvey Island punched him full on the nose. The crunch of the blow resounded across the yard and the assailant stood briskly back, his jaw dropping. Silence fell in the yard and Beef stepped forward, said something to the con that made his face turn grey. That night, an ambulance came, went, and the armed robber from Canvey hasn't been seen since.

Pulford peers over Beef's shoulder, sees Mister Crawshaw withdraw onto the landing.

'What the fuck you got to be scared about, sergeant? Or do you need to watch your tongue?' Beef puts his hand to Pulford's mouth and grabs it, like you would an apple from a tree. He breaks Pulford's skin where the window had grazed him.

Crawshaw sneers, 'Careful, Salmon, he's bleeding. Don't catch AIDS.'

Beef puts his face right up to Pulford's. He licks the blood from his wound and whispers, 'I ain't 'fraid of fuckin' nothing, me. You get me? I'm an animal. Everyone says so.' With one hand still squeezing Pulford's mouth, Beef reaches behind him, pulls a piece of paper from his waistband and holds it up to Pulford. 'See this? I gave you a copy.'

Pulford focuses on the piece of paper, sees it is the printout from Google Earth. He raises a hand, grabbing Beef's neck, but he makes no impression.

Beef says, 'Mummy's house. We been there and her next door, Jean, she reckons your mummy thinks you're wasting yourself in the police. Maybe it's 'cos you can't do your fuckin' job. People like us, we're above the law and you can do fuck all about it.' Beef drops the piece of paper and takes something from his pocket. He squeezes Pulford's mouth even tighter until his lips part. His jaw cranks open and Beef presses his handful into Pulford's mouth, puts his hand over and holds it there as Pulford gags.

After ten seconds, he lets Pulford go and steps back, laughing as Pulford spits out the mouthful of dog hair.

He spits and spits, but his mouth is dry and he has swallowed some. The taste is rank and it spikes all the way down his throat.

'Simba,' says Beef. 'That's mummy's dog, right?'

'You cunt,' says Pulford, rushing at Beef, but just before he gets to him, Beef shouts, 'Thor!'

Now, Crawshaw steps in.

Pulford has his hands on Beef's throat again, but barely covers half the circumference.

'Don't use that language, Pulford,' says Crawshaw, stepping up and twisting him.

'Thor,' says Beef. 'That's the name of my dog. A proper name for a dog.'

The PO has Pulford bent double, his arm up the back and his shoulder right on the edge of its socket. His bleeding cheek is pressed to the cold floor and Mister Crawshaw says, 'You're on a Governor's. See how that looks in the case for the defence.'

Eight

Earnest waiters glide through Les Ambassadeurs, heads erect like Deco silhouettes. 'You remember the first time we came here?' says Finbar Hare.

The bar is softly lit, and crystal glasses and bottles of Armagnac glisten like jewels. Beyond, through the dining room, a private garden deludes you into thinking you are not in London at all. 'We were younger then.'

'And wild.'

'Some of us still are,' says Staffe.

'Quite an admission from the Inspector.'

'I meant you. Now, about Fahd Jahmood?'

'There's a chap I know was sent into the Jahmoods to check out what the sons were up to. Young Fahd over there had fifty million in a checking account in Miami, not even getting interest. A two per cent return on that would bring in a million a year. Enough for most of us.'

Staffe watches Fahd and Attilio. Fahd talks to the wine waitress with his hand on her hip. Attilio fidgets, sipping wine then water and looking around constantly, not exactly at home here; Staffe wonders what would be enough for Attilio these days. What does it cost to be in his new club?

When the wine waitress has put the bottle back in its silver bucket and left them to it, Attilio leans across the table, grabs Fahd by the arm.

Fahd laughs, waving at Attilio dismissively as if he was a fly on his cuff.

Attilio stands, swings an amateur punch at Fahd, which glances off his handsome head, but is enough to have the Arab covering up like a boxer on the ropes.

A butler raises a white-gloved hand and through a door beyond the bar, a tall, athletic man in a suit emerges. He moves slowly, calmly. Staffe shifts in his chair and the leather squeaks. Attilio is standing over his Arab companion, his back arched and his arms outstretched, hands around Fahd Jahmood's neck.

Fahd's own protectors converge on Attilio, systematically laying hands on him, kicking him sharply behind the knees. They do it in tandem and Attilio falls like a caber, smashing his head on the table. The heavies get Attilio on his stomach, arms behind the back and fit him up in a pair of zip-tie cuffs, in the manner of secret police.

'You lying bastard!' shouts Attilio as the heavies carry him out. He writhes and kicks, and as they carry him past Staffe, Attilio looks up at him with pleading eyes. But his anger is spent; in its place, fear – as he recognises Staffe.

'Where are you taking him?' says Staffe.

The man in the suit says, 'Steer clear,' and when Staffe shows his warrant card, he swats it away.

Staffe follows them towards the room behind the bar but another man in a suit appears, blocking his path. 'I'll come back, with uniforms and warrants.'

The man in the suit looks down at Staffe, shakes his head slowly. 'I don't think so' – and the door closes, onto its private world.

*

Josie looks up at the Attlee Estate, whose concrete is stained by the rain, as if it had been weeping from its windows. Some crosses of St George flap in the breeze alongside drying *salwar kameez*. Weed is in the air, and phug hip-hop. Somewhere, 'Redemption Song' breaks through.

A young teen in a black trackie comes towards the electric gate which buzzes open. He has the pall of crack about him.

'Wait! I'm coming in,' says Josie.

'Fuck off!' he says, trying to shut the door on her, but Josie is quick off the mark and pushes him back through the door into the estate and flashes her card.

He comes at her and Josie's heart stutters, but she plants her feet wide apart and lowers her centre, watches his trainers. You can read the next move by watching their feet, and she kicks out at his knee. Not so hard that he would require an ambulance, but it fells him. She tries not to take any pleasure as his face turns grim.

He looks up at her from the ground, cussing. He is white as unbaked pastry but sounds Afro-Caribbean. She reaches out and pulls a handful of wraps from his pocket. He is a handsome boy with blue eyes and long, dark lashes.

Josie empties a wrap and crunches the small rock with her shoe. 'What flat is Shawne Haddaway in?'

'Give me my stuff.'

Josie empties another wrap onto the floor, grinds the rock to dust with her foot.

'C thirty-four.'

'Have you seen him today?'

He blinks his eyes slowly, to suggest 'Yes'. Suddenly, he looks his age. Acts it, too, as the adrenaline must ebb and he holds his knee.

Josie bends down, feels the ligaments around the knee. 'You'll be OK, just make sure you rest up a day or so.' She drops the remaining wraps onto his shallow chest, knowing that if she doesn't return his narcotics, his future will darken, not brighten. 'And stop using this stuff.' She puts a hand to his cheek. 'You're a good lad. You can't hide it from me.'

'Suck me,' he says.

She laughs, clocks his fake ID on the floor. 'Shut up, Louis.'

'How you know my name?'

She puts the toe of her foot on the corner of the ID.

'Don't mess with Haddaway, miss.' He struggles to his feet, bends his leg, rubs his knee and picks up his ID. He stands in the doorway and watches Josie all the way into the lift, stays there as she gets in. As the doors close, he says, 'Serious. Don't go.'

The lift rattles and jolts, the storeys counting up slowly. The stench of humanity is thick and Josie puts a hand over her mouth and nose, takes in the smell of soap between her fingers, thinks about how officially there are only two e.gang members living on the Attlee. One is Brandon Latymer, invisible to the police since Jadus Golding was shot. The other is Shawne Haddaway and she is here to see if Shawne has a computer and if he does, to see what footprints he has left in the virtual world.

Josie gets out at Level Three and steps over the discarded box of a fifty-inch TV. From up here you can see the City glisten not so far away. Dogs bark and the mother-freaking hip-hop is louder. She works her way around the deck until she gets to the Cs.

A drawl of music leaks from inside number thirty-four and

Josie peers through a gap in the curtains of the front room, can see nothing, so she knocks, lightly. Waits. She knocks again and takes out her ring of keys, checks the likely candidates and tries one. Along the deck, a young woman pushes a baby out of her flat. She must be fifteen, but looks younger, and as she passes Josie she curls her lip. The key turns and Josie opens the door, says softly, 'Haddaway. Shawne Haddaway?'

No response.

She follows the low drone of music down the dark hall, chipboard for floor, and darkly stained in places. It could be blood. At the end of the hall, she pushes open the door and the sound of Marvin Gaye spreads joyously from a boombox on the window-ledge. 'What's Goin' On.' Between her and the music, a young man is flat on his back on a bare mattress. On the floor by his dangling hand, the rudiments of an afternoon on the crack pipe. She taps him on the shoulder and steps back, warrant card in hand. He doesn't move.

Josie backs tenderly out of Haddaway's bedroom, easing the door closed and looking anxiously over her shoulder. She checks the bathroom and goes into the open-plan living area, which has a rusting two-ring hob next to a sink piled high with pizza boxes and bottles of Courvoisier. On the floor is a brand-spanking AirBook with its screen up. She powers it up and immediately a screensaver of Rihanna appears. There is no end of choice for unsecured wireless connections and within seconds, Josie is scrolling through Shawne's web history: an unglittering profile of music downloads, weaponry sites and porn.

In amongst them, Google Earth. When she hovers over the search predictors, only one item comes up. Right-clicking, her stomach turns over.

Josie and Pulford had a thing once. It was three years ago and unsatisfactory and they each laugh about it now, an unrequited petting frenzy and a wordless breakfast at a greasy spoon in Southgate, but she remembers quite vividly the few minutes Pulford spent talking about his mother. His mother who, when her only son moved to the Big Smoke, stayed put. Josie hadn't known the place she stayed put and Pulford had to tell her it was near Newcastle.

Now, she reads 'Whitley Bay' and remembers.

Shawne Haddaway had summoned Google's might down from the sky and trained a bead on 24 McIvor Street, Whitley Bay. Josie inserts her memory stick, saves, closes down and retires, but she hears a bang from the bedroom and she hears Shawne cursing. Her heart misses one and she makes for the door, but as she opens it, a familiar young man looks Josie in the eye.

It's obvious that Louis Consadine doesn't want to be there, but he has three mates with him. One of them has his hand down his trousers. Josie thinks he's probably holding his heat and she says to Louis, 'I know you. Remember? I know your name, so don't do anything stupid.' Her heart beats double-time and she looks at the youth with the hand down his trousers. He's barely fifteen. 'Louis, don't do anything stupid.'

Louis forces a broad smile but his eyes seem dead. 'Suck me,' he says.

'Suck him,' says the one with the heat.

'Grow up,' says Josie, pushing past them, walking as slowly as she dare, back to the stairwell. She won't chance the lift, and as soon as she is round the corner she bolts down the stairs, two at a time – chased by her own echo.

Maurice swelters in his coat. Its tweed collar snags the hairs on the nape of his neck and the band on the inside of his hat tacks to his forehead with sweat. The rain has gone but the evening air is still muggy.

He puts his hands on the iron bars of the gate to Palazzo Adriano – this wonderful mix of English and Dutch with its curved gables and stained glass. But something is definitely in the rarefied air. Perhaps he was naïve to have come. Tatiana often says he is naïve.

A car drives by and Maurice can tell from the sound of the engine that it is slowing, so he pulls down his hat, waits for it to pass, but the engine peters quickly to nothing. He wants to look over his shoulder but resists. The handbrake clicks and Maurice plunges his hands deep into his pockets, still damp from the rainstorm earlier. The car door opens and slams shut; then another. He holds his breath.

Footsteps get close and Maurice knows he shouldn't have come – not so soon. He wishes everything could be the way it used to be. He prays for Carmelo's soul.

'Excuse me, sir.'

Without looking, Maurice knows the voice is police. He wants to be home, with his books and the Olivetti Lettera 35 that his father, Claudio, gave him. It was supposedly an heirloom, but he later discovered his father had won it in a game of cards.

'Sir? Turn round please, sir.'

Maurice looks at the house, thinks what truths might lie within.

'Sir!' It is a different voice.

Maurice turns round.

Each of the policemen seems shocked to see how young he is. Maurice resents his youth. It bows his shoulders. It shortens his stride but it is the one thing he knows can mend itself. He will be old – soon, he hopes. And Tatiana says she will still love him. He wishes her young, for ever.

'Why are you here?'

Maurice intuits that the least harm will ensue from his being totally co-operative, and by staying as close to the truth as he dares.

*

They pull into Leadengate and Maurice recalls that this is where they investigated Calvi. He wasn't even born then, but Maurice is well schooled in all aspects of his rich heritage. It would be fair to say it is something of an obsession with him and has been ever since his father first balanced him on his knee, telling him tales.

Now, he feels momentarily afraid as he is checked in by a kindly immigrant called Jombaugh, who regards him as if he can't possibly have done something terrible. Then a weary inspector with hair an inch too long and clothes a cut too casual takes him into a room. Maurice tells Inspector Wagstaffe where he lives and that he will talk through his lawyer and only his lawyer. His lawyer, a gentleman by the name of Goldman.

The unkempt inspector is given an envelope, says, 'There's no need to keep you here, Mister Greene. We can get our answers at your place.'

'Isn't that irregular?'

The inspector wafts the paper he has removed from the envelope. 'We're authorised to conduct a search, so I'd say it suits us all. Unless you'd rather not. It would be irregular, surely, if you preferred it here to the comfort of your home.'

'I have nothing to hide,' says Maurice. 'Quite the reverse.' He smiles and sees the inspector's mouth turn down at the edges, as if some upperness of hand has been wrested.

Nine

Maurice's flat is housed within a slim, early Victorian affair that looks onto London Fields. A gentle stroll would get you to Carmelo's home in a quarter of an hour.

Staffe shows the young fogey a photograph taken outside Carmelo Trapani's house on the day Carmelo disappeared. It has been lifted from the CCTV footage and is taken from above, slightly behind, and is grainy and blurred, the perspective warped. Maurice doesn't bat a lash. He stares straight ahead, pale-eyed.

Martin Goldman says, 'That's not Maurice. Unless you can prove it, which you can't, and as we have said, Maurice was in his house from eight o'clock in the morning on the day of Signor Trapani's most regrettable disappearance until noon the following day.'

Staffe reappraises Maurice, a fine-featured, oddly handsome man. He sports an educated voice but every now and then a hint of Italian singsongs through. His fiancée came to live with him after a trip to Siberia two springs ago. Maurice fell in love with Tatiana the instant he saw her and in her broken English she verifies that Maurice was home for all the requisite hours. Tatiana's crystal beauty takes the breath away.

It appears that Maurice has no job; hasn't worked a day nor claimed any kind of benefit since he left York University with a first in English and Carmelo gave him this flat.

Staffe regards Maurice long and hard, and he just can't imagine

Maurice having what it took to account for Carmelo Trapani. 'Carmelo took good care of you?'

'I fend for myself now, inspector, though I do concede this might be a mystery to you.'

The slant of the sun catches the dust in long bugles of light. There is something of the Havisham about it, and though the flat is furnished in perfect keeping with its age, this is clearly an abode of the young. Magazines, from *Grazia* to the *New Statesman,* litter the coffee table and there is the paraphernalia that goes with recreational drugs. Books are piled everywhere and Staffe spots a *Karenina* in Russian.

'There are too many mysteries associated with Carmelo's disappearance.' Staffe thinks about a mystery closer to home: why Carmelo was so keen to speak with Pennington.

'Maurice loves Carmelo very,' says Tatiana. They look at each other with the utmost quizzical intensity, like two curious, incarcerated and besotted creatures of similar, but distinct, species. Staffe cannot fathom them at all.

'What do you do for a living, Maurice?'

'That would be a private matter. I can't see how—'

'I consider it germane to this investigation. As is Carmelo's relationship with Attilio. He appears to treat you more like a son.'

'He's my uncle, that is all.'

'This is a nice place,' says Josie, browsing Maurice's papers. 'But it has overheads.'

Maurice hands Josie a bank statement, says, 'Minimal.' Two sheets cover the whole year, the balance diminishing infinitesimally from £28,000.16 at the end of January to £27,904.87 at the end of July. A tenner in cash here, a modest cheque there. 'No direct debits,' says Josie.

Maurice nods. 'I'm old-fashioned. I like to go to the town hall, hand over the lucre for the privilege of having my rubbish removed; my safety secured by our fine police.'

'You live well, it seems to me, without working.'

'Maurice is a writer,' says Tatiana.

Staffe looks at the bookshelves. 'Not published, yet.'

'Verse,' says Tatiana. 'And a play. Maurice has a gift for words.'

'It nourishes us,' says Maurice, smiling encouragement at his girlfriend.

'And he has a beautiful voice. He is truly an artist.'

Staffe reaches down the side of a Regency framed couch and hefts a large stack of loose papers. 'The play?' he says, reading the title page: *A Russian Doll.*

'It will be performed soon,' says Tatiana, pride writ large across her face.

'As yet unfinished.'

'Sing for us all, Maurice,' says Tatiana.

Everybody looks at Maurice, awaiting his excuse, but without hesitation, he places a hand on his heart, sings a refrain from 'Tears Dry on Their Own'. Staffe and Josie look at each other as the words soar and swoon. In the sepia, fading study of this Victorian room, surrounded by musty leather volumes of Byron and Brooke, Staffe thinks for a moment that anything is possible. Maurice's voice shimmers to a close.

'I love you, Maurice,' says Tatiana, flopping down onto the threadbare divan settee and clapping her hands.

'Very nice, Maurice, but I don't think you're signed with CBS or EMI, are you? So, you're going to have to tell us where your money comes from,' says Staffe.

'If that is the law, it's a strange one. I think I will not comply.'

'Because you have something to hide.'

'I have my privacy to maintain. That is all.' He gazes at Tatiana and she leans all the way back on the divan, her little skirt ruching up in her lap, legs slightly apart.

Staffe spots two tulip-shaped shot glasses in a glass-fronted secretaire. He turns an evidence bag inside out, using it as a mitten to pick up the glasses, but the moment he lifts them, he realises they are no help to him. They leave two perfectly clear circles in the dust of the shelf, have clearly been there, unused, for several months, if not years. 'Jacobo has some of these,' says Staffe, riffing with what he thinks might be the truth. 'They are from Murano. I think Carmelo must have given them to all his favourite people. Your Jacobo must be one of them.'

'*My* Jacobo?'

'Tell me about Jacobo, Maurice. He is missing, too. His wife is afraid.'

'I can't.'

'Her spirit is broken, Maurice. She's a lonely old lady. Have a heart.'

'He has a heart,' says Tatiana, standing. She wraps her arms around him and they kiss, long and deep, leaving Staffe and Josie to look at each other, nonplussed – there being no law against it. When she is done, Tatiana says, 'A good heart.'

*

Rimmer takes a sip of his pint and asks the landlord of the Crooked Billet if Attilio frequents the place.

'Lord Snooty? Nah.'

Attilio wasn't at Ockingham Manor earlier, when Rimmer

had finished taking the statements. Typically, Staffe doesn't fancy Attilio for this. He never fancies the obvious, which gives Rimmer a position to adopt. 'Will you join me?'

It is quiet, the pub, and the landlord says, 'No harm, while we're quiet. I'm Rodney.' He thrusts his hand at Rimmer and they shake.

Rodney pretty much fills the whole of the space behind the bar and he rests his foot up on a keg of Old Rosie cider, pulls off a half for himself.

'Powerful stuff,' says Rimmer, recognising the drinker's glint too well. 'I know it of old.' He mimes the tightening of a noose around a hanged man's neck. They both laugh, and idly chitchat, but all the time, Rimmer is thinking about how Pennington said he wanted Rimmer's intuition brought to bear. Pennington had tapped the side of his nose when he said 'intuition': 'Like your old man, hey?'

He gets Rodney another half of Old Rosie, says, 'Bloody awful business, though – at the Manor.'

'You a journalist?'

Rimmer proudly pulls the lapel of his jacket to one side, revealing his warrant card.

'The real deal,' says Rodney, clearly impressed, and he refuses the money for the round. 'You know, her last husband, Lord Dominic, was a real gentleman. And handsome? He could knock 'em for six. Mind you—'

'Yes?'

'I can't say.'

'You'd be amazed how the smallest detail can sometimes crack a case like this.'

Rodney looks around the pub and lowers his voice. 'You'll

have heard they're on their arse up at the Manor. It's always family in these cases,' says Rodney.

'You know, Rodney, you really are one step ahead.'

Rodney's proud face smiles and he finishes his Old Rosie. 'A bottle of Bushmills says it's the bloody son.'

'You think so?' Rimmer takes a swig of the pint. His mind shifts maybe five degrees and he feels less sad – as if a better outcome is becoming available. It's a weakness, this fondness, it did for his father, and his father was a better man. 'How did you know Bushmills is my weakness?'

'You can see these things, in my game.'

Rimmer stretches a hand across the bar. 'We're on.' It's a bet he wants to lose.

A way down the line, as the night draws all the way in, Rimmer asks Rodney if they do rooms and the landlord's smile rips his face in two. 'Oh yes, my friend.' And much later, long after the last local has been shoehorned out onto the hedgerowed lane, Rodney says, 'I tricked you.'

'What?'

'With the bet. I've got an inside track, see.' He raises a finger to his lips. 'First rule, we don't gossip, but that bastard, that Italian fucker—' Rodney hiccups. 'Six months ago, she left him. And a mate of mine's an accountant . . .'

'You mean Helena left Attilio Trapani?'

'Yes! And my mate, he's a right big-bollocks in the City and he deals with bankrupts and the big firms and he says to me, "Any day now, Rodney". That's what he says to me one night.'

'He meant "any day" for the Trapanis?'

'No. For the lady. For the dowager. Ha! She was going to lose the lot. The whole shebang. She bangs. Ha! My God, how she

69

bangs, like a lav door in a gale, for all her airs and graces.' Rodney pours them each another Bushmills.

'But they're still going strong from what I can see.'

'Let's just say she has a knack with the towelheads.'

'The Arabs?'

'There ain't such a thing as a secret in the country, you know.'

*

Pennington finishes jotting and he sips from his Leadengate machine tea, which is cold and spiked with a whisky. It has been dark for hours and his computer beeps an email at him. It is from Rimmer's mongroid phone saying he has made good progress and had to stay down there. He can tell from the upbeat mood of the message that Rimmer has had a drink. Pennington knows where that weakness comes from, knows too that Rimmer's dad set an impossible standard – the best copper Pennington ever worked with and taken way before time.

He spins his chair, looks out on the City's riches, glimmering in the east and capped by the Gherkin. He slowly rotates back for his tea and drinks the lot in one, looks at the three lines on his piece of paper.

PULFORD – INTERNAL INVESTIGATIONS ??

BUDGET CUTS – STAFFE vs RIMMER

CARMELO APPOINTMENT?

Pennington scrunches the paper into a ball and the problems become one.

Internal Investigations called earlier to say they are recommending the Crown is given its trial date for the case against DS Pulford in the murder of Jadus Golding.

In the scheme of things, whether he should make Rimmer or Wagstaffe redundant seems trivial, but it's not. That's how deep the shit just got.

He calls his wife, tells her he has to put in an all-nighter. Then he pours a whisky, this time without the tea and drinks it in one, dialling Cassandra's number from memory. She says he can come round in an hour; she just has to get rid of someone first. So he pours another.

Ten

Staffe sits opposite Martin Goldman in the front room of Goldman's modestly furnished, semi-detached house in Stamford Hill. 'Strange, I manage to get through all these years in the police, yet I never came across you, Martin. Now here you are, representing a missing man and the two prime suspects in his disappearance.'

'Perhaps the lazy policeman keeps his investigations close to home.'

'History tells us these things are usually close to home.' Graduation pictures of two boys sit on top of the old, analogue TV. One is of a handsome youth, looking cool and smiling. The other is not and Staffe thinks how Martin seems to be the reverse of everything his brother is. 'Anthony's something else, isn't he?'

Martin regards Staffe as if he might be from the Revenue and picks through his words like a man playing straws. 'Anthony took the accountancy business in directions I couldn't. He sees the world in straight lines. I envy him very much.'

'But yours isn't a world with straight lines. The law can be long and very winding. You changed direction late in life.'

'There is still plenty for me to accomplish.'

Staffe notices a large pile of papers on a bureau in the corner. It is neat and looks as if it has not been disturbed in some time. Beside it sits a yellowed reel-to-reel tape recorder. 'You employ old methods.'

'Aaah. No, that is a different life's work.' Martin's face brightens. 'My father's life.'

'You're compiling his memoirs?'

'Forgotten histories. He was in the East End when they turned on us. At least they tried.'

'Cable Street? A triumph,' says Staffe.

'Cable Street disguised the reality as a triumph.' Martin leans back in his chair and after a few moments, a shallow smile spreads into his face, as if he might be somewhere more exotic.

'Is that when your father first met Carmelo Trapani?'

'Ask him yourself.' Martin stands, goes into the hallway and calls, 'Father!'

When he returns, Martin comes into the room like a servant, deferential, his hands clasped behind his back, and as he speaks, he bows his head a little. 'Inspector, this is Leon Goldman. My father.'

Leon appears in the doorway. He is the same height as his son, with slightly less hair but brighter eyes. He eases himself into the chair with a creak and a happy gasp. 'Terrible business about Carmelo. Any news?'

'I'm afraid not.'

'You haven't had a note yet? For ransom.'

'I can't discuss that.' Staffe gives Leon his most respectful look. The old boy has a happy, whiskery face, a smile permanently creased in his grey jowls. 'But I feel as if I won't get anywhere in this case if I don't trust somebody.' He pauses. 'No, we haven't had a note yet, and I fear we won't get one now.'

'He's worth more than a few bob.'

'That is my assumption. I saw your other son yesterday but he wasn't very forthcoming.'

73

'Carmelo is the most talented businessman I ever met. He can tell a bad idea from good in a fraction of a second. He can tell a man is lying by the way he blinks, but Anthony is correct. We can't discuss his affairs without authority.'

'A dead client is no use to anybody.'

'That's not true. The estate will prevail and the investments, actually, go nowhere. Are you close to finding him?'

'It would help if people would answer my questions. Perhaps you could tell me about Jacobo.'

'Jacobo loves Carmelo like a brother and vice versa, but I don't know where he is.'

'Did I say he is missing?' says Staffe, going to the desk. 'I don't recall saying that.' He puts an index finger on the tight pile of typescript, at least eight reams thick. 'Your memoir is intended for the public domain, I take it.'

'Of course. That's why I have employed a lawyer to draft it for me,' laughs Leon, a little mischief in his bright, watery eyes.

Martin looks hurt.

'It would do no harm if I read this?' says Staffe. 'Nothing to hide?'

Leon's smile beams a little broader. 'It is a memoir, not a diary. It requires an audience of more than one.'

'It's unfinished, and flawed,' says Martin.

Leon looks at his doting son as if he is a buffoon. 'You will make a copy for the inspector, Martin. I can see he has a little wisdom.'

'I really don't think it is ready, father.'

'It's my life to give away.' Leon winks at Staffe, unseen by his son. 'I hope you find Carmelo. He has a heart as big as the moon, as heavy as the seas.'

'That's quite an image. I look forward to reading your story.'

'I will bring it tomorrow, if that is what father wants.'

Staffe says, 'You must be very proud of both your sons,' watching Martin's eyes darken.

'Anthony is like me. He has a gift for money.'

'For figures?' says Staffe.

'In my business they are the same thing, as Martin knows,' says Leon. 'It wasn't your cup of tea, was it, Martin?'

Martin says nothing.

Staffe says, 'I dread to think of the conditions Carmelo is being kept in.'

'We should tell the inspector,' says Leon.

'Tell me what?'

Martin Goldman sighs heavily at the writing desk. He leafs through a diary, says, 'It hasn't even been a week yet.'

'The inspector said that time is of the essence in a case like this.'

'There is nothing to tell, father, not if we haven't even convened.'

'Convened what?'

Leon Goldman says, 'Carmelo came to us last week.'

'I'm his lawyer, father.'

'And I'm his friend. He came to see both of us,' says Leon.

Martin says, 'Carmelo said he had made some changes to his will. He wouldn't discuss them, nor would he sanction my even perusing them, but he is provenly sound of mind and the codicil is witnessed and certified, he assures me.'

'He went to a third party?'

'Tell him everything, Martin,' says Leon.

'It gives me the strangest feeling.' Martin removes his spectacles and looks at Staffe. 'Just several days prior to his disappearance, Carmelo came to me with the amended will and instructed me, in the event of anything materially untoward – and I asked him to define "untoward", upon which he said I would immediately know – that I was to convene a reading of his will.'

'I can assure you, this is untoward,' says Staffe.

'He was very specific. He said I was to wait a week.'

Leon Goldman says, 'And there is one more thing.'

'Carmelo said that I was to arrange for the presence of the police.'

'At the reading?' says Staffe, thinking about the appointment Carmelo made and never kept with Pennington. 'He knew what was coming.'

*

Today, Rimmer woke with his first hangover in three years. Halfway through his usual twenty-minute routine of sit-ups and star-jumps, Rodney's wife brought his breakfast and bill, saying Rodney had gone out, but he knew Rodney hadn't gone out at all. He was in purdah, for shooting his mouth off.

Now, in Leadengate, Rimmer tells Pennington what Rodney had told him about Attilio Trapani and Helena Ballantyne and the filthy-rich Arab in the middle, and about the Ballantynes' teetering bankruptcy, but before he can get to the end of his story, Pennington cuts him dead.

'Christ, Rimmer! Is that what you were excited about? I want evidence; hard bastard evidence, not tittle-tattle.' Pennington sighs. 'The Ockingham Stud might be on its arse, but we can't use what that landlord said to you,' says Pennington.

'But Trapani's wife is having an affair with Jahmood,' says Rimmer.

76

'So?'

'So it undermines Attilio's position completely. A man has to provide. He'd do anything to raise the cash to save his business and his wife's stately home.'

'Including abducting his own father?' Pennington swivels his chair, looks out of his window across the City tops to the Gherkin. A view he loves dearly. 'Can you imagine doing that to your own father? Maybe. Stranger things have happened. God knows, in this job you get to see what families are capable of.'

'Precisely, sir.'

Pennington swivels back, says, 'Let's say you can have a proper run at Trapani. But don't rattle Staffe's cage, hey? He's got plenty on his plate and I'd like the two of you to work side by side on this – like equals, not at each other's throats.'

*

Josie is in the snug of the Hand and Shears, sharing a plate of corned-beef hash with a sinuous man with a sleeve tattoo on his left arm and hair cut into a bob like a woman's. He has dark rings around his eyes. Josie, too, is short of a couple of hours' sleep. She and Staffe clock each other and her eyes avert, as if she has been caught mid-mischief.

Staffe extends his hand to the man, says, 'I'm Will.'

'Conor,' says the man, shaking his hand and smiling easily.

'My boss,' says Josie.

'I'm going to see Pulford,' says Staffe.

'Now?'

'That's the guy in jail, isn't it?' says Conor.

Staffe looks daggers at Josie and she busies herself with another forkful of the corned-beef hash. She chews it and the men talk about what Conor does for a living. He is a video film-maker and Staffe makes a fine fist of showing interest while Josie eats. Conor doesn't touch the food and when Staffe stands, they shake hands again. Josie puts a fiver down and stands, too.

Staffe says, 'No, you stay. Stay with Conor.'

'It's OK, Will. I understand. The job comes with her. I'm cool with that,' says Conor, smiling benignly. He kisses her on the mouth. 'Just cool.'

When they get out onto Cloth Fair, Josie says, 'You could have called me. I'd have met you at Pentonville.'

'You'd have been cool with that?'

'Don't take the piss, sir.'

'He just seems different.'

'Different to what?'

'Never mind.' Staffe hails a cab, asks for Pentonville. Once they're on the Farringdon Road, he says to Josie, 'Do you have the printout from Haddaway's computer?'

Josie plucks a piece of paper from her bag. 'How did you know that he'd been on Google Earth?'

'I saw the logo sticking up from Pulford's file. Let's put the rest down to guesswork.'

'You know the significance of Whitley Bay?'

'His mother lives there. It's what I feared as soon as I saw the logo. They're threatening him – to keep him quiet.'

'Shouldn't we lay off? Imagine if it was you. Wouldn't you want to make your own call on something like this? I know I would.'

'I can't watch Pulford go down for this, Josie. You know that.'

'And you think the rest of us want it?'

'It was me who Golding shot.'

78

'It's not your fault that Golding is dead, or that Pulford's on remand for it.'

'Pulford didn't do it. There is a murderer to find here, but our hands are tied because of bloody Internal Investigations. It stinks. Pennington's shitting his St Michaels in case there's a backlash. You can see it: "Policeman remanded on murder charge. Despite rising crime figures, City prioritise clearing killer's name." That's why we're working on scraps. It comes down to people building their bastard careers. That's why we have to look like we're just working the Trapani case.'

'But you can see where Pennington's coming from.' Josie looks out of the window, watches the Grays Inn Road roll by. 'Pulford crossed a line, the way he hounded Jasmine Cash, and now the father of her little girl is dead. Pulford was up to something, sir. I know it. You weren't here, but I saw him. He was unhinged.'

'And we should have helped him. He was being loyal. Pennington sent you to Spain to get me, and now you're being reticent.'

'All I'm saying is, it has to be Pulford's decision. It's his mother.' Josie reaches into her bag again, pulls out the photocopy of an itemised phone bill. 'This is from Pulford's phone.' A series of calls have been highlighted in luminous yellow. Alongside the seventeen items are two names: 'Golding' and 'Latymer'.

Staffe says, 'Brandon Latymer is e.gang, and they're putting the pressure on Pulford from the inside. And they can manipulate the mood on the Limekiln and Attlee, on the streets in Hackney.' He taps the satellite printout of Pulford's mother's house. 'What in God's name is Pulford up against? Poor bastard. If we don't help him, who will?'

Josie shakes her head. 'This Brandon Latymer, they call him B-Lat. We never had his phone number. We tried a hundred times to get him in for questioning. He's like a ghost, and what's worse – he's got no history. He's clean as a whistle.'

'But Pulford was talking to him,' says Staffe.

'The lease for Cutz is in his name.'

'Cutz? Shit.'

Cutz, the barber shop that rinses the e.gang's ill-gottens. Cutz, the place Jadus Golding put two bullets into the torso of DI Will Wagstaffe.

Staffe turns the printout over, looks down the list again. 'And Pulford was talking to Haddaway, too.'

'The very gangster who is Google-Earthing Pulford's mother's house,' says Josie.

'They've got him by the balls.'

Eleven

Jacobo Sartori looks out of his hotel room. From here, he can see the exotic onion domes of the Brighton Pavilion through the thickening sea fret. Seagulls swoop and call to each other. Salt is in the air and so are memories. What a life he has had. For the most part vicarious, of necessity, but nobody could question it has been a rich one.

Down the phone, the caller says, 'You should be present at the reading, Jacobo.'

Jacobo holds the phone away from his ear and thinks of Appolina. He must stay away. Over the decades, he came to love her and now he can't remember the time he didn't and it is breaking his heart – flake by flake, like the flesh of fish the way they cook it in the Regency. The gulls call and Jacobo puts the phone back to his ear, says, 'When is it?'

'Tomorrow.'

'But the police will be there.'

'You have nothing to hide, surely?'

'Can any of us say that?'

'The longer you stay away the worse it looks.'

'I hear they have been questioning Maurice,' says Jacobo.

'There's no evidence against him.'

'He has done no wrong.'

'How can you know that, Jacobo?'

'I am certain.'

'They would say there is only one way you could know that,' says Martin Goldman.

'You mean if I did it?'

'I mean, if you know who did it. Carmelo was your friend as well as your master, Jacobo. You were like brothers, and I need to know what to do if you are a beneficiary?'

'Do as you would if I were dead. Consider what is mine to be Appolina's.'

'It would devastate her, to hear you talk like this.'

'Now, can you tell me what is in this damned will?'

'I haven't opened it yet. I made my promise.'

'A promise, from a lawyer? You may as well sign the sea.'

The line falls silent. 'I can hear gulls.'

Which deduction induces Jacobo to hang up – a little too late, he fears.

*

Crawshaw pats Pulford down and vets the *Journal of Criminal Studies* that Staffe has brought in with him.

Pulford sits heavily opposite Staffe and Josie, his shoulders bowed. If you didn't know him from Adam, you would say he is a broken man.

Staffe watches Crawshaw move away and looks at the duty PO, says, 'Can't we have some privacy? He is one of us, you know.'

The PO looks across at Crawshaw, says, 'I have to be by the alarm, in case it kicks off.'

'Please, just give us a few minutes of privacy.'

'Are you the one they shot?' says the PO.

Staffe nods.

The PO looks around, to see he's not being observed, and moves away, pats Pulford on the shoulder as he goes, making sure Crawshaw doesn't see.

'They're letting you study?' says Josie as Staffe hands him the journal.

Pulford mumbles, 'It's the only thing they can't stop me doing.'

'What's the subject?'

'Recurring histories of gangland crime.'

'Christ! Just a bit of light relief, then.'

'The old times are coming back.' A glint returns to his eyes. 'Back in the twenties and thirties, different minority groups formed cartels, and now that's happening again, with eastern Europeans and Asians, and north Africans.'

'How heart-warming; a league of nations coming together to keep us in work.' Josie looks around the room. 'And this is research, I suppose?'

For an instant, Pulford smiles, like a door swinging open and closing immediately.

Staffe says, 'We need a viable suspect for Jadus Golding's murder. You know who did it – am I right?'

Pulford shakes his head.

Josie says, 'We know they're threatening you.' She reaches into her bag. 'God knows what I would do in your position.' She places the printout of Google Earth on the table.

Pulford's mouth drops open. His lip quivers. 'Leave this to me. Please.' He looks past Staffe and Josie and his eyes flit.

'What were you talking to Shawne Haddaway about, David? You were phoning him the week before Jadus Golding was shot.'

But Pulford is looking away now, distracted by Levi Salmon, who has a visitor on the far side of the room.

83

Josie turns to see what Pulford is looking at, but she doesn't register Levi Salmon. She sees his visitor, says, 'Louis.'

'What?' says Staffe.

'What the hell is Louis Consadine doing here?'

Staffe says, 'Is he the one who's threatening you? That big fella over there?'

Pulford shakes his head and the three of them look at Beef and the young lad, sporting a black eye and a mouth like splattered fruit.

Josie says, 'You were talking to Brandon Latymer, too. We didn't even have a number for him.'

Louis stands up, lollops across the visitor centre and starts shouting, 'Grass! You fuckin' grass!' He points at a table in the opposite corner.

The PO says to Staffe, 'First sign of trouble, you press that alarm, right?' But by the time the PO gets to Louis, it is too late.

Louis shouts, 'Fuckin' frag!' and kicks away the chair of the seated visitor and kicks again, once to the ribs, then a full swing to the head as the visitor squeals. All around the room, inmates and visitors crowd in on the action.

Pulford's eyes flit left and right, wide with horror, and Staffe registers it, sees that his nerves are withered, his spirit shot to bits. Staffe rushes to the alarm button and presses it.

Pulford cowers at the sound, hunching over and putting his palms over his ears as the thunder of dozens of POs gathers, running towards the incident from all directions.

Inmates and visitors are getting involved in Louis's fight on the far side, and eventually Louis is dragged away by a PO. The brawling inmates are twisted by officers, their faces pressed to the floor. Some female visitors scream and others appear to be getting off on it. In the midst of it all, Beef has made his way to Pulford's table and is now beating a retreat, taunting Pulford, pointing at his lap.

Pulford stares down, into his lap, at the dog's tail, dried clots of blood at its stem; looking at it as if it might blow up in his face. Eventually he picks it up. He says, 'Simba.' He strokes the dog's tail, says, 'The bastards did for Simba.'

*

Jombaugh says, 'You have a visitor.'

Staffe clocks the enormous pile of paper at the end of Leadengate's reception desk, says, 'Martin Goldman by any chance?'

Jombaugh laughs. 'Some bedtime reading! He's in Two. Been waiting over an hour, said he had something important to tell you.'

When Staffe enters the interview room, Martin Goldman says, 'Father wanted you to have his memoir.'

'I have seen. Is there something else?'

'It's the reading of the will tomorrow. Father is quite insistent that I told you in person. This must be conducted precisely in ac-cordance with Carmelo's instructions, but we are also concerned for our family's professional reputation. You do understand, we have to keep confidential matters confidential – unless directed by the estate.'

'Will Maurice Greene be at the reading?'

Martin says, 'He has been invited. That is all I can say. Now, as regards the memoir, father is very proud of his work, and it has also become something of a life's work for me, so I implore you to tread softly. This is a family affair. It is in sections. There is a list of the sections on the top, but it is told thematically, not by chronology, and there will be some typographical errors. Nonetheless, father said he is anxious to know what you think of it. My favourite episodes are the early years; the events surrounding the Battle of Cable Street. My father was a very young man, and so were Carmelo and Jacobo.'

'Jacobo? Will he be there tomorrow?'

'It would benefit everyone concerned if he was. But I'm afraid to say, I doubt it.'

Twelve

Staffe follows Rimmer into the boardroom at Martin Goldman's premises in Half Moon Street, a grand confection of a room and something beyond what you might expect of a one-man show.

He still can't understand why Rimmer is here. Pennington said Rimmer has done some excellent background work on Attilio Trapani and deserves the chance to see his man in the headlights. And after all, he and Rimmer are equals. 'You are aware of that, aren't you, Will?' Pennington had said, pinning Staffe to the Leadengate floor with one of his stares. 'I can't do anything about that.'

Martin Goldman says, 'We are here at the request of our good friend and devoted father, Carmelo Trapani. Carmelo is missing and, God forbid he actually expected this, but he came to me just a week ago, with specific instructions.'

'My God,' says Attilio Trapani.

'This is very strange,' says Anthony Goldman.

'It's very Carmelo,' says Maurice Greene. 'Very Carmelo.'

Martin Goldman breaks the seal of an envelope. 'Carmelo specified that I was not to know the outcome in advance.'

'But you're his lawyer,' says Attilio.

'When he came to see me, Carmelo advised that he had just changed his will. It was verified by Northcotes, in Stamford.'

'That's outrageous,' says Helena. 'You're his solicitor.'

'He wouldn't discuss the contents, merely the people he

wanted present. Northcotes have an impeccable reputation and they have confirmed everything is above board. The soundness of mind is, as we know, beyond question. The revised will and the codicil will be the last word, should a last word be necessary. And let us pray that it is not necessary. Any testaments will, please, be unopposed.'

'What is a codicil?' asks Appolina Sartori.

'A variation to the terms of a will,' says Maurice Greene.

Martin Goldman's eyes widen as he scans the documents. He reads quickly, occasionally clasping the muzzle of his mouth and jaw; other times he scratches his head, rubs his temples. When he is done, he exhales loudly.

Attilio Trapani says, 'Come on. Let's have it.'

Helena says, 'Surely, it's a minor change.'

Maurice Greene smiles to himself, hunched in his tweed coat and rubbing the end of his turned-up nose.

Martin Goldman reads aloud, slowly, mechanically. '"As my accountant will be aware, my investments have been complex and wide-ranging and with this in mind, I engaged a Guernsey firm to simplify my affairs."'

'It's a damned insult,' says Anthony Goldman.

'You knew about this?' says Leon Goldman.

'I tried to dissuade him!'

'However,' continues Martin, '"in recognition of his advice and assistance so far beyond duty, I wish to bequeath my oldest portfolio to Anthony Goldman. He receives one hundred per cent of the shares in Dundee Investments."'

'The bastard,' says Anthony.

'Anthony!' booms Leon.

'It's a hotchpotch of all those failed venture capital projects and some half-built apartments on Corfu with more debt than equity. It's a liability!'

Martin continues, "Palazzo Adriano, my home in Beauvoir Place, is bequeathed to my nephew Maurice Greene and my lifelong friend Jacobo Sartori, and it shall be jointly enjoyed by them in equal measure, not disposed of while either remains alive."'

At this, Appolina begins to weep. She raises a kerchief to her nose, saying, 'Where is my Jacobo?'

Maurice Greene takes out a piece of paper from his overcoat, begins to scribble.

Attilio Trapani says, 'What about me? What about us?'

Martin raises a finger to his lips, waits for quiet and says, 'I beseech you all to pray that this is nothing more than an academic exercise and that the police here can find Carmelo, and none of this may come to pass. The only thing available to any of us today is the fondness of our memories; or a little shame. I urge the former.

'Now, returning to the will,' Martin smiles. "'My boat, *San Angelo* – so enjoyed by my good friend Martin Goldman – is bequeathed to him and his family. It will remain in Ischia and Martin will find that a mooring has been purchased in perpetuity. I will laugh when he laughs, will take a sip of grappa when he sips."' Martin wipes a tear from his eye.

Attilio Trapani drums the desk with his fingers, exhales loudly. His wife, Helena, has turned a greyish white. She holds her mouth, as if she is unwell.

Maurice Greene leans forward. 'Whilst everybody is here, I would like to register an interest in purchasing outright the interests of the other beneficiaries in Palazzo Adriano – at the market value, of course. I would like to live in it.'

'Where would you get the money for that?' says Attilio. 'You are a layabout. You've never worked a day in your whole life. How the hell did you even get to be here today?'

'I have my flat, and some savings. I can borrow against the house itself.'

'You're not even proper family,' says Helena.

'Please. Everybody please exercise a little restraint,' says Martin. 'The will is quite clear. The house is to be jointly enjoyed.'

Appolina says, 'We need to move on, to forget. How can we do that if there remains a connection?'

'Forget?' says Maurice.

Appolina says, 'That house contains all his memories. None of us should be burdened by that.'

Burdened? thinks Staffe. An inappropriate word, you might think.

'What about the cash?' says Attilio. 'He had lots of cash.'

'Not so,' says Anthony Goldman.

'The Guernsey investments, then,' says Helena.

'There is a little cash,' says Martin.

'How much?' says Attilio.

'Eight hundred thousand pounds.'

'Not to be sniffed at,' says Helena.

'Half of which will endow the school in Cefalù. Carmelo wished his son, Attilio, to be the trustee of the endowment,' says Martin.

'Trustee? For someone else's benefit?'

'And the other half of the cash is bequeathed to Bogdan and Vanya Livorski.'

'Who the hell are they?' says Helena.

'His bloody conscience,' says Attilio. 'This is a joke; the devil's joke.'

'Which brings us to the final item of significance. There are a few minor affairs, such as the settlement of outstanding commitments, and the funeral, but let us pray that is unnecessary.'

'Do we know precisely when he made those arrangements?' says Staffe.

'Just three days before he disappeared.'

Maurice Greene says, 'He knew he was going. My God, he knew.'

'What of the Guernsey investments?' says Leon Goldman, 'I'm most intrigued. They must be substantial.'

'Carmelo has indeed simplified his affairs,' says Martin, leafing purposefully through the document. 'His investments are: US Treasury Bonds, value seven million dollars; Cable Portfolios, value sixteen million pounds and comprising minority holdings in twelve different investment trusts.'

'Sweet Jesus,' says Helena, clutching Attilio's arm. 'That's over twenty million pounds.'

'There'll be death duties,' says Attilio Trapani. He leans back, hands in his hair. He is sweating profusely now, looking sidelong at Goldman with a curled lip, daring to smile.

'Who is the beneficiary?' says Leon Goldman.

'Isn't it obvious?' says Helena Ballantyne.

Staffe looks at Anthony Goldman, then around the table, readying himself for the reactions.

'Abraham Myers,' says Martin.

'Abie?' says Appolina, a wry smile upon her face.

Anthony Goldman's expression doesn't budge.

'Abie Myers,' says Leon Goldman. 'The wily dog.'

'It's an error,' says Helena.

'Like Attilio said, the devil's joke,' says Anthony Goldman.

Attilio Trapani clutches his heart, leans forward on the table and wheezes.

Helena says, 'He has these things.' She looks at him contemptuously. 'The doctors say it's asthma.'

'We need to speak to Abraham Myers,' says Staffe.

'Good luck with that,' says Anthony Goldman.

'Does anyone have an address?'

Martin Goldman writes the address for Staffe and the meeting falls into a near silence. Attilio and Helena stare into a void and Leon Goldman shares a confidence with Appolina Sartori. Maurice Greene says nothing, surprisingly underwhelmed for a young man whose future has just been secured.

Slowly, under firm encouragement from Martin Goldman, everybody leaves, save Staffe and Rimmer, who says, 'The nephew gets more than the son.'

Martin says, 'Carmelo had strong emotions and the most steadfast morals, so whatever his reason for finding such kindnesses for that boy, and for the Polish family, they will be benign.'

'But Maurice Greene was right – when he said that Carmelo knew what was going to happen to him, before it happened.'

'Which means it is somebody who knows him,' says Staffe. 'If Carmelo could see it coming, the abductor—'

'Or the murderer,' says Rimmer.

'They planned it – way ahead of time.'

'Could it be Carmelo himself?' says Rimmer.

Staffe looks around at his colleague, impressed with that odd train of thought.

Martin Goldman says, 'I think, today, Carmelo took the earth from beneath all our feet.'

'He put the wind in your sails,' says Staffe.

Martin smiles, tight-lipped, and hands Staffe Abie Myers' address.

As they leave, Rimmer says, 'I don't get it. Attilio doesn't stand to get a penny.'

But Staffe is elsewhere already, deciding how to play Abraham Myers, and wondering if the address can be correct.

Thirteen

Staffe walks east, across the Commercial Road. He picks up the lunchtime edition of *The News*.

Six arrests have been made for public order offences in Hackney. A burnt-out police car was found on Hackney High Street where the officers had attended a bogus domestic incident. All six arrested men are black and the Police Commissioner has issued a statement denying that London is on the verge of a late summer of riots.

Staffe quickly flicks through the paper, skims a 'Where Are They Now?' article by Nick Absolom featuring four rioters from the summer 2011 riots.

When he reaches Stepney Green, Staffe sits in the gardens opposite the Arbour Youth Boys Club. The street where Abie Myers lives was once at the hub of London's sweatshops. This is where the Communists thrived, where they and the Jews pushed back Mosley's Fascists on the day the people said 'Enough!' and a quarter of a million people took to the streets to stop the Fascists coming. The police came to protect the Blackshirts and the East End's children threw pepper in their eyes, tossed marbles under the horses' hooves. And the people won.

Slowly, surely, favoured sons of the East End moved away from the Mile End Road to Hampstead and the north's gentle woods and village high streets. Staffe appraises Abie's slender, three-storey house.

Abraham Myers has just come into twenty million pounds and by all accounts that won't even get close to doubling his wealth, yet he lives amongst the poor, still. Abraham Myers will know by now of the vast increment to his vaster capital. Might he have been aware of the contents of Carmelo's will already?

At Leadengate, Staffe had invested an hour, discovered that Myers made his first bob or two running a razor gang down in Brighton, enforcing his illegal gambling books. Only later did he move into property, housing immigrants in slum dwellings in good areas and waiting for values to drop before buying more. He changed the complexion of parts of Notting Hill, for example, and waited for the area he dragged down to rise again. And Abie has always liked the nags. As the years progressed, he built quite a string. Even now, he still has horses in training.

The twenty million from Carmelo isn't to be sniffed at, of course, but it won't change Abie's life. So why on God's earth did Carmelo Trapani snub his own son to heap yet more millions on Abie?

A Bentley pulls up outside Abie's house on Stepney Green and a slender, athletic man in a shiny grey suit gets out, leans against the car. He has a suedehead and cheekbones like hammer-heads. Staffe perceives a look of the ex-army about him: the straight back and the loose, relaxed hands – ready.

Staffe clocks the registration plate and makes a call as Josie appears, parking up on the other side of a large skip.

Rimmer picks up, and after he's taken the Bentley's details, he says, 'I've just finished talking to Northcotes, and Carmelo Trapani saw them four times in the last month. He was even in the day before he disappeared, and that's when Cable Portfolios was fully endowed with its trusts. He was switching his money all over the place, right up until he disappeared. So Attilio would have still thought he was in for the lion's share.'

'Is Cable Portfolios an off-the-shelf company?'

'No. There's a Certificate of Incorporation of Change of Name,' says Rimmer, sounding pleased with himself.

'How did you get on at the funeral directors?' says Staffe, thinking about the name Cable Portfolios.

'Carmelo gave them ten thousand pounds last week and told them exactly what he wanted. They said he was jovial.'

'They said "jovial"?'

'Jovial.'

An elderly man emerges from the slender house, walking with a stick and pausing on the step to his front door. The suedehead rushes to help but the elderly man shrugs him away. The old man is scrawny but has bright eyes. His face is wrinkled, like a St Bernard. Wisps of grey hair float beneath the band of his fedora.

'Where are you? What are you up to, Staffe?'

Staffe hangs up, watches Abie Myers get into the back of his veteran car. His face isn't that of a man who has just become twenty million richer. His eyebrows pinch and he talks constantly, spitting venom. He buckles up and they move off, slowly. Staffe steps to the kerb and Josie picks him up, saying, 'We follow the Bentley?'

'Wherever it goes, and for however long it takes to get there.'

'Pulford called. I was going to see him later.'

'Is he going to disclose to us? Maybe we should go now.'

'There was an incident, but I'm trying to get us a visit.' She puts her hand on Staffe's knee, smiles across. 'He's going to be all right.'

'Do you think he's cracking up?' says Staffe.

'I called North Yorkshire Police. They're doing a knock on his mother's street, saying there's been a cable TV scam; just to keep an eye. They were really good about it.'

'We should lean on those young pricks on the Attlee Estate. If we can prove who exactly is putting pressure on Pulford, that will get us closer to the evidence for who really killed Jadus.'

'You don't think there's any chance it was Pulford, do you, sir?'

'No way!' As he says this, Staffe's words fail him a little. But this is what he must believe.

'If we put pressure on those boys in the Attlee, word will get back to Pentonville. You saw what happened in the visitor centre, and if anything happens to Pulford's mother . . . Christ, sir, I'm not sure I could live with myself. And imagine what Pennington would do! We can't move on them until Pulford opens up.'

Staffe knows she is right, knows also that there is a law to uphold in the midst of this. Pulford strayed – somehow – and these are the consequences, but he is innocent. He must be.

Josie drives one-handed, reaches out with her gear-change hand and she clasps Staffe's hand tight. 'It'll be all right, won't it, sir?'

'It's a bloody mess.' He squeezes her hand, puts it on the gear stick. 'Now, tell me what you know about our new friend Abie, with his designer bodyguard.'

Josie weaves in and out of the traffic on the A23. She says, 'Abie was born in Lublin, eastern Poland, in 1920. His father came over here in 1929, with his wife, their elder son Benjamin, and Abie. Benjamin died a few years later. Abie married a woman called Esther who nobody knows about. He built up quite a property empire – housing immigrants – but before that he was a bit of a rogue, something to do with betting.'

'I knew that. There's nothing more? What about the wife?'

'You called me away, remember?' Josie lets the Bentley get away from them on the dual carriageway sections. 'Rimmer is looking into it.'

He puts the radio on low and a Joni Mitchell song comes on. Even though he thinks she must be too young to know it, Josie sings along. She can carry a tune but is kind of out of key. He watches her mouth saying the words and smiles.

Many songs later, Josie's mobile rings and she takes it on hands-free. He recognises the voice from the other day in the Hand and Shears. She's been seeing him since before Staffe got back from Spain, and Staffe wonders whether this Conor will hurt her. He wants them to go to Dublin for the weekend. When she says she can't, he says they should go to Borough Market on Saturday instead and he'll get some Dublin Bays. He'll make dinner for her. Staffe looks ahead, can't see the Bentley. In a raised voice, he says, 'Where's the Bentley?'

Conor says, 'Oh, you're with—'

'I'd better go,' says Josie.

'You're going to have to floor it,' says Staffe.

'Drive safe,' says Conor.

Josie cuts him off, pulls them back into third and presses her foot to the floor of the souped Mondeo. It has 210 brake horsepower camouflaged beneath its blue bonnet and it throws them back into their seats as Josie thrashes it to eighty along Preston Road, just going into Brighton, but the road forks and she can't see the Bentley any more.

'Ease up,' says Staffe.

'I can't see them.'

Staffe points up and to the left. 'Go up here.'

The Bentley is waiting at the lights by a park, one brake light glowing red; the other out.

'Sorry about that, sir.'

Staffe puts the music back and Joni Mitchell is replaced by Tracey Thorn. He says, 'I like this one.'

'I won't ruin it by singing then,' she says, slipping the amber, slowing as soon as she sees the brown sign to the 'Racecourse'.

'You can sing if you want,' says Staffe. 'I like it when you sing.'

Josie turns and her eyes seem soft.

'He's good to you, this Conor?'

She nods and they take it slow, Staffe closing his eyes, wishing the world would go away, for just a day or so.

*

Levi Salmon scrubs down after luncheon service. He is alone in the kitchen with the knives, which he shouldn't be, but Mister Crawshaw likes a fag after service and Levi can be trusted. Mister Crawshaw will be back soon with Chef and Roadknight, the other orderly, and then they will painstakingly return the knives to their cabinet, which will be locked tight. Each knife has a white outline of itself so even an idiot can tell if a knife has been taken because its white outline will be glaringly unconcealed.

Levi scrubs some more. You can never quite get rid of the smell of fish fingers, nor the cooking fat, which Chef never changes because he's got to try and do a fiddle somehow. Everyone has a fiddle, even if it's only saving twenty quid a month on cooking oil.

Yesterday, they sent in that young scrote Louis with the tail of poor Pulford's dog. Levi thinks he might not be able to bear this cruelty much longer, but then he thinks about how his mother is being looked after by Brandon and Haddaway, and how they have to develop fresh talent like Louis so the older gangsters, like him, can get a higher ride. You've got to keep building layers of fodder between yourself and the law, but bringing in the tail of that dog – fucksakes. He hated to see that copper's face break up the way it did.

He will have to put more heat on the copper, so he takes out the sachet of black paint that Louis brought him and he smears out the shape of the paring knife in the cabinet – his favourite knife. He uses it to chop onions and peel potatoes. He is mustard, according to Chef – but if Chef knew anything, why the fuck would he be working in Pentonville nick with Levi and a prick like Mister Crawshaw?

There are good screws and bad screws, and Mister Crawshaw is one of the worst screws. Levi shouldn't be left alone with the knives. What if he was a slasher? And he knows for sure that Crawshaw brings in smack and it's him that sorts out access to that poor copper. They say the POs are worse than the inmates: they choose to come into jail. Some of them think they can do some good, can heal, or at least stem a tide – but not Crawshaw. And it makes a difference when you have a man's teenage daughter in the palm of your fist.

He can hear them coming, so Beef blows on the black paint where the paring knife should be, and he puts the knife back. Tomorrow, or the next day, when he takes the knife and wraps it in baking paper and slips it between his butt cheeks so they can't feel it when they pat him down, they won't see white where the knife should be.

'Come on, Salmon, put your fuckin' yoghurt gun back in your

Calvins and let's get you back to your pad, you cunt,' shouts Crawshaw.

Roadknight and Chef laugh and Crawshaw locks the cabinet and comes up close to Levi. 'Beef,' he whispers, patting him down lazily and stinking of smoke, 'I've had word to take you to see our friend again.'

Levi's heart sinks but he puts on his soldier face and flexes, nods slow. 'Bring it.'

'They say you've to fucking take him to the edge. But don't get all gangster. Don't spoil it for fucking everybody.'

Crawshaw pushes him out of the door and together they slope back to the wing. Everyone else is locked down and as they walk along the fire road between the wings, they get abuse and whistles and catcalls. Levi puts an extra roll to his walk, buffs up his chest and gives his sign when he passes the pads of his soldiers, who call out to him, 'Beef'! It makes him look big, but each day of bird he flies in here, he feels a little smaller. What can a man do, when all he's good for is being big and bringing hurt?

Fourteen

'Ahaa. Abie Myers revisits his past,' says Josie, watching the old boy amble from the parked Bentley towards the grandstand.

Flicking through the racecard, Staffe says, 'He's got a horse in the three-fifty – View From Above.'

'Not trained by Attilio Trapani?' says Josie.

'I'm afraid not.' He scans the rest of the meetings at the back of the racecard to see if Abie Myers has any other horses running today. 'He's got another, at Newmarket in a Group Two race. This one is a seller.'

'What language are you speaking?'

'He's come here with an outsider's chance of winning £1,300, rather than go to Newmarket to see probably the best horse he has got racing for a first prize of nearly £100,000.'

'It's not the money that matters, though, surely. Not for Abie, when he's just come into twenty million quid.'

'It's about the winning.' Staffe locks the car, parked up at the side of the Fox on the Downs pub, opposite Brighton's racecourse high above the town. You can see the sea, a smear of battleship grey today, and a hint of Europe. A steward on the door of the Prince Regent Suite actually bows as Abie and his minder pass.

Staffe punches a number into his phone as he and Josie join the scant midweek gathering. 'Fin?' Staffe keeps an eye on the balcony of the Prince Regent Suite, sees Abie's minder checking the place out. Finbar Hare answers and Staffe says, 'Abie Myers? How much of a player is he in the racing game these days?'

'Hang on.' The line clicks off and a few seconds later, Finbar Hare is back – Finbar Hare whose spread-betting firm sold out to a big boy five years ago, netting Fin a few million. 'Twenty-five horses in training, down from over sixty a few years back.'

'I don't suppose he's got any with Attilio Trapani.'

'Wait.'

Staffe borrows a brush from Josie and grooms his hair.

Finbar says, 'Myers has six horses with Trapani. All promising two-year-olds and switched there from Ransome's yard just a month or so back. There's bad feeling in the game against Trapani, so my boys say. For what it's worth, Abie's horses are a class above anything else in Trapani's yard. You in Brighton?'

'How do you know?'

'Seagulls. Who's the detective now? Abie's got one down there today. View From Above.'

'Do you fancy it?' The suede-head clocks him from the balcony.

'No.'

Staffe hangs up and buys a trilby and a tie from the Brockle-hurst stall, to which Josie says, 'Oh my, doesn't sir brush up mighty fine?' She hooks her arm through his and says, with a nod of the head and a pucker of the mouth, 'Shall we?'

In the bar upstairs, overlooking the winning post, Abie Myers is surrounded by a group of men in suits, binoculars festooned with racing badges, and on their arms pretty, younger women, with exceptional legs and cheekbones like wing mirrors. This is not-so-new money maintaining an ascendancy.

Abie's gang stand around a large wine barrel and drink from

flutes charged by two bottles of Veuve Clicquot. Someone toasts Carmelo Trapani and for a moment the laughter subsides and they nod, earnestly, chink glasses and slowly resume. Abie is centre of attention and his eyes are bright, his voice strong. When he speaks to the women, Abie places his thick-veined fingers on their arms and makes them smile even more brightly. Here, thinks Staffe, is a man absolutely in his element: at the centre of his world.

At three o'clock the gang drain their drinks and follow Abie to the parade ring. They laugh and joke as they go, any problems in the world reduced to a few known elements. Are the odds right? Is the horse being sent out to win? Are you on or are you not? All of which is not known to everyone on the track.

In the ring, the trainer, Ralph Hambro, a quintessence of the English country gentleman, introduces his jockey to Abie. The jockey is a young one and he removes his riding helmet, pats down his hair. As Abie whispers in his ear, Hambro looks away. The young jockey smiles – quickly covers it up.

Staffe and Josie take up a position in the stands and can see onto the balcony of Abie Myers' box. From the start, View From Above is settled in behind the front horse and for the first three furlongs the jockey has his work cut out in holding the horse up. 'He's got a double handful there,' says Staffe.

'What?' says Josie. 'Does that mean he's going to win?' She pulls out a ticket from her pocket. 'Look, a fiver at five to one.'

'He *should* wipe the floor with them.'

Entering the last furlong six lengths behind the leader, the jockey on View lets his reins out an inch or so and Abie Myers' horse accelerates, but the leader gets a slap down the shoulder from its jockey.

'Come on, View!' shouts Josie, her call drowned as the crowd thunders its encouragement for the favourite, which holds View From Above at bay all the way to the line. Five yards past the post, View From Above surges ahead. Too late. 'Damn! He should have won.'

'Should,' says Staffe, looking across to Abie Myers' box, where the gathered contingent isn't unduly downcast. 'That's a big word.'

'Abie will be pissed off.'

Staffe looks down at the ring as queues form to get paid out on the favourite. Down on the rails, where the big money moves, Abie's suede-headed heavy sidles up to Vinty Chamberlaine, one of the old school bookies. Vinty hands across a wad and shoots the sharpest knowing glance up to Abie's box, to say, 'I'll get you another day, you old bastard.'

Abie raises his flute an inch or so and smiles, then turns slowly around, in response to someone addressing him from behind: Maurice Greene.

Maurice shakes Abie by the hand as if they are business acquaintances, and within seconds the rest of the box empties, leaving the two beneficiaries of Carmelo's estate alone.

*

Maureen Pulford bows her head into the north wind on McIvor Street. She hasn't been out of the house in days and knows she shouldn't let things get her down, but since David went to work in London . . . That was six years ago, and before that he was at university and before that away at school. Just thinking about him makes her both joyous and sad. Maureen looks to the sky, sees the sun is lighting the thin edge of a cloud. It will soon break through.

As she walks, she calls, 'Simba!' but more in hope than anything. He has been gone three days now. In the fourteen years she has had him – to replace David when he won his scholarship to that wonderful school – Simba has never strayed more than twenty feet. She fears he has taken himself off somewhere. The vet said he had a cancer and was too old to operate on but he had at least a year left in him. 'Simba!' she calls, passing a large car that reverberates with deep bass music. She thinks it is hip-hop, which is unusual for round here. It's a decent area and mostly the young ones behave. The two men in the car pull their baseball caps down.

She turns left onto Salt Street and the sun breaks through. On the corner just before the police station, she fixes her tights and puffs her hair, takes a deep breath, not wanting to know.

Ray Greaves is on the desk. She hasn't seen Ray in a long while. When David first started talking about going into the police, it was Ray who Maureen asked to dissuade him. That failed.

When Ray sees her, his face drops. Perhaps he thinks she blames him for David going into the police, but she doesn't. Ray was a friend of Maureen's husband, Bill, and he was very kind to Maureen when Bill deserted her. Ray turned his back on Bill and for a while dropped in on Maureen. Once, when Ray came round, he said he had the day off and was going for a drive, just down to Seahouses and would she like to come? She said 'No' without thinking. She was only forty. She's fifty-two now and she thinks how young she was then, so young to be putting herself on a shelf.

Ray looks at Maureen as if he is about to break bad news and

106

she can't help herself. She bursts into tears and Ray rushes from behind his counter, wraps his arms around her.

'I'm so sorry,' says Ray. 'I should have come round.'

'I feel so alone,' she says to Ray.

'We're keeping an eye on you.'

Maureen looks up, says, 'You are?'

'I'm responsible, in a way.'

'That's ridiculous,' says Maureen.

'You came to me. You asked me to talk him out of it.'

'What's happened, Ray?' says Maureen, seeing something in his eyes, feeling deep in her heart that something is wrong. She clutches her stomach and Ray reaches for her. 'Is it David?' Even before Ray answers, she feels as if she will be sick.

'I'm so sorry, Mo. It looks as if there's going to be a trial.'

Which is when Maureen's legs give way and Ray Greaves stoops down to catch her.

Fifteen

Emma Thyssen-Wills, of whom there is only one on the electoral registers for the inner London boroughs, lives in Kensington and Chelsea. Specifically, she chose 5 Launceston Mews on the sweetest row you ever did see, just around the corner from Staffe's own place and worlds removed from the seamier spots in this great city. Outside number five, a yellow Porsche Boxster is parked on the cobbles.

As the handle turns, Staffe expects to see the jet-black hair, green eyes and porcelain skin that will turn heads in any street. But this evening, Emma holds a packet of Waitrose frozen peas to her eye and when she says, 'Hello,' she shows a broken tooth. 'Lacrosse,' she says, in explanation.

'Really?'

'I used to play county,' says Emma, stepping to one side, inviting Staffe to enter. 'I was just going to have a gin.' She removes the frozen peas to reveal a closed eye, puffed maroon. It looks like the satin cushion that rings are boxed in.

'Did Anthony tell you about the reading of the will?'

'Anthony? The bastard is what I call him now. Yes, the bastard told me the gist of it.'

'He's upset you?'

'He's sacked me, the bastard.' Emma cuts a curl of lemon zest with a paring knife, pops it in his gin and hands Staffe his drink, plonking herself heavily beside him on the sofa, crossing her legs.

'Carmelo was his main client, you see.'

'Surely he saw it coming, that Carmelo wouldn't last for ever.'

'That's why he feathered his nest with Attilio.' When she says 'Attilio' her voice cracks. 'Poor Attilio.'

'You like him?'

'I don't see why he was cut out of the will like that. From what I saw, he adored his father.'

'Tell me about Abie Myers.'

Emma takes a sip of her gin, grimaces and looks at her watch. 'I have to go to the dentist. It's a friend of my father's and he's fitting me in after his last patient. I'm sorry, a girl has got to put her looks first.' She beams a broad smile and shows her broken tooth.

'You do know Abie, don't you, Emma?' says Staffe.

Her smile goes out, like a slap.

'I think you probably know him rather well.'

Emma prods the little cut on her lip with the end of her tongue.

'How did you really come to have a broken tooth?'

'I'm a bright girl. I'm not such a fool as to ignore the fact that this' – she points to her face – 'is my best asset. It's what I call my gun.'

'Your gun?'

'And my brain is a kind word.'

'Aah,' says Staffe. 'A kind word will get you so far, but a kind word and a gun will get you further.'

They both laugh.

'But seriously,' says Staffe.

'Seriously! I have got a brain and it tells me not to say anything, except . . .'

'Go on,' urges Staffe.

Emma looks pensive and her meticulously crafted eyebrows

pinch together, as if calculating whether something might damage her. 'It's the servant they seem to be worried about.'

'Jacobo? What would Jacobo tell me?'

'Anthony said something about a secret to his father, Leon. No. Actually, he said, "the secret".'

'*The* secret?'

'I think maybe it's sometimes better not to find some things out.' She takes Staffe's untouched gin and tonic, drinks it in one.

'You should take it easy,' says Staffe. 'They'll be giving you an anaesthetic.'

'No, they won't. Didn't I tell you, inspector? I like the pain.'

*

Vanya Livorski's jaw drops an inch. Holding baby Gustav in the doorway of her flat, she gawps at Staffe's warrant card. Within, a smell of vinegar.

Staffe suspects the Livorskis' legality and is curious as to how the husband, Bogdan, makes ends meet. 'Don't worry,' he says. 'It's not what you think, but I need to see your husband, too.'

Vanya shakes her head, the way a guilty child would.

'I know he's here.' Staffe puts the middle knuckle of his index finger on baby Gustav's podgy cheek and rubs it, gently. Baby Gustav chortles. 'You're blessed, Vanya. Please let me in so we can all sit down and you can hear my good news.'

'What is it you want?'

'I'm here on Carmelo's behalf.'

Over her shoulder, Bogdan appears. He is not so tall but stocky and with a wide face. When he turns to close the kitchen door behind him, Staffe sees his head is flat at the back. Flat as a chopping board.

'He's been kind to us. Very kind,' says Vanya.

'We have our papers. We're legal,' says Bogdan.

'Is Mister Trapani all right?' says Vanya. 'He is a very kind man.'

'I'm afraid he is not all right.' Staffe keeps his eyes on Bogdan as he says it. Vanya is scared of life, but Bogdan is scared of something very particular. 'When was the last time you saw him? We'll have to check it out, so there's no point telling me lies.'

'I heard you from the kitchen,' says Bogdan. 'You said there was good news. This doesn't sound like good news.'

'Can I come in?'

Bogdan says something in Polish and Vanya nods, quickly, like a child accepting a punishment, and Bogdan leads them through one of four doors in the flat into a small lounge-diner, no more than twelve by twelve. They have a nice TV and the place is kitted out with good stuff – courtesy of Carmelo, perhaps. In the corner, a low table has a wooden crucifix on it and a figurine of the Virgin. Church candles flicker and on the wall above, a picture of the Pietà taken from a book.

'How did you come to know Carmelo?'

'What makes you think we know him?' says Bogdan.

'You're choosing to lie to me, Mister Livorski. Carmelo has left you a large sum of money in his will, so I know you know him. And now I also know you have something to hide.'

'A *lot* of money?' says Bogdan.

'When was the last time you saw him?'

'A few days ago,' says Vanya. 'He liked to come to see Gustav.' She strokes the baby's downy head. 'He wished he had a grandson of his own. Carmelo *is* all right. You said something about a will.'

'What day?'

'It was a Tuesday. He always came on a Tuesday.'

'Aaah.' Staffe goes to Vanya. Down on his haunches, he takes a hold of both her hands. 'He is missing. He went missing last Tuesday.'

Bogdan says, 'A large sum of money?'

'If he is dead, you inherit four hundred thousand pounds.'

'My God! That's too much.'

'It's far too much,' says Bogdan, with meaning.

'Tell me everything about that last visit of his.'

Vanya looks across at her husband and seems on the verge of tears. 'My mother has never seen the baby. We didn't even tell her about the baby until he was born.' She clutches baby Gustav so tight Staffe fears the infant might not be able to breathe. 'We didn't dare hope he would survive. I still can't believe he won't be taken from us, and it's all because of Carmelo.'

'You really are in Carmelo's debt,' says Staffe.

Bogdan looks ashamed as Vanya tells Staffe precisely when Carmelo came and went on that Tuesday. When she is done, Vanya shows him out, down the narrow stairs that leads to the front door, sandwiched between AB Taxis and Kenny's Fried Chicken.

Vanya tugs at his sleeve, whispers, 'Bogdan is a good man. He is anxious because he can't believe that the harm in his life will not be visited on Gustav.'

'What harm?' Staffe enquires.

Vanya looks anxiously back up the stairs, lowers her voice even more. 'His father was a doctor, but they didn't like what he said. I tell Bogdan it's a different world now.'

'What happened to his father?'

'They put him on the bins, as you say here.'

'A dustbin man?'

She nods. 'And Bogdan was training to be a doctor, too. He wanted to be a surgeon. He's an intelligent man with a good heart.'

'So why did you come to England?'

'His brother was sick. He has three nephews and a niece and they had no money.'

'He wanted to be a surgeon?' says Staffe. 'Lucky Carmelo, to have such a qualified man in his pay.'

Staffe strokes baby Gustav's head and says he hopes Vanya can take her son to visit his grandmother soon. 'You must,' he says, turning.

Opposite Bethnal Green's fine Edwardian tube station, just past the Beef and Salmon pub, Staffe can make out the tower of the Limekiln Estate and he makes an adjustment to his day, decides to call on another mother.

Sixteen

Jasmine Cash holds Millie tight. The little girl is in nursery now, but Jasmine cuddles her like she would a baby. She looks at Staffe as if he is the enemy, even though he tried to put her Jadus on the straight and narrow and took two bullets for his troubles. She says, 'I've said everything to you.' As she talks, she puts a hand over Millie's ear.

'The last time you saw Jadus, was he back with the e.gang? You have nothing to lose by telling me – unless they're still looking after you, of course, which we could soon establish; and that would mean you're receiving, and that's not good.'

'Millie's dad was murdered. Even your own people think your sidekick killed him and you come asking me questions?'

Staffe looks at the fifty-inch TV. On the sideboard as he came in, he saw a set of keys for a Range Rover. 'The night Jadus shot me, he was scared. I looked into his eyes and he chose to pull a trigger twice. We were stood as close as you and I right now when he decided he wasn't going to be man enough to face the problems he made, for himself and for you and Millie. He took the coward's way.'

'That doesn't mean someone can take his life in revenge.'

'Jadus was scared that night and you know it. Had he become a liability? He wasn't bringing in, but he was still taking out. And he knew everything. He was a risk to the gang.'

'That's shit.'

'What about his bank-draft scam that backfired? Who's at the top, Jasmine?'

Jasmine looks at Millie, says, 'I need to put her down.'

'I don't think it's Shawne Haddaway. Is it Brandon Latymer?'

Jasmine turns her back on the question, takes Millie through to her bedroom and Staffe picks up the keys for the Range Rover, clocks the registration still written in the dealer's hand on the fob. When Jasmine returns, she says, 'I was told you couldn't come round here no more. Not with your sergeant friend going down.'

'He didn't do it. So, I have to do what I can for my sergeant, even though he is a friend. The person who killed Jadus is close to home. I think you know that, too.' He jangles the Range Rover's keys. 'This can't be the value of a man's life, can it? Or an innocent man's freedom?'

Millie yells out and Jasmine rushes through.

Staffe phones the registration details of the Range Rover to Jombaugh and opens the fridge; two bottles of vintage champagne in the door. When Jasmine comes back, he asks if he can use the bathroom, goes in and runs a tap. The bathroom cabinet reveals a combination of what a woman needs and what a child needs, and a little of what a man needs. Staffe removes the top from the shaving foam and sees the nozzle has an excess of fresh foam around it. He flushes the toilet, goes back in.

'I can see you'd need a man in your life, Jasmine.'

'You think I need a man? You're wrong.'

'I will find whatever I need to find, but I don't want to have to call on your mother over in Plaistow. I don't want to have to get Millie's teachers to call me whenever it's not you who picks her up. I don't want to dig up Jadus's past, find out where he was every

115

time he wasn't here.' He presses his phone for the text and reads the message from Jombaugh, holds it out so Jasmine can see that her Range Rover is registered to a Reuben Haddaway, Shawne's father. 'It was bought the week after Jadus was killed. Its MOT was paid for in cash at a garage in Bethnal Green just last week and the brake pads and rear wiper needed doing. It came to four hundred and thirty quid. Where did you get that cash, Jasmine? Give me ninety seconds with that garage man and he'll tell me you didn't pay for that service. He'll tell me who did and they'll give me a convincing story about where the money came from – maybe the dogs. And I might not get so far, but pretty soon, you'll be more trouble than you're worth – just like Jadus was.'

'You used to be so kind to me.' Jasmine's voice cracks.

'You're hiding the man who killed Jadus.'

'He's on remand in Pentonville. His name is DS Pulford.'

'In that case, whatever you tell me will just help prove that.'

'All you care about is getting your man off the hook.'

'You'd better get someone to look after Millie.'

'She's only just gone down. You can't do this!'

'I'll have a WPC come for you. We'll probably have to detain you overnight.'

Jasmine and Staffe each look disappointed with the other. They always were quite fond, but Jadus did what he did and Staffe is what he is. No matter how hard you try, sometimes people are just too different. Staffe says, 'You can take a better road, Jasmine. No one will ever know it came from you. All I need is the name.' And he can tell by the way she sets her jaw that she is lost. 'You will be absolutely immune. I promise you.'

She crosses her arms and as she looks at him, her expression changes, slowly, until her eyes have narrowed and her lip has curled to the point where, indisputably, she hates him. Her decision is made.

On his way down the stairwell, he gets glimpses of the Attlee Estate, just a few hundred yards away.

He will call on Shawne Haddaway, see how he or his father paid for the Range Rover. Josie can check out the garage who MOT'd it. They will squeeze everyone around the e.gang, see what oozes out.

First, he waits for the WPC to collect Jasmine Cash, but twenty minutes later, he's still waiting so he calls Jombaugh to check where she is. Jombaugh's voice falters. 'They're not coming, Will. Pennington has said you've to lay off Jasmine Cash, says there's no way in the world he can let you question her in custody.'

'She could be harbouring the man who killed Golding. She could be about to send Pulford away, for God's sake.'

'You're going to have to find another way. And when you come in, he wants to see you.'

In the Limekiln's quadrangle, a gang of teenagers slouch in a circle, on their iPhones, but when they see Staffe, they galvanise, start moving. 'I'll be in later, Jom.' He clicks off.

The youths all wear baseball caps and their hoods pulled up and he recognises one from the visitor centre at Pentonville the other day. Staffe takes a deep breath, and walks up to the youth, his nerves twitching and his heart racing. Every now and again, he feels a flutter at the top of his stomach. With the young ones, you never know. They don't always know the score. He bends down, whispers to Louis, 'Got your name, Consadine. I've got your number, too.'

Louis looks afraid. His face is swollen, yellowing, and his mouth is cut and tender. He says, 'You're a fuckin' nutter, man.'

'Fuckin' muppet,' says one of the others.

They're all under age and full of themselves, valuable to their elders in the light of the reduced tariffs their crimes attract. Staffe looks in their eyes and sees what they've got to enable them to hurt him the most: no hope. But Louis, he looks like he might be able to glimpse a different life, a better outcome.

Staffe feels them watching him walk up to the Attlee. They follow him for a while and then he loses track of them, but as he enters the estate, a low-rise affair with brightly coloured fascias to the decks, he knows for sure he is being followed by someone. It gives him the shivers and he feels the eyes all the way up to Haddaway's floor. His heart pumps. Again, he is sure he can hear steps behind him but not a whole gang. Maybe just one person.

At the top of the stairs, he is short of breath and has a shooting pain in his chest, so he pauses. All he can hear, through the murmur of distant beats, is Louis and his mates laughing, far away. Then they stop and he makes his way along the concrete deck to Shawne Haddaway's place. The Attlee is dead quiet now.

Haddaway opens the door straight off. His eyes are heavy and his mouth hangs open. He smiles, clearly stoned, says, 'You the fuckin' pussy, man. Am I right?' He takes a step back and puts his hands down the front of his Sean Pauls, suggesting he might be carrying.

'Tell me about Jasmine Cash's Range Rover.'

'She's got fuckin' wheels, so fuckin' what?'

'We know you bought it for her.'

'You know shit.'

'She got it three days after Jadus was shot. Is that the price of silence these days?'

'Your sergeant fuckin' killed J. Fuckin' execution, man. You lucky there isn't more trouble on the streets.'

'I think it's time we brought you in. You want to call your brief?'

'Fuck off. You're not even supposed to be here. See, we know more than you think. We see the whole picture – like a map. Like Google fuckin' Earth.'

'That Range Rover of Jasmine's is ringed. Your boys have a history for ringing.'

'Come back when you *know* it's fuckin' ringed. Cos you know what? It's fuckin' not and if word's out you're harassing the friend of a man you executed, there'll be murders.' Shawne takes a step closer and beckons Staffe to him with a curl of the fingers of both hands. He has fat gold rings on every finger of his right hand. He smiles, sly, and looks past Staffe, who looks over his shoulder, sees the gang of boys from earlier: Louis, plus four.

Staffe's heart flutters fast and misses. A searing pain skewers his chest and he must grimace because the gang snigger. He wants to clutch his chest, but resists, and the four from behind close in on him. Haddaway says, 'Officer enters without warrant; we didn't fuckin' invite him in. He didn't show any ID. He coulda been anybody.'

'Stupid fucker comes without back-up.'

'I'm just asking about Jasmine's car.'

'He is a copper,' says Louis. 'Maybe we shouldn't—'

'Shouldn't what, Louis?' Haddaway goes up to Louis, hands behind his back. He's broader than Louis, and the back of his head is mapped with scars. Next to Haddaway, Louis is like an infant.

Louis lowers his voice, but Staffe can just hear him when he says, 'Just, maybe we should talk to Brandon before we do anything to a copper.'

119

'You fuckin' muppet.' Haddaway slaps Louis across the face with the back of his right hand and the big rings make four tramlines. Blood comes straight up to the surface of Louis's already broken face. Haddaway turns to Staffe. 'You still want me to come to the station?'

The pain shoots into Staffe's chest again and Haddaway takes a step closer. This time Staffe can't help himself. His head sags and he gulps for air, sinking to his knees.

Haddaway lays his hands on Staffe and pushes him backwards, puts his foot on his chest, presses down with all his weight.

'Leave him.'

'Who the fuck?' says Haddaway.

'Leave him,' says the man, again. And it is a man, not a boy. Staffe looks up from the floor. In the doorway, Abie Myers' suede-headed minder.

Haddaway moves back and Louis and his mates disperse. Abie's man holds a telescopic steel in one hand. His other hand is knuckle-dusted with large, angular rings. Staffe sits up, the pain abating.

'Mister Myers wants a word, lucky man.' He has perfect teeth and luminescent blue eyes. He turns to Haddaway and says, 'You help this gentleman to his feet.'

Haddaway thinks twice, evaluating his prospects. After a few seconds, he holds out a hand and Staffe takes it, pulls himself up and they stand chest to chest. One on one, he's not so sure if these days he could take Haddaway. On the way out, he says to himself, 'Brandon. Brandon. Brandon.'

Seventeen

The Cavendish would be easy to underestimate, hunkered down in one of the city's groins, off the Tottenham Court Road. The lighting is dim and Staffe glimpses a couple of women in long black dresses through a curtain beyond the small stage, but otherwise it's only men.

Abie's minder offers the cashier the name 'Miles Hennigan' and leads Staffe to where Abie is sitting in on a blackjack game. He folds. Looking at the players, you can't tell who is winning, which suggests to Staffe that these are serious hands.

'You seem to like your gambling,' says Abie. His eyes are cloudy but he has a kind face, with bushy brows and a strong jaw. He beckons Staffe, who draws up a chair.

'I don't dabble.'

'But you like to watch.' Abie taps his nose. 'Taking a View From Above.'

Staffe laughs. 'I'll wager it wins next time out. Not quite at the races today.'

Abie laughs. 'You have a job to do, inspector. I appreciate that, but if I can help in any way, I'd rather you asked me straight. I have nothing to hide.'

'There'll be some direct questions if Carmelo Trapani dies.'

'Carmelo will die, of course. As will I. Even you, inspector. I heard you were at the reading of the will. I wasn't invited. What do you make of that?' Abie looks around the table, raising his bushy brows. Within seconds, everyone in the hand folds, leaves the table – including the dealer. Abie lowers his voice. 'Carmelo's idea of a joke, is what it is.'

'It's a shame for poor Attilio. From what I can gather, he needs the money.'

'Poor Attilio doesn't need to worry. I know right from wrong.'

'You already have horses with him – but that's not enough to keep him above water.'

'I will say this once, inspector, because I am feeling generous. You can forget about casting aspersions on Attilio. Look closer to home.'

'Closer to Carmelo's home? Are you talking about Jacobo Sartori?'

'You catch on quick, inspector.'

'I can spot a secret when people clam up.'

'I didn't say anything about a secret,' says Abie Myers, his eyes narrowing.

'Do you want me to find Jacobo Sartori for you, Mister Myers?'

'I simply want my good friend Carmelo to be found.'

'Carmelo shifted his money around, these last few weeks – he knew something was going to happen.'

Abie Myers beckons Staffe closer. 'Me and Carmelo, we used to be tight, but this bequeathing came out of the blue. You shouldn't read anything into it and it certainly won't help you find him. I guarantee it.'

'He had a stake in one of your investment trusts and pulled out not so long ago. Then he leaves you all his money. So you understand why I come to you.'

'It was I who brought you here. Good job for you that I did.'

'Every time I dig into Carmelo's past, something stops me. Attilio is tight-lipped, which I can understand. Jacobo is gone. No wives. Not even Esther.'

Abie Myers' eyes darken. 'You've no business bringing my wife into this, inspector. Watch your step.'

'Where is she, Abie?'

'The honest truth? I don't know. She left the house forty years ago without saying a word. She didn't take a penny, or even so much as a toothbrush. Once, a couple of years after, she let me know she was safe. I pray for her every day. Now, Jacobo Sartori, inspector – he's the one you need, don't doubt it.'

Abie Myers stands, stiff-limbed, but he somehow cuts an imposing figure. As he walks slowly across the casino, people turn, smile benignly, and one of the women comes from behind the curtain, skirts around the stage to take his arm, lead him into a room.

Miles Hennigan reappears, says to Staffe, 'I'll show you out.' At the door, he says, 'Try Brighton.'

'To find Jacobo?' says Staffe, turning.

But Miles closes the door, smiles through the glass as if he knows something the inspector doesn't, and something in the empty, mercenary eyes that accompany his smile gives Staffe the chills.

*

Staffe walks through Bloomsbury's tidy Georgian squares into studiously dishevelled Clerkenwell. When he reaches Leadengate, he asks Jombaugh to send Brighton and Hove CID a copy of the photograph of Jacobo Sartori.

As soon as he gets to his office, he puts a hand to his heart, feels the memory of what happened on the Attlee and he calls Janine up at City Royal, to see if there is someone she knows who can give him a quick once-over.

'What's happened, Will?'

'Nothing.'

'Is it your wounds again?'

'No. Just a pain I had.'

'In your chest?'

'I don't want a fuss.'

Janine says she will make a call. A friend of hers is a chest specialist and she thinks he is working tonight.

'Thanks, but keep this to yourself.' He hangs up, looks out on the quiet city and feels his way along the threads Carmelo Trapani has left for him to weave.

Ever since he disappeared, the old man has been whispering into the void he left behind: shifting his money and squeezing out Attilio; deserting Anthony Goldman and urging him on in the direction of Abie Myers. And now, all points seem to want to lead him to Jacobo Sartori.

But are Abie and Jacobo in cahoots, sending him on a goose chase? And what of the long-missing Esther Myers, never actually reported missing?

Rimmer is in the incident room, tapping away at his computer keyboard. His desk is clear and he sits with his back to the window. They are the only ones in.

'Where is everyone?' says Staffe.

'There's a black alert. Some trouble up Hackney.'

'Damn.' Staffe knows that any tension on the streets will be bad for Pulford. Over Rimmer's shoulder, the City's glass peaks twinkle in the night.

He needs to get on with the business of tracking down Brandon Latymer, but also needs to get to Brighton, and to try to find Esther Myers. He says to Rimmer, 'We really could do with tracking down Abie Myers' wife. She left him forty years ago.'

'I know. You're not sending me off on a wild-goose chase, are you, Staffe?'

'If I was, would I tell you?' he laughs, but he feels a stitch, puts his hand to his chest.

'You all right, Staffe?'

'I'm fine.' He grimaces. 'I just need to prioritise. Pulford is innocent and I can't do everything. Your loyalties are in the right place, aren't they, Rimmer?'

'There is a bigger picture here.'

'No, there's not,' says Staffe, leaving. In the corridor, he sees Josie coming out of his office and she says, 'Your phone was going. It's Janine up at City Royal. She says you've to see a Doctor Wellbeck at ten tonight. What's going on, sir?'

'Nothing. Call her back and say I can't make it.'

'What are you seeing a doctor about?'

'Tell me about Brandon. That lad Louis Consadine mentioned his name tonight.'

'You're not supposed to—'

'Just tell me!'

'There's nothing to tell. Like I said to you before, he's clean. We've no live connections to him. He's like a ghost.'

'Yet Pulford was on his case. He was calling him. Do you still have a key to Pulford's place?'

Josie nods.

'Come on, let's go over there.'

'You should see that doctor.' Josie looks at him disapprovingly.

'I can go to Pulford's on my own.'

Rimmer pokes his head into the corridor, calls to Staffe, 'You'd better come in. Smet's just sent something over from the Met. They've got a CCTV match on Carmelo's car from the night he was taken.'

Staffe and Josie go into Rimmer's office and the three of them look at the screen, watch the Daimler pull up to a set of lights. Text in the top right tells them it is Brompton Road, looking east. The image in the car is vague and the driver wears a hat and a big coat. A figure sits in the back and the driver turns to talk to the passenger.

'They're travelling west out of London. The way I'd go home if I lived in Ockingham,' says Rimmer. 'But wait.' He clicks the mouse twice and brings up a new image of the same car at a set of lights. 'Tibbets Corner,' says the text. 'Facing West.'

This time, they see into the rear of the car. There is no glare on the rear window now and the image is clear enough for them all to say, as one, 'Carmelo Trapani.'

'What time was this?' says Staffe.

'Six minutes past ten,' says Rimmer. 'And he's still alive. They didn't kill him at Beauvoir Place.'

'They're taking him somewhere to persuade him to do something,' says Staffe.

'Or dissuade him from doing something,' says Josie. 'Maybe the money he was moving around?'

'Who the hell's driving?' says Rimmer.

'You can't tell.'

'Send it to the techies.'

'We should pay Attilio another visit, though,' says Staffe. 'Carmelo's car was going that way.'

126

'I'll do it. I'm on that track,' says Rimmer.

Staffe turns to Josie, winks at her and says to Rimmer, 'Can we do it together? You take the lead, naturally.'

Rimmer looks bemused, and more than a little delighted. As they leave, Josie whispers, 'I'll do Pulford's place.'

'Look for anything at all to do with the e.gang, and especially Brandon Latymer,' says Staffe, and for some reason, he is suddenly touched by the realisation that evidence can incriminate, as well as redeem.

Eighteen

Ockingham Manor appears to have retired early for the evening, with just a solitary orange glow from an upstairs room. There are three cars in the driveway: Attilio's Range Rover Sport, a workhorse Land Cruiser and a yellow Porsche Boxster that Staffe recognises.

Rimmer parks up and says, 'Looks like they're in bed.'

'I don't doubt it,' says Staffe. 'How do you want to play this?'

'We'll talk to Attilio and Helena separately, to start with.'

'You'll be lucky.'

'We'll do this my way. We agreed.' Rimmer rings the bell and they wait a while before Attilio opens up, saying, 'What the hell do you think you are up to, calling unannounced at this hour?'

'We have new information relating to your father,' says Rimmer. 'I would like to talk to you. And DI Wagstaffe here will ask your wife a few questions, too.'

'He won't.'

'I'm afraid I insist,' says Rimmer.

'She's not here,' says Staffe. 'But we still need to talk about the night your father was taken.'

'I was entertaining friends. You know that.'

'Your father was still alive when you were entertaining your friends,' says Rimmer.

'How do you know he is still alive?' says Attilio, standing to one side, showing the two policeman in, watching Staffe as he clocks a pair of slingback shoes in the doorway to the drawing room.

'We didn't say he *is* still alive. We said he was alive that night.'

'After the reading of the will, surely you can't think I had anything to do with my father's abduction? I had nothing to gain.'

'Money isn't the only motive,' says Rimmer.

'It's late to be doing your books,' says Staffe.

'What?' says Rimmer.

'Goldman and Son provide quite a service.'

'Emma!' Attilio calls, up the stairs. 'When you've reconciled the balance sheet, you can go.'

Staffe says, 'Will Abie Myers be pushing a bit more your way now he stands to benefit so?'

'We have a small string of his horses. That's all,' says Attilio.

Rimmer takes out a notebook, says, 'I have some questions.'

'I'll wait here,' says Staffe, watching Rimmer follow Attilio into the drawing room.

Within a couple of minutes, Emma Thyssen-Wills appears at the top of the wood-panelled staircase. Her hair is dishevelled and she pads down the stairs barefooted even though she is wearing a cocktail dress that shows her fine legs off to their full. When she is near, Staffe says, 'I thought Anthony Goldman had released you.'

'Don't be clever, it doesn't suit. Let's go in the kitchen.' Up close, her bruising has subsided a little and her tooth has been capped. There are pinpricks of perspiration above her broken top lip.

'Dark horse,' he says.

'I've had a rough ride. He's a kind man and I can help him. There's nothing to this. Nothing at all.'

'The rough ride?' says Staffe. 'That wasn't him?'

129

'Attilio couldn't hurt a fly.'

'Your life hasn't exactly improved since his father disappeared.'

Emma touches the broken skin of her lip with the tip of her tongue.

Staffe looks at her attaché case, says, 'Attilio can't look after you, but I can, and that's a promise.'

'I don't need protecting. But I am very fond of Carmelo. He has a good heart.' She opens her small case and pulls out two sheets of A4. 'This didn't come from me,' she says, handing him the sheets. 'A balance sheet only paints a picture of a given day. With the Trapanis, you need a grasp of history. It all goes way back, and believe me, there are far too many given days for me to ever understand them.'

Staffe reads through the summary of Ockingham Stud's assets and liabilities, then its management accounts for the last quarter. The company is just about solvent, thanks to a handsome profit in the last month. Training fees were heavily reliant on Fahd Jahmood, but projections for the next quarter show these to be reduced to nil. This, however, is more than balanced by a vast increase in training income from Abie Myers.

In the balance sheet, the capital value of the stud attracts an accountant's note, referring to a contracted sale of the Ockingham Stud to Blackfriars Holdings, just weeks ago, resulting in an increased valuation from £750,000 to £2.75 million. Without this, the company would have lost two million pounds.

Staffe says, 'Blackfriars. I can find out with a few searches – but would you just save me half a day?'

'As a taxpayer, shouldn't I want to see you putting your back into this investigation, inspector?' Her eyes crinkle.

'You want to improve the odds of me finding Carmelo alive?'

She nods.

'I bet Blackfriars Holdings is owned by Abraham Myers' trust.'

'Save yourself a morning at Companies House. It's Abie, all right. You've got my back, haven't you?'

'Do I need to?'

'What do you think?'

Rimmer comes into the kitchen, says, 'I'm done.'

'I'd like a word with Attilio.'

'Pennington said this is my lead. I don't want you undermining my authority. Now, let's go.'

Outside, on the Ockingham gravel, Staffe says, 'Was Carmelo brought here the night he died?'

'No.' Rimmer's jaw is set.

'I'd still like to talk to Attilio.'

'No!'

Staffe steps back, says, 'Are you all right, Rimmer?'

'Can't you call me Frank? Can't you treat me as an equal, for crying out loud?'

'Did he give you the impression his father came here that night?'

'He did everything to give me the opposite impression. But Fahd Jahmood was here. We'll ask him.'

'You think you can get Jahmood to talk?'

'I'm pretty sure he's been having an affair with Attilio's wife, Helena.'

'What! How the hell do you know that?'

'I fancy a pint. There's a pub down the road called the Crooked Billet.'

'It's almost closing,' says Staffe.

'I took the trouble to befriend the landlord. He has no time for the new lord of the manor and a few whiskies down the line, his tongue loosened up. We're good for a late one.'

'Oh my, Frank.'

'And you can tell me all about Ms Thyssen-Wills.'

*

Josie hasn't been in Pulford's flat since they remanded him for the murder of Jadus Golding. No one at Leadengate, Pennington included, had seriously considered the possibility of Pulford not getting bail, but they got that idiot Judge Hislop who had clearly got a call from the Home Office. A young black man dead, a policeman suspected, an election round the corner.

Pulford was on the ragged edge when Josie came here that last time. He had a stack of papers on his table. If only she knew where they are now, they might tell her who Pulford was trailing in those weeks before Jadus was murdered, but as she begins to take the flat to pieces, yard of carpet by length of floorboard, she prays it doesn't lead her all the way back here.

Josie moves up to the loft, accessed from the bathroom. It is hot and the small fibres from the insulation prick her skin. She works along the joists, checking in boxes and lifting up the insulation to see if anything is hidden, but finds only a few bundles of essays from university and Hendon.

She sits on the edge of the loft hatch and looks down onto the old-fashioned Victorian toilet with its high cistern. The floorboards are stripped and all the nails are undisturbed. The only place he could hide something down there would be in the cistern, so she eases herself down, feeling for the chair with her pointed toe. It reminds her of doing ballet. She used to love those Saturday mornings, before her mother became ill; before she realised what a bastard her father was.

Josie lifts the lid, surprised how clean it is. She feels sad, thinking how Pulford must have done his housework, how happy he was to get this place after his struggle against the demons of gambling. Peering into the cistern, there is nothing inside, so she replaces the lid, climbs down and braces herself for the worst part, reaching into the toilet. She runs her index and middle fingers under the rim of the bowl, where the water feeds. It is dry, unsurprisingly, and she scrubs her hands vigorously in Pulford's lime-scaled basin.

While she is here, she may as well have a pee, so she takes a seat and looks out into the hall. She dabs, pulls up her pants and straightens her skirt, then flushes and returns to the basin to wash her hands again. Leaving the bathroom, something seems absent, but she can't tell what it is.

Josie peers down the hallway. Pulford's bedroom is one way, the open-plan living room the other. It is so tidy compared to the last time she was here. He was such a mess, yet it is pristine now. Then it strikes her. The flat is silent, totally silent.

There is no watery hum from the flush being pulled and she looks back at his toilet, returns to pull the chain a second time; then a third, just the faintest trickle of water coming through where her fingers had been. Yet the cistern had been full before. She climbs back on the chair, steadying herself by gripping the long pipe that serves the toilet from the cistern. Sure enough, the cistern is full. The pipe, clearly, is obstructed and now she sees where the join in the pipe is discoloured. A canny place to stuff something you want secreted.

Nineteen

Josie unfurls the papers which Pulford had rolled tightly, wrapped in cling film and then taped up in a bin liner and stuffed into the downpipe to his toilet.

The photocopies of the forensic reports are here, proving the gun which fired the bullet killing Jadus Golding had also been used to discharge two rounds into Staffe. There are also accounts of the meetings with Shawne Haddaway and Brandon Latymer who each have stonewall alibis, having been at a rap concert in Manchester the night of Jadus's murder. And there is a copy of the official interview with Louis Consadine, a juvenile. 'Louis,' says Josie, to herself. Louis, of whom Pulford wrote in the margin: 'dodgy alibi' and 'check brother. Curtis.'

Amongst the papers is a photograph of Brandon, taken on a telephoto lens, judging from the depth of field. Brandon is leaning against his Cherokee Jeep and with him is a woman Josie last met in the City Royal morgue, Jasmine Cash. Jasmine and Brandon are embracing – to put it politely. Jasmine, the grieving mother of Jadus Golding's daughter, seemingly happy in the clutch of Jadus's friend and associate.

Lastly, there is a handwritten printout of times and locations, headed 'BL Tracker', which appears to describe the precise movements of Latymer for a week: from the evening before Jadus's murder until the day before Pulford was arrested on suspicion of Golding's murder. Josie knows for a fact that Pulford had neither sought nor obtained official sanction for the use of such a device.

She calls Staffe. Judging by the choral music in the background, he is in Rimmer's car. 'Pulford was on Brandon Latymer's case. I've found the forensics report, a photograph of Brandon with Jasmine Cash—'

'Are you sure?'

'Absolutely, and there's an unauthorised tracker on Brandon – from before Jadus Golding was murdered and after, too.'

'That could be good. Or not,' says Staffe.

'You mean he could have been baiting Brandon Latymer to get to Jadus.'

'You can imagine what Latymer's lawyer would say.'

'And Louis Consadine was on his radar. Seems Pulford thought his alibi for the night Jadus was killed wasn't quite waterproof.'

Josie picks up the photo of Brandon with Jasmine Cash, examines its back. 'The photo of the best mate and the widow was printed at Jessops on Tottenham Court Road, three days before Jadus was killed.'

'So they were already together before Jadus was killed.'

'And Pulford mentions Louis's brother. I didn't know he had a brother. Curtis. What do we do with it all, sir? We're going to have to show it to Pennington sooner or later.'

'There's some due diligence first.' He lowers his voice. 'Before we go putting the wind up the DCI.'

He sounds distant, kind of lost, and Josie wishes he was here, so they could work it out together.

Staffe turns away from Rimmer, shields the phone, says, 'Look after yourself, Josie.' He hangs up and watches the road ahead shift, Rimmer's headlights panning across the Crooked Billet, with ivy growing up its half-timbered frontage. They pull into the car park, past a clutch of smoking locals who give them the evils as they park up.

Rimmer introduces Staffe to Rodney, who clearly has mixed feelings about seeing Rimmer again, having had his tongue so liberally loosened the last time, but as they sit down in the snug, Staffe senses that Rodney cannot resist a swelling of pride at being visited by not one, but two police inspectors.

Staffe looks across at the locals, coming in from a smoke, and after a while, says to Rodney, 'Would these chaps have been in, the night Carmelo disappeared?'

'Bilbo's in every night, and Fran is a brainiac. It was quiz night.'

'And who is the other fellow?'

'Gavin's a lad at Trapani's yard.' Rodney looks at his diary. 'It was Epsom. Just down the road, so I'd say he was in.'

'I'll have a quick word, if that's all right.'

'Don't scare the horses,' quips Rodney.

Staffe explains to the three locals that he is up from London and investigating the disappearance of Attilio Trapani's father, and two of them look at him warily, but Fran, the mechanic, says, 'Has he got something to do with it, then, that arrogant bastard? I used to work on the estate, for Mister Ballantyne. Now he was a gentleman, but that eyetie, my godmothers!'

The other two stand up, ready their fags, and Fran says, 'Smoke?' jiggling his packet of Regals towards Staffe, and even though he doesn't, Staffe takes one, goes with them.

The door is on the crest of a bend in the road. Staffe draws on his Regal and they all watch a car as it slows, changing gear for the bend. The locals raise their hands to salute the driver.

'Fuckin' Mitch. Dirty bastard, still slipping Slowcombe's wife while he's away,' says Gavin, the lad.

'Can't blame him,' says Bilbo.

'You work with cars,' Staffe says to Fran.

'Who's told you that?'

Staffe nods down to Fran's oily fingers, the nails stained black as boot polish. 'I saw a Boxster in the drive just now,' says Staffe, scathingly.

'That'd be that piece he's been seeing,' says Bilbo.

'The accountant woman,' says Gavin.

Gavin, the lad, stubs out his cigarette and says, 'I'm off.' He drunkenly climbs a stile on the other side of the entrance to the car park, stumbling down, and staggers into the night.

'He's gone off without his bike, again,' says Fran, nodding to an old butcher's bike leaning against the wall. They stub their fags underfoot and go back inside.

When Staffe sits back down, Rimmer says, 'We need to find out why Fahd Jahmood really withdrew his horses from Attilio Trapani's yard.'

Staffe's thoughts turn to Brighton and the past. He slaps Rimmer on his shoulder and says, 'Good man.' Rodney beckons them to the bar with the wiggle of a fine bottle of malt and Rimmer goes across. Staffe watches from afar, nods his agreement when Rimmer suggests they stay the night.

Twenty

Staffe rises before six. He is in a tiny guest room in the eaves of the Crooked Billet and the rising sun slants in through the Velux window. He has a quick wash, climbs quickly into his clothes and sneaks down the stairs, hearing Rimmer snore through the walls of the neighbouring room. Rodney's dog yaps twice, but Staffe lets himself out into the yard, gets Gavin the Lad's bike and pedals down Tippets Lane to the Ockingham gallops. Attilio and his small staff make silhouettes on the folded outlines of the gentle Surrey hills.

Attilio directs affairs and Staffe waits for the last piece of work to be done. Judging from the way the last horse's work is watched intently by everyone, this must be Gemstone – the jewel in Attilio's string and owned by Abie Myers. Slowly, the string is taken back to the yard. The morning has become brilliant.

'I've told you and your damned colleague everything I know,' barks Attilio as he hacks past Staffe. The horse's sweat is sweet and deep. Staffe freewheels through the dew in Attilio's wake and Attilio pulls up, looking down on Staffe. 'What do you want?'

'I can see you're upset, but I just wanted to say—' Staffe waits as Attilio's hack rears up. Attilio calms the horse expertly and the string gets further away 'You can't escape what you don't say; what you don't do. I only realised after my father died, all the things he did for me. The duty he paid. He was a different man to what he wanted to be, and I never thanked him for being a father. The best he could be.'

Attilio dismounts. 'Don't try to trick me.'

'I left too much unsaid. When my father was suddenly not there any more, I was angry with myself.'

'I haven't even said goodbye to him,' says Attilio. He leans with his back to a large yew tree. 'There are things about my father I will never know. Carmelo is the last of the line. His story will disappear with him.'

'And then you will be last of the line.'

Attilio shakes his head. 'I was never going to be that. You were there, at the reading of the will. Unacknowledged, that's what I am.'

'He changed his will very close to the end. You could challenge it.'

'Oh no, I couldn't do that. You have to let an old man go the way he wants to go. There is something called honour. This is a matter of doing the right thing. You won't find me digging it all over.'

'Digging it all over?' Staffe thinks this a strange phrase.

'Digging. That's what you do.'

'I'm digging into Jacobo but not getting anywhere. I have to consider the possibility that he was involved in your father's abduction.'

'As another victim, you mean?'

'Or otherwise.'

'Jacobo is fiercely loyal to my father – in a way I have never understood.' Attilio watches his string come round a last time and head back to the training yard, led by Helena now. She looks daggers at them. 'He was always around, when my father was not. Jacobo and Appolina were like a mother and father to me.'

'Why might Abie Myers think Jacobo is responsible for what happened to your father?'

'I can't believe he would say such a thing, and I won't speculate.'

Attilio continues to watch Helena.

'You're reliant on Abie now. Is that what your father wanted?'

'How am I reliant upon Abie Myers?'

'I know about Blackfriars Holdings and the deal with the estate. Abie's saved your bacon. And Helena's.'

'That was a good deal for everybody. Now, if you're finished—'

'What about Maurice? Your father obviously took quite a shine to him.'

'It would be easy for me to point a finger.'

'He has a foot in Abie's camp, too. I saw them at the races just the other day.'

'You can't drag me down that road. I will try to do the honourable thing; for the family and its name. I am under no illusion, I have to fight for my life.'

'Fight for your business, and your marriage, you mean?'

'My marriage has nothing to do with this, you hear.' Attilio remounts his hack. 'Nothing whatsoever.'

'How does Helena feel about selling out to new money?'

'We still have the house.'

'For how long?' says Staffe, watching Attilio kick his hack's quarters, and the steed accelerates away, hooves heavy in the ancient Surrey turf. Time was, Henry the Eighth came a-hunting in these parts.

The mist rises from the meadow between them and the manor, its Jacobean chimney stacks rising like something from a fairy tale.

This is the best time of day. The sun catches the dew on the football pitches and the fields are covered in vapour. The air is still and the shadow from the chapel's ugly spire is cast long and fine. The curses and threats are still between sheets.

Pulford rises at five-thirty each morning. He likes an hour to study and think. In this hour, he could be anywhere. Every other time in jail, even when he closes his eyes, there's nowhere else he might be.

He will run out of material if he doesn't slow down, so he rations this final article, chews long on the ideas and facts, digesting what Hutchison is saying about the Afghan and the Albanian gangs and how it was ever thus in the East End, when Jews and Italians, Turks and Jamaicans would join hands across all their oceans, in the name of organised crime.

All the time, in the back of his mind, the danger his mother is in taunts Pulford. It turns his stomach and fogs his thoughts. For hours every day he curls on the thin mattress and feels himself slowly churn. He should tell Staffe, but if the e.gang get word the police know, the danger she is in will escalate. He can't help imagining how she must have reacted to the killing of Simba. She bought the dog fourteen years ago as a puppy when Pulford had first left home to take up his scholarship at that school. Look at him now.

He reverts to a potted biography he is compiling of Charles Sabini, and he sifts through the footnotes, reading about Sabini's Brighton years when he passed under the name of Fred Handley – setting new standards for viciousness in the businesses of extortion and illegal gambling. He marks the text and makes an entry in his bibliography, then refers back to his notes from the article Staffe had brought in: 'Colour-blind Crooks'.

Someone is outside his door. In prison, your instinct for the abnormal is hypersensitive, so Pulford rapidly finishes his sentence, noting: 'The ethnic diversity, the social inclusiveness of crime in London today simply mirrors the halcyon period of pre-war gangland London.' He writes 'Melting Pot' just as the knock comes on the door. A thought occurs to him and he writes 'Carmelo? Age. Sabini.'

The knock is louder and accompanied by Mister Crawshaw's sneering welcome to the new day. He quickly puts his pile of papers away and watches the door open, sees Levi Salmon, large as a bear and smiling, stepping into his cell. Levi carries a tray. The door closes behind him and from outside, a key turns; the bolt shoots.

Levi Salmon has a gold tooth and shoulders wider than an armchair. 'You ought to keep your nut down, Pulford. And your mouth shut. So when your mom comes—'

'What!'

'My peeps in the north say she knows all about you now. Knows you're coming to trial. We keep an eye on her. We keep an eye just like the police up there. Who you think told the police up there to keep an eye on your mummy? Your uncle Ray? He's been tending her close. Tending *all* her needs, is what my soldiers tell me. How's that sound?'

'You bastard!' Pulford swings for Beef but the big man sways back, fast as a middleweight. Pulford lunges again, but Beef brings the tray up, catching Pulford on the chin. He yelps with pain, has bitten into his tongue, not all the way through but enough for the blood to sluice, and Pulford stops, tries to talk but it hurts too much.

Beef lets the tray fall to the floor, and as it clatters, Pulford sees what magic Beef might perform. In his right hand, he holds a paring knife, and he backs Pulford up to the wall. He puts the tip of the knife to Pulford's Adam's apple. 'Open your mouth.'

Pulford opens his mouth, closing his eyes.

'That's nasty, man. But anyone can see, they's teeth marks done that, you clumsy motherfucker.' Beef whistles and the bolt shoots. Crawshaw steps in, tosses the morning edition of *The News* onto his bed, folded open to a picture of hooded youths in Hackney. In the bottom right corner, a small, inset portrait of Jadus Golding.

*

The train picks out a high-hat rhythm as it chunters along the track. Staffe remembers the first time he made this trip, with his father and his sister, Marie, speeding through cuttings and along bridges over meandering rivers.

He flicks through a sample he lifted from Leon Goldman's vast memoir, looking for something on Brighton. The memoir jumps back and forth in time and the sections are arranged thematically, on the subjects of Heritage, Beginnings, Commerce, Heart, Hedon, Homeland and a final, incomplete collection of notes on Legacy. Martin Goldman hasn't compiled an index yet and Staffe has only brought the parts in which he saw mention of Carmelo on the quick flick-through – mainly from 'Hedon'. Goldman writes:

We would attend Brighton for racehorses and Hove for greyhounds, rendez-vousing the evening prior to laying final plans for the sojourn. The British Queen was our favoured establishment and the gathered throng would imbibe whisky and soda, save Carmelo, whose penchant was for pep with a shot of rum, in deference to his delicate stomach. In all our years as client and advisor, I was never aware of Carmelo visiting a doctor with his supposed ailment and I suspect he had an aversion to whisky. Grappa was his tipple of choice, but this wasn't available in the British Queen, where gin was considered exotica.

It was ever the case that the plans for the south coast trips would accommodate an evening in which Carmelo went unaccompanied. We all had our suspicions what this might involve. Carmelo's libido was certainly quite enviable for a man like myself, contentedly married and not endowed with the most handsome of faces. I envied Carmelo neither his wealth nor the power it wielded, but the regard he was afforded by the most beautiful, sought after and mischievous women, sometimes made me a little green.

We would always travel by train, reserving an entire first-class carriage. If Abie Myers was with us...

Staffe rereads this section, makes a pencil mark in the margin and folds down the top corner of the page.

...If Abie Myers was with us, we would smoke cigars. This began in the days before Castro, when Abie would return from his voyages, renewing investments in Cuba, with the tallest tales of the Cuban women and the music, and, of course, a box of Cohibas. In summer, we would gravitate towards the Regency and partake of oysters and lobster, before retiring to the casino. There would be the same complexion of people in the casino as at the course and the gambling would escalate. The winners from the course had money to reinvest. The losers had losses to recoup. In such circumstances, something has to yield, and invariably a confrontation would ensue. On one occasion...

Staffe rubs his temples. Goldman's archaic style is hard to bear but he conjures images of what it must have been like when Carmelo was in his pomp and first met Abie Myers.

He takes out the photograph of Jacobo Sartori and reverts to the text, seeking mention of Jacobo, but there is none. Even the most turgid memoir doesn't dwell on a manservant.

Staffe determines to visit the Regency and have the lobster, a taste Abie Myers perhaps acquired in Cuba, and Staffe thinks back to the journey he made around Carmelo's house in Beauvoir Place and the oil painting of the fishermen on the promenade. He knows what is depicted now. It is the Malecon in Havana, with the sea crashing high against the sea wall and the vintage American cars cruising by. Carmelo must have visited Cuba in the fifties, which puts him in a new league. He went with Abie Myers, which puts them in the same boat, from an early time, and he remembers what Emma Thyssen-Wills had said to him, about the Trapani history and too many given days.

Twenty-one

Inspector Wagstaffe has a good face, just as Appolina described, though his appearance is somewhat dishevelled. He has a face of burden, as his father used to say. Jacobo saw his father for the last time waving him off from the port at Trapani for a brave new start. He was a different person then.

Four days later, when he passed through customs at Tilbury, Jacobo was taken to one side by a policeman with a lop-sided face and informed that his father was dead. He asked the policeman if it was an execution and the man said he didn't know. Walking to the East End that day, he knew there was no way back. He had to become a man and put his past behind him.

Every now and again the inspector stops to regard his surroundings with a long gaze. Once they are on the seafront, it becomes clear that Wagstaffe is heading for the Regency where on any other given lunchtime it is where Jacobo might be found, in the window seat with his whitebait and a glass of Sangiovese. Better a bird in the trees than a duck, sitting. Clearly, the inspector's instincts are good.

It might serve Jacobo well to walk in there now, introduce himself and put himself utterly at the police's disposal. But he shan't do that whilst there is still a chance things might come his way.

The inspector takes a tucked-away seat, from where he can see everything in the place. He orders lobster which he eats expertly, and at leisure. As he slowly chews, he reads from a pile of loose papers on the table.

When the waiter clears the table, the inspector engages him in conversation, shows him something that he takes from his inside pocket – presumably a photograph of Jacobo. He wonders if it is the one of him by the bandstand. The inspector would have asked Appolina where Jacobo is likely to be and she will have told him nothing. Always, she has known nothing, and he hopes that is sufficient to assure her safety. Looking briefly away, he sees the bandstand.

After a little more than an hour, the inspector pays and in the doorway, leaving, he receives a call.

Jacobo knows that if the inspector knew to come to the Regency, then he will probably find his way to the dog track, and later to the Rendezvous. But if they knew the inspector was coming, they would know that by watching the inspector they may find him. Jacobo is easing that process, so he walks into the Lanes, winding and narrow where you can easily lose yourself.

He knows he can catch up with the inspector later, by conforming to old habits, old places: the Lord Nelson, Hove dogs, the Burlington tea rooms, or even the Rendezvous. Lost now in the Lanes, Jacobo wonders how Maurice is faring. He looks in an old jewellery shop, Fraenkel and Son. Old man Fraenkel was their fence, those years ago. He looks and he sees himself amongst the pearls and stones, half-sees and half-imagines a pale outline of Maurice's grandfather and old times. Poor Maurice.

*

Josie traces her finger along the mapped landmarks on the enlarged street map of the East End. She has charted all the points Brandon Latymer made on Pulford's unauthorised tracker and, sitting in Hoxton Square, she waits, poised to follow his Cherokee Jeep. He's behind his routine so she calls Staffe, listens to him wax about Brighton. It's a lovely day, apparently. She says, 'Well, I'm hoping it just got a little lovelier.' Brandon's Jeep enters the square, passing the White Cube. 'Brandon's head just poked above the parapet.' She can't see beyond the smoked windows but it is definitely him. Her blood pumps and she moves in behind him as they process out of the square, driving east. 'I think I know where he's going, sir.'

'Where?'

'The Limekiln.'

'Wait for me to get back.'

'I'll set up – in the flat we sorted,' she says. 'You know where I'll be.' She hangs up, calls into Leadengate and as soon as she sees Brandon's brake lights glow on the approach to the Limekiln, she veers away, parks underground down at Old Street and changes into her velour track suit. She makes a ponytail and pulls it through her Lakers cap, checks herself out in the mirror and calls the caretaker of the Limekiln Estate for the keys to the empty flat.

She walks back to the Limekiln with her iBuds in. Once inside the empty flat opposite Jasmine Cash's place, one floor up, Josie puts up the net curtains and seats herself at the window, prepared for a long haul.

*

The dogs come out, led towards the traps by their handlers. There is one in particular that appeals to Staffe, but he is distracted by the sound of Martin Goldman in his ear.

People often lie when they talk to police. Most often, it is down

148

to a fear of authority – not lying to conceal a guilt, rather to tell you what they think you want to know. Goldman is plain lying, though. 'My father is asleep, I can't disturb him. He's a frail man.'

Staffe says, 'It would really help the investigation if you could send me an electronic version of your father's memoir.'

'You're lucky to have the script at all. It's a personal document and cannot be relied upon, of course.'

'I'm enjoying it, but there is no timeline, and there are over a thousand pages. It's impossible to follow.'

'It's a first draft.'

'I think it could be published, you know,' says Staffe. 'These histories are important.'

'I will ask him when he wakes, but I think he might regret giving you the memoir in the first place.' Martin hangs up.

The dogs are being loaded into the traps now. His father took him to Wimbledon dogs where they would meet 'Uncle John'. Once, Uncle John had a beautiful woman with him, in a short skirt and with big hair. She was called Cynthia and fussed over young Will. His father said, 'Will's going to pick you a winner. Which one, Will?' His father's breath was sweet with drink.

Staffe knew from previous trips with his father and Uncle John to choose the dog led by the prettiest girl and he pointed to a girl he thought looked like Olivia Newton-John. Will loved Olivia Newton-John with all his young heart and his father and uncle guffawed and piled on the dog with big old fivers.

The dog won and everybody gave Will all their change. The beautiful woman kissed him and went 'hmm' as she did it, saying, 'You're going to break some hearts.' When they got home, his father said, 'Jangle for your mum,' and they all laughed. Will went to bed thinking that one day he would be just like Uncle

John and he wonders, now, why that didn't come to pass.

The starting bell rings for the race he came for. According to the *Racing Post*, the Trap Two dog, Dowager Dawn, should go off at 6-1. Now, it is 5-2. It is trained just up the road and owned by Greene, M. Though 'Greene' is by no means the uncommonest of names, Staffe reckons the 'M' is for Maurice. He works his way down to the rails as Dowager Dawn hardens even further, to 2-1. He puts fifty quid on and takes his ticket, says to the bookie, 'Is Maurice here?'

The bookie takes someone else's money and nods up to the restaurant above them. 'He loves this fuckin' dog. He's on big style.'

Staffe doesn't look up, but works his way through the throng of people huddling around the bookie stands. The air is thick with the smell of frying hot dogs and cigarette smoke.

The crowd soon thins to nothing in the old, rickety, iron-roofed stand, where the lights aren't even on. In the grandstand, the restaurant is brilliantly lit with its Tote girls and office out-ings. Beyond, the track has an ellipse of high lights, like badly strung pearls.

Staffe takes out his binoculars and pans up to the boxes. In the third along just one person stands at the front, his binoculars trained on Staffe. The two sets of lenses couple and Maurice Greene raises his arm, smiles broadly.

The gun goes off and the dogs power past, clattering the earth with dull paradiddles, tilting at an impossible camber and in an instant it is over. The dogs turn on the rabbit and a handler throws them a tatty rib of beef. The winner is fussed, put on a lead, and led away – by the prettiest handler of them all. Staffe looks at his ticket, which says 'Trap Five'. He looks up at Maurice Greene, who is glum.

Staffe picks up his winnings, courtesy of Trap Five, and as he hands across the twenty twenty-pound notes, the bookie smiles, from which Staffe gleans that had Maurice's Dowager Dawn come in, he would have taken a bit of a pasting. 'Have you seen Jacobo?' asks Staffe.

The bookie reaches past Staffe, pays out the man behind him, flashing a suspicious look and shaking his head without looking him in the eye. He shouts, 'Move along the bus if you're paid out,' and busies himself in his leather Gladstone bag of loose notes.

Staffe turns and wafts the wad in the air, in the direction of the boxes, not looking up, but knowing he is seen.

*

Josie takes a swig from her last can of Red Bull and readjusts the cushions on the dining chair she has set up by the window of the flat. It is dark now and the concrete decks of the Limekiln are lit here and there. Some windows glow behind drawn curtains and a compendium of urban music booms around the estate. On the decks, they hang out, in young, unsupervised huddles.

A man in a hood swaggers up from the stairwell, and Josie leans forward, the net curtain rough on her forehead, between her and the window. The man walks as if he has a limp, but with a defined rhythm. She can't be sure, but from CCTV footage she has seen, he has the hallmarks of Brandon Latymer. Sure enough, he doesn't break his stride until he knocks on the door to Jasmine Cash's flat. Within moments, Jasmine appears and he goes in. Josie sees them kiss – longer than friends.

As soon as the door closes on them, she calls Staffe. When he answers, she can hear he is in a crowd. 'Are you still at the dog track?'

'I'm just leaving. There's one more thing I have to do.'

'Brandon Latymer is on the Limekiln, sir.'

'Don't go near him. Wait for me.'

'But you're in Brighton and he's here now.'

'"Here?"'

'Brandon Latymer has called on Jasmine Cash. They kissed. He's in there now.'

'My God.'

'We need to take advantage of this, sir, but we don't want uniforms up here.'

'I'll come up as soon as I can and if he's staying the night, we can deal with it in the morning. If he's not staying the night, I can't get there anyway. Just promise me you'll stay put.'

'I could call Rimmer.'

'No! You mustn't call Rimmer. Promise me that.'

'Why?'

The phone goes quiet, then Staffe says, 'He's somewhere else tonight. Remember, we don't know exactly what Pulford was talking to Latymer about, and we haven't written up the new evidence from Pulford's flat yet. Just keep me posted, and stay put.'

She watches Staffe's name fizzle to nothing on her screen and finishes the Red Bull, refixing her attention on the door to Jasmine Cash's flat, but as Josie scans the Limekiln's concrete deck, she sees a tall, skinny, familiar youth with a skulking gait and badly bruised face. Louis Consadine pauses at Jasmine's door, gives it a couple of knocks and the door opens. Louis moves quickly inside.

Josie quickly puts on her Lakers cap and pulls her ponytail through. She folds down the waistband of her trackie bottoms and goes out. Weed hangs in the air and the estate is busier now than when she got here in the afternoon. As she works her way to the stairwell, she has to pass a group of girls. One of them pushes a thin-framed pushchair. They look her up and down with suspicion – as if she represents competition. One of them says something in a deep city patois and Josie readjusts her iBuds, which aren't receiving, and goes down the dark, empty stairwell, the way Louis came up.

She waits there, every sound amplified; every second feeling like a minute. She tries to look as if she is waiting for a dealer. A drunken man comes past, reeking of all-day pub. A woman in a Morrisons blouse with hooded, sad eyes struggles by and Louis comes out of Jasmine's place. He knocks into the woman with the sad eyes and helps pick up her shopping, saying he is sorry but he does it one-handed. All the time, his other hand stuck down his grey trainer bottoms.

When he is done, he looks up, sees Josie and walks towards her, tuning his walk into a swagger and looking at her breasts, quickly at her face, then away. He doesn't recognise her, so Josie says, 'I said I'd come see you, Louis.'

He double-takes, looks her up and down again and keeps the one hand down his trousers, stiffens his slouch into a hard-man's pose. 'And now you here.' He talks to the flesh between the waist-bands of her top and bottoms, still doesn't recognise her, so she takes a step closer, watches him flinch, then correct himself, and now he looks her in the face. He squints. 'Miss?'

'That's right,' says Josie. 'I've got a place here, now.'

He looks her up and down again. 'You live *here*.'

'That's right.'

Louis checks behind, concerned he might be caught with her. 'We should go there, Louis, if we're going to talk.'

'I don't want to talk.'

'It's best for you that we talk in my place and not out here. We don't want Brandon and Jasmine to hear.'

'Fuck!'

'And you need to tell me about your brother, Curtis.'

'The fuck?'

'Come on, Louis. I don't look like police tonight, do I? Nobody needs to know, just when we walk past those girls on my deck, just look like we're – you know.'

'Fuck, man,' says Louis, his hand moving inside his bottoms. And his expression changes, as if a penny is dropping. 'All right.'

They walk back past the group of girls and Josie puts an extra few degrees of shunt to the roll of her hips. At her empty place, she removes her cap, welcomes Louis into her world, but as he comes in, brushing past her, he seems to have discovered a proper swagger. He seems different, in control, and she realises he succumbed too easily.

Twenty-two

Staffe shaves at the pink basin with a one-blade scraper he bought from the all-night store on the corner. He draws his wet hair back and fashions a parting with his fingertips, picks up his phone and goes to the window of his hotel room, lifts the sash. The night is balmy and has salt on its sea breath.

He makes the call, fearful this could backfire. 'Jacobo is here,' he says. 'I'm damn sure of it. We're on.'

Although they have agreed a plan, Staffe is uneasy as he walks to the Rendezvous. When he gets to the casino, he pauses on the steps, is tempted to turn around, but resists. He feels eyes on him. It's what he wants, and he calls Josie, but she doesn't answer. He hopes that this is because she is sleeping, so he texts her to say he can't be contacted for at least two hours and he'll see her in the morning. He reiterates that she should lie low until he gets there.

Going inside, he makes the final call, gets a final thumbs-up, and at the desk, where members sign in, he sees himself again, on a monitor. The commissionaire is a handsome woman who shows him all her teeth. Looking over his shoulder, via the monitor, he sees an old man waiting in the doorway. Jacobo Sartori.

The main room is low-lit with a balcony running in a horse-shoe above the tables. Staffe sits at the bar, sees Maurice Greene playing blackjack on a mid-rollers' table. He chats to the croupier and bets casually, winning more than he loses. Staffe nurses a coffee, unable to tell if Maurice knows he is there.

He fixes a hard gaze onto Maurice, the way you can sometimes make a person feel they are being watched. It's something you can achieve beyond the five senses and, sure enough, when the hand finishes and the dealer pushes a teetering column of chips in Maurice's direction, the young fop turns and looks at Staffe who walks to Maurice's table and pulls up a chair alongside. Without turning, Maurice pushes across a small pile of low-denomination chips. They are playing a fiver a pop and Staffe takes his cards. 'Where's Jacobo, Maurice?'

'Jacobo?' says Maurice, raising his voice slightly. He turns, looks around the room and says, 'Jacobo?' again, so anybody keeping an eye on them might see what he is saying.

Staffe turns, too, but you can see little of the room beyond their immediate sphere of light. It's a place to be on the outside looking in.

'You seem intent on being with me tonight, inspector,' says Maurice, folding his cards. 'First the dog track . . .'

Staffe takes another card, raises, and Maurice folds. Staffe wins and the dealer pushes across a modest pile of chips. 'You're in the public domain.'

'And so are you. Haven't you considered that in following me, you might be being watched?'

In this instant, Staffe has an instinct – that Maurice is a force for good. He knows better than to trust these instincts and, lo, beyond the tables, a commotion erupts.

A glass smashes and a deeper rumble sounds as if a table might be overturned. A woman shrieks and Staffe turns to see a congress of bouncers slowly trundling through the room. Some punters turn to see, but most keep their eyes on their hands. This is not so unusual, when money and greed and defeat come together at the end of long days.

The house lights come up and a brace of men in overcoats, clearly not bouncers, accompany a frail, elderly gentleman. Staffe recognises one of them as Miles Hennigan. The old man is Jacobo Sartori, with his turned-up nose and big jowls. His hat is askew.

Maurice says, 'I fear you have been used, inspector.'

'I was lured here to bring Jacobo out, wasn't I?'

'He worked for Carmelo long enough to know that the best way not to be watched, is to watch.' Maurice looks Staffe in the eye and weighs him up. 'But you might have known that. Did you know that and come here anyway?'

'Let's go outside, see what's happening.' Staffe walks towards the door, in no particular hurry and he flashes his warrant card to the head doorman. He lets Maurice go first, to keep an eye on him.

Two squad cars point full beam at the Rendezvous's golden entrance. Four uniformed officers have a hold of suede-headed Miles and a police dog snaps at his legs. A WPC holds Jacobo Sartori's arm, the way an attentive niece might accompany an elderly uncle. His eyes are wide with excitement, flitting one way and then the other, possibly trying to calculate who presents the greater threat.

Alongside Jacobo, Rimmer smiles broadly at Staffe, who says to Maurice Greene, 'Don't you just love it when a plan comes together?'

'You expected this?'

'I'm sorry, Maurice. I think I like you.' He clasps a strong hand around Maurice's thin forearm. 'But you're going to have to come with us.'

'I admire your style,' says Maurice. He smiles, and shrugs, spins free of Staffe's clasp, taking a fast step back against the door of the Rendezvous and karate-kicking Staffe in the balls. As Staffe hunches double, Maurice brings down the full weight of his two small fists on the back of Staffe's neck.

Staffe's head whiplashes and he falls heavily to the ground, his face smashing into the flagstones. He watches Maurice's shoes, a high-end pair of side-buckled brogues, skip fast across the ground, deep into the dark.

*

Louis Consadine chain-smokes his L&B silvers. Josie can tell he is coming down from something and she says, 'If you help us, I'll make sure they can't touch you. And whatever it is you need, I can get it for you.'

'Fuck off.' He says it with a broken spirit.

'Brandon killed Jadus. You know that, don't you, Louis?'

Louis stubs his cigarette out on the cracked linoleum of the kitchen-diner. He avoids looking at Josie and fidgets with his pack of L&B. He has one left and chooses to save it.

'If you think they're going to protect you, Louis, you're wrong and if you don't help me, there'll be two squad cars round here in five minutes, and uniformed officers marching you past Jasmine's flat, with Brandon watching you go into custody. What's it going to be like for you then? And Curtis.'

'Curtis? What you talkin' about?'

'Curtis is involved, isn't he, Louis?'

'You don't know Curtis. He's not like me.'

'I asked around. He's just started Uni.'

Louis plunges his hand deeper into his trackie bottoms.

'They've all got alibis for the night Jadus was murdered. Yours isn't so good, is it?'

'I was with my girlfriend – in Margate.'

'Do you think she'll stand by you once you're remanded in custody and Brandon pays her a visit? Do you want Brandon to pay her a visit?'

'That fuckin' copper killed J.'

'You know he didn't. I know you know.'

Louis looks up at Josie, then at the door. His eyes go wide and Josie feels a chill in her stomach. Louis looks as if he's trying to work something out and his forehead crinkles, his tongue pokes out the corner of his mouth. She has backed the dog into the corner. 'Will you let me help you, Louis? I can help you and Curtis.'

'You're right. It wasn't that copper. It was me. I killed him, miss. I killed J.'

Louis Consadine pulls the Browning from his trackie bottoms. He looks at the gun and backs away from Josie, extending his arm. He looks at the gun in his hand as if it might damage him and he turns the gun ninety degrees, so it is horizontal, the way he has seen in films, and out on the silt flats of the estuary, past Tilbury, learning to use the thing.

'Louis, don't. Don't ruin your life.'

'You're the one ruining it. You should have let me be, but you didn't and now it's all fucked up.'

'You didn't kill Jadus, Louis. I know that.'

'I fuckin' did.'

'Where d'you get the gun from, Louis?'

'I fuckin' killed him, man. Brap! Brap!'

'Where did you shoot him, Louis?'

'Down the fuckin' canal.'

'Where in his body did you shoot him?'

'You know that.'

'But you don't, Louis. And how many times did you shoot him?'

Louis steps towards Josie. He reaches out with the gun and pushes it into her face. 'Open your mouth.'

'Please, Louis. I want to—'

'Open your fuckin' mouth, you bitch.'

Josie opens her mouth. She tastes the metal of the barrel and it bangs hard against her teeth. He pushes the barrel in further and she gags, convulsing, and the gun bangs into her teeth harder. With his other hand, he picks his last cigarette from the pack, puts it in his mouth and scrunches the pack, drops it to the floor, then lights the cigarette and blows smoke in her face. She closes her eyes, keeps them closed and breathes smoke in through her nose. The metal harshness of the gun withdraws. When she opens her eyes, Louis is further away, the gun by his side.

'I'm sorry,' he says, and he turns the gun around, holds it by the barrel and hands it to her.

Josie takes hold of the pistol butt, and together, they are each gripping it. Josie pulls the gun away from Louis, but he keeps hold of the barrel. She tugs again and he tugs back and they each look at Josie's hand, one finger on the trigger. Louis takes a long draw on his cigarette, holds the smoke in his mouth, the burning tip glowing red, then he blows into her face again and fast as a flash, plunges the glowing cigarette into the soft flesh of her hand.

Josie can't help herself. She clenches and the trigger snaps heavily. She waits for the bang, but it doesn't come and then pain sears into her hand. Louis pulls the gun away.

'Not fuckin' loaded, man.'

She wrings her hand, instinctively puts the soft flesh to her mouth, sucks on the burn as Louis walks away, letting himself out and taking the gun with him, her prints on it now.

Twenty-three

Leadengate's strip lights buzz in the bleary night and the coffee machine gurgles. Far away, a photocopier whirrs.

Staffe issues his instructions to the uniforms and SOCOs for the exercise of warrants at Maurice Greene's flat, both Abie Myers' houses, Ockingham Manor and Jacobo Sartori's house. Uniformed officers will simultaneously enter each of the premises, and the SOCOs will work in two teams, taking Greene's place and Abie's Stepney Green house first. Staffe tells Josie to call on Appolina Sartori and stay with her. It might be some time before they get there.

Josie smiles thinly and looks at her hands, covering the burn on one with the palm of the other. She looks up at him and together they think about the prints those hands left, on the gun that probably killed Jadus Golding. For now, nobody else in the room knows about that.

As everybody leaves, Staffe catches Josie, says, 'When we're done with these interviews and searches, we'll catch up with that scrote Louis Consadine.'

'I'm so sorry. I was an idiot.'

'For now, get Appolina Sartori talking about the past. She knows something. She might not even think it's important, but Jacobo and Carmelo share a secret, I'm sure of it.'

*

Jacobo Sartori asks if he can see Appolina and Staffe tells him that will have to wait, which saddens both. In the meantime, Jacobo refuses to answer the questions asked of him: why did he go into hiding; why was he in the Rendezvous; when was the last time he saw Carmelo; did anybody come to the house that day; why would Abie Myers wish to lure Jacobo to a public place and then try to abscond with him?

'Everything you have done links you to the abduction of Carmelo Trapani,' says Staffe. The strip lights in the Leadengate interview room flicker and Jacobo wipes his milky eyes. Tiny triangles of creamy saliva collect in the corners of his mouth. 'We have a warrant to search every fibre of your home.'

'That would be very upsetting for my wife, but she is strong.'

'Perhaps she loves you more.'

Jacobo looks away. 'You're not entitled to judge me.'

'You don't seem concerned about Carmelo, considering how long you have been together. I understand he introduced you to Appolina.'

Jacobo passes one hand through the other in looping figures of eight and chews his lip, the triangles of creamy saliva licked away. 'Do you think he's still alive?'

Staffe can't tell what response might please Jacobo. 'I know you bear a burden. I'll be speaking to Appolina about it before you see her next. It would help your cause if the information came from you.'

'I want to speak to Martin Goldman.'

'You can't. He would have a conflict of interest.'

He looks up at Staffe. 'In that case, I can't say anything.'

'And you're happy to remain here in custody? I can see that.' Staffe buzzes through to Jombaugh. 'Sergeant, would you make up some release papers for Mister Sartori and bring them through?'

'You can't just let me go.'

'If you won't talk, what's the point of keeping you here? You said you wanted to see Appolina. You can be there when we conduct our search.'

'I wanted her to come here. I just want to see her.'

'I can see why you wouldn't want us to release you into the world of Abie Myers,' says Staffe, going to the door, greeting Jombaugh and directing him to hand back the items on the inventory of possessions: a wallet containing an American Express card and one thousand six hundred pounds; a hunter pocket watch; a white plastic keycard for the Kings Hotel, Brighton; two tote betting slips from Brighton Greyhound Stadium. Staffe picks up the pocket watch. 'Hmm. Smith and Sons. Very nice. Eighteenth century.' He hands it back to Jombaugh, says, 'Now, sergeant, you'd better get back to Mister Hennigan. I think we can release him, too. Perhaps the two of you could share a cab. You know Miles Hennigan, don't you, Jacobo? You met in the Rendezvous casino. From what I saw, the two of you have unfinished business.'

'Very clever,' says Jacobo, playing with the end of his turned-up nose. 'I suppose I could make a statement.'

'I think you're going to be a great help to us, Jacobo.' He says to Jombaugh, 'Perhaps you'd be kind enough to take Mister Sartori's statement, sergeant, whilst I tell Mister Hennigan he will need to get a cab home on his own.'

'You can't release him,' says Jacobo.

'You really don't want to be anywhere near Abie Myers and his gang, do you, Jacobo? You either have something they want, or something they fear.'

Whilst Jacobo Sartori writes his version of everything he's done and seen since he last left his house in Muswell Hill five days ago, Staffe makes his way down Leadengate's musty corridors towards Miles Hennigan, stewing in Interview Room Three – except, when Staffe checks on the monitor before he goes in, Miles isn't stewing. He stares at the camera with a contented smile. He doesn't blink, simply exudes a professional's calm.

When Staffe enters the room, Miles says, 'I know what this must look like to you, inspector, but Mister Myers is very fond of Jacobo Sartori and we were only trying to save him from himself. I promise you, with all my heart, I wouldn't harm a hair; or let anyone else. When Mister Myers heard what happened to Carmelo, and we discovered Jacobo was missing, he felt he had to do everything he could to find Jacobo.'

'So why is Jacobo afraid at the prospect of having his liberty restored? The poor man is desperate to see his wife, yet he doesn't want to be released. He is afraid that you and Abie are waiting for him.'

'Some people don't know what's good for them.'

'Like the Nigerians?'

Still, Miles Hennigan doesn't bat an eye. His smile widens a little, as if out of respect for Staffe's research. 'You might think I am a mercenary, but I choose my causes carefully.'

'What does Jacobo know that might hurt your cause so badly?' Now, Miles Hennigan does blink. Just once, but it tells Staffe more than everything else he has said: Jacobo Sartori does know something. Perhaps it is what Appolina refers to as 'his burden'. 'I'll come back as soon as you decide you've got something to say.' He pats Miles on the shoulder.

'I saved your neck. Remember?'

'I'm trying to save Carmelo's.'

'We're all very fond of Carmelo. Why else would he remember Mister Myers so generously in his will?'

'What would you know? You're just the hired hand.'

'Never use the word "just", inspector. I never "just" do anything. I embrace a mission with commitment and unfailing loyalty.'

'You consider your work for Abie a mission?'

'It is my mission to employ my skills for good causes. This cause, I assure you, is a good one.'

'Where had you been when you were recommended to him?'

'I won't say.'

'Palestine?'

'Some would say that's not a place,' says Miles, his mouth pursing to deadly seriousness, which gives Staffe his answer.

'Tell me what Jacobo knows, Miles. Tell me his burden.'

Miles stares into a distance, not blinking.

*

Jacobo Sartori wipes the corners of his mouth and takes the small microphone from Jombaugh.

'It was a cold day. Appolina called me back from the gate and gave me the ushanka hat. It was a gift from her the time we went to St Petersburg. That was twenty years ago. She asked me again why I had to stay over, and I told her again that I didn't know, but Carmelo was insisting.

'When I got to the house, he sent the housekeeper away and cancelled the gardener for the next day while I made risotto. My risotto takes eighteen minutes and that's all the time we spent apart the whole night. We had two

grappas each and retired early – by ten, I would say, and in the morning he was already up and about by the time I was dressed and soon after he disappeared into his room. He was there for an hour or so and he phoned down to me to say he wanted veal for lunch. The only place we trust the veal is down on Jamaica Road, so I had to go down there and it's dreadful for buses.

'I was gone two hours and as soon as I got back with the veal, he told me he was going out later, to see the Livorskis. I don't know what hold they have on him, but Bogdan Livorski was in the square when I came back with the veal. He was on a bench in the far corner of the square. I'm sure it was him but my eyes sometimes let me down. I started to cook the veal and Carmelo took a phone call.

'He was raising his voice and when he was finished, he came into the kitchen and turned off the stove. He told me to get packed and he gave me some money, a couple of thousand, and he said to get away. He said there was nothing to worry about but I should not be in London for a day or so. He looked very concerned for me and I said I would get Appolina but he was insistent that I said nothing to anyone about where I was going. He made me promise.

'I have known Carmelo all my life and sometimes it seems we have shared one life not had two separate ones. I trust him absolutely. He has never acted against my interests. Not ever, so I eventually agreed to go. I told him that I would go to Brighton. It is close and I am very fond of it, and it is busy enough to go unnoticed. I stayed on the Hove side, at the Lancaster.

'Carmelo called me a taxi for London Bridge and we left the house together. He drove the Daimler round to the Livorskis and I went to get the train and that is the last time we saw each other or spoke.'

Jombaugh takes the microphone from Jacobo and saves the audio file, emails it to the office, copying it to himself.

Back at his desk, Jombaugh logs in the contents of Jacobo Sartori's small suitcase that has been delivered from the Lancaster Hotel. It contains everything that was in his room there. As he makes the inventory, Staffe emerges from his interview with Miles Hennigan.

Staffe looks into the open suitcase. Lying on top, in a clear plastic evidence bag, labelled 'Found in bin, Lancaster Hotel Room 19', is a photograph of himself. He picks it up, scrutinises it and asks Jombaugh to run Jacobo's audio file. As he listens through headphones, every word that Jacobo says is distinct. His recollection is clear, a little too clear. Staffe squints at the photograph of himself, sees something in the background. When the audio file is played out, he says to Jombaugh, 'I don't really look that rough, do I, Jom?'

'Where was it taken?'

Staffe taps the photo, just above his right shoulder. 'This is Carmelo's place. The morning after he disappeared.'

'The only person who knew Carmelo was missing then, was Attilio,' says Jombaugh. 'And Helena.'

'Or the person who abducted him.' Staffe flips the photo over, sees written, in a large, meticulous hand: 'An Inspector Calls.'

'Which means we know precisely where they were the morning after Carmelo Trapani was taken.'

'Let's have one last small chat with Jacobo, then I'm going to take him home. We'll let Hennigan stew. Keep him fed and watered and don't let Myers anywhere near him.'

'There's something else for you.' Jombaugh hands Staffe an envelope, embossed with the logo of the National Archives.

As he gets into his car, Staffe thinks about the contents of the bin at the Lancaster Hotel, and something undefined niggles him. 'Lancaster Hotel,' he says to himself, aloud. It sounds wrong but he doesn't know why. He reverses the car out in a wide arc, sees Jombaugh striding towards him, waving a piece of paper, saying, 'Lancaster Hotel.'

'What about it?'

Jom goes into his breast pocket, pulls out a card, wrapped in an evidence bag. 'Why would Jacobo have a key for the Kings Hotel?'

Twenty-four

Louis Consadine's brother, Curtis, has perfect caramel skin and luscious locks of dark brown hair, tousled from the night. His eyes are still puffy from sleep and he blinks at Staffe, says 'What the fuck?'

Beyond, in his student flat, a tiny, beautiful Japanese woman gets out of bed wearing just a T-shirt. When she bends to get juice from the fridge, her butt cheeks show. She turns, smiling, wiggling a carton of apple juice. Curtis is a very lucky young man. Looking back at Curtis, Staffe thinks, *And so are you, young lady*.

He shows his warrant card to Curtis, who merely shrugs. Clearly, this is not the first time for Curtis, even though he has no criminal record and he has just started a BA in economics and statistics at LSE. He got straight A*s from Ernest Bevin in Hackney and is on one of the most competitive undergraduate courses in the country.

'The fuck you want?' he says, sounding out of context; sounding just like his little brother.

Staffe says, 'I'm worried about your little brother, Curtis.'

'Who are you?' says the girl, coming up to Staffe and peering at him. Her eyes are like tiny pillows made from silk, to take jewels. She studies him as if he is a rarity. 'I have to practice.'

'He won't be here long, Mako,' says Curtis, kissing her away. The two men watch her pick up a violin and pad into the ensuite. Once she closes the bathroom door, Curtis says, 'There's nothing wrong with Louis. He's a good boy.'

'He's got a different life to you.'

'I got to the plaudits first, is all. They run out fast where we're from. Can you *imagine* that? Only space for one freak, man.'

'I can see trouble coming for Louis. You know Louis is tangled in that Golding murder. You'll have known Jadus, and Brandon Latymer.'

Curtis shakes his head, slowly, extravagantly. 'Why exactly are you here, harassing me?'

'This isn't harassment, Curtis. I just need to know where Louis was on 18 August.'

'The fuck would I know?'

'He says he was with his girlfriend, Leilah Frankland.'

'She's a crackhead. Anyone will tell you. But if she says she was with him, she was with him.'

'Let's hope so. Where were you, Curtis?'

'I was out Margate. It was results day, see? You can check that out, and I went to the sea with a bottle of rum and I drank the fuckin' lot and gave thanks to my mother. I promised her I'd make it and I did. I keep my promises. The Consadines keep their promises.'

'Your mother passed away?'

He nods his head.

'And it was just you and Louis?'

'That was then. He's old enough to be on his own.'

'You're going to be a rich young man is my guess. This city's going to be your oyster in three years' time – so long as your brother doesn't muddy the waters.'

'I think it's about time you fucked off, don't you, inspector?'

The sound of a violin emerges from beyond the door and

both men stand dead still, their mouths slightly open as they listen to Mako's music soar and swoon. Eventually, Staffe says, 'Bartók.'

'Number five,' says Curtis.

'I can never get the numbers,' says Staffe.

'You can't make two and two make five.'

'How do you mean?'

'This is no political environment to be parking your man's murder on innocent black boys.'

'Louis isn't black.'

'Brandon Latymer is. Jadus Golding was. You know the desired outcome here.'

'Did Brandon do it, Curtis? Louis could help himself if he just told us what he knows.'

Curtis's eyes narrow and his fists clench. 'You can't force statements like that on innocents. You've enough blood on your hands.' Curtis unclenches his fists and wiggles his fingers, like a boxer.

'You seem to find this a touchy subject.'

'I'll tell you this for fuck all – my Louis did bits and bobs once-upon, but those days are over. See, he couldn't hurt a flea, my Louis, that's why he needs to get out of there. That's the plan. We just need three years while I get the letters after my name and we're out – so you bear that in mind when you're trampling innocents underfoot.' He looks up to the ceiling, as if talking to someone not here. He closes his eyes, takes in the music. It seems to calm him and after half a dozen bars, he says, 'Listen to that. She's loose, isn't she? So fuckin' loose, man.'

*

172

Birdsong flutters from the trees in Appolina and Jacobo Sartori's garden. It is a compact, nurtured garden and the early sun paddles soft light on it, as if this place might belong to René and Georgia Magritte.

Appolina leans on her stick, drowned in her dressing gown. She says to Josie, 'So, Jacobo is safe, but you won't let me see him.'

'This is a serious situation – for both of you. We want you both to feel safe.'

'Safe? This is my home, why wouldn't I be safe?'

'Because of what Jacobo knows.'

'What do you mean?'

'Like I told you, Abie Myers was trying to abduct Jacobo when we intervened.'

'Why would he do that?'

Josie pours tea and adds lemon for Appolina. 'I would love to hear your story – what it was like in Sicily, all those years ago.'

Appolina sits in a wingback chair that faces the garden. 'I wouldn't know. I'm a Roman girl.'

'Tell me about the first time you met Jacobo.'

'It was here, in London. We met through Carmelo. I worked for him and I can remember the first time Jacobo looked at me. Do you have a husband?'

'I am with someone – sort of.'

'Give him time. It's not what people say, you know. Not always.'

'It sounds to me like you were lucky.'

'They say you make your own luck. We have a responsibility to our heart, but we're not beholden to it.'

'Jacobo has been a loyal husband.'

'He put me first, you might say. To begin with, he had to go

173

away with Carmelo but gradually he put a stop to that. He never told me anything, though.' Appolina talks to Josie about life after the war and how gradually everything began to change for the better and Carmelo made more and more money and they came by this house and Jacobo became more and more content as the years passed.

'But then Carmelo's wife died. And he never found love again?'

'Love was never such a thing for Carmelo. I never saw a person who could control his heart the way Carmelo did. He never lost his temper, you know. He always acted with his head. Ice in his veins. Not a bad man, but he didn't feel things like Jacobo. He spent all his love on Mary and God.'

'And what about Abie? I heard his wife moved on.'

'Moved on?' Appolina stares into the garden. She looks startled and her teacup shakes in its saucer. She holds the cup by its rim and Josie goes to her, takes it from her.

'It might help, if we could talk to her. It could help Carmelo.'

'I owe Carmelo nothing. He will take his chances with St Peter. That's what he always said.'

'We need to eliminate Jacobo from our enquiries, so you can resume your life. You won't be at peace until we find who took Carmelo, and Esther could help.'

'She was crazy, that Esther Myers. She had to move on.'

'Crazy?'

'Oh yes,' says Appolina, turning away from her garden. Her jaw is set and her chin raised, resolute. 'Really crazy, that's all I know; but I can tell you I wasn't sad when I heard we'd seen the back of her.'

*

In Leadengate, Staffe signs the papers for Jacobo's release and as they walk to the car park, he says, 'We need to know why you were watching me in Brighton. Who sent you the photograph?'

'It arrived at the hotel. I don't know who from and that's the God's honest truth. Then a phone message at the Lancaster to say which train you were on.'

'You put yourself in the firing line, following me. Not such a good outcome as it turned out.'

'Well, that's the truth.'

'From what I've read of Leon Goldman's memoir, Abie Myers would have known you might be at the Lancaster. But why would Abie come looking for you?'

'Because I have something he wants.' Jacobo is faltering now. 'I don't know what it is, but you must protect me, inspector. You promised you would.'

'And you must tell me the truth. You say you stayed in the Lancaster. You're sure about that?'

'You've seen my statement.'

'You're getting tired, Jacobo. Let's get you home.'

Staffe drives Jacobo home and the motion of the car soon lulls the old man to sleep, but after a while, Staffe pumps the brake, twice and fast, which jolts Jacobo from sleep and he looks warily out of the window. They are driving past Spitalfields Market. 'This isn't the way home.'

'But it is.' A few trendy revellers smoke outside the Lion as Staffe turns onto Cable Street towards Shadwell station with the overground tracks running above them on the left. On the right, St George's Town Hall and its enormous mural of the Battle of Cable Street; the plaque for the men and women who joined the International Brigade: 'They went because their open eyes could see no other way.'

'I brought you the scenic route.' He slows the car down as they pass the high, proud tenements on the left, just where you would turn up to Stepney Green and Abie's place. He watches in the rear view as he makes the turn and slowly, ever slower, they crawl past Abie Myers' house where the lights are on. Outside, a couple of SOCOs load their gear into a van. 'He didn't move far, did he?'

'Who?' Jacobo's voice is weak. He is clearly afraid to be here.

'Abie. He has a fancy place up in Stanmore, but he chooses to live here.' Up ahead, the non-stop traffic of the Mile End Road rumbles by, hammering in and out of the city. A short distance across the East End is Carmelo's home. 'Times change, but they didn't move on.' Staffe turns off the engine.

'We can't stop here.'

'Tell me about Cable Street, Jacobo.' Staffe jabs his thumb over his shoulder. 'You were there, weren't you?'

'I don't remember.'

'A quarter of a million people came. They rose up against fascism. It was one of our greatest days. Are you sure you weren't there? You'd remember.'

'I wasn't there.'

'OK.' Staffe turns on the engine and they move slowly away. As they go, a frail figure comes to the first-floor window, peering out. 'If you say so.' Staffe puts a hand on his heart, feels the papers that came through from the Archive, confirming that Jacobo Sartori had come from Sicily to England on Sunday 23 September 1936, just two weeks before the Battle of Cable Street gladdened the heart of the free world. The address he gave to Customs? 45 Cable Street. His home town? Siracusa, the opposite side of the island from Carmelo Trapani.

Maurice pulls up the collar of his overcoat against the sea wind. He takes out his phone and looks at the photograph of Tatiana on its screen. His stomach is hollow and his thoughts meander, always turning back to her. He watches people board the boat and makes up his mind. He is so close to the end, he can't take flight yet, so he tears the ticket in two and makes his way back to town.

As a final group of people rush past him towards the Dieppe crossing, dragging cases and children, Maurice unwraps the memories of his father, Claudio, and plays back the old story he told him: too old to be sitting on his old man's knee, but happy nonetheless to smell the fat of the ham in his sweater and let the gravelly words slip into each other. The story changed a little every time. He always expected a proper ending but he never got one and now he pauses, takes out the photograph of his father's father and Carmelo Trapani and Jacobo Sartori, in Tilbury dock, October 1936.

His blood courses a little faster and his mind becomes clear.

Twenty-five

Pennington hands Staffe the three files and leans back. As Staffe flicks through the papers, Pennington feels the cases and the criminals from all down the years pressing down on him as if the ether is heavy with paper and dark souls.

One file contains the original immigration papers for Maurizio Verdetti, the grandfather of Maurice Greene, who arrived in England on 7 September, a couple of weeks before Carmelo Trapani and Jacobo Sartori. Maurizio, born in Palermo, just like Carmelo.

In another file, the births and deaths of the families are all detailed. In a third and final file, the academic records of Maurice himself, there being no criminal records, nor employment history. He doesn't own a car, has never troubled the Revenue.

'Has Rimmer seen these?' asks Staffe.

'Don't you worry about Rimmer. Stay focused on finding Carmelo Trapani.'

'While Rome burns.'

'What? Aah. Pulford. There's news, I'm afraid. We have a date for trial.'

'He can't be going to trial.'

'The evidence is all one way, Will. Maybe this will shake the tree and he'll spill some beans. Internal Investigations have done all they can to help him, believe me.'

'Bollocks! They're hanging him out to dry, trying to show we're whiter than white. He's being threatened, for God's sake.'

'He hasn't filed a complaint. Internal Investigations sent a man down there, but Pulford refused to speak to him.'

'They killed his mother's dog.'

'Can you prove that?'

'Brandon Latymer is back in circulation. It's only a matter of time before he gives himself away. We've already sighted him with the mother of Jadus's child. He wanted Jadus out of the way.'

'His lawyer will say it is a tryst born of loyalty and shared grief. It's not uncommon.'

'My arse.'

'The CPS are prepared to play ball. Everybody wants a swift conclusion.'

'You're not talking about a deal?'

'It's what's best for Pulford. You know it's like tinder out there on the estates. We can't have another Summer '11 on our hands.'

'Not with people's careers at stake.'

'Look, Will. If Pulford didn't do it and he's holding out on us for whatever reason, he is bringing this on himself. Don't blame me. Don't blame anyone else.'

'I'll blame the people who killed Jadus Golding. And I'll catch them. If you'd forgotten, that's what we're supposed to do. Pulford didn't kill Golding.'

'You can't know that.'

Staffe doesn't want to tell Pennington, but knows he has to. Every hour he delays, the greater the repercussions will become. 'We've seen the gun. The e.gang has the gun. It's a Browning, the one Golding used on me.'

'Where the hell is it?'

'They have it.'

'How do you know this? I told you to stay away.'

'We just know it, sir. We've seen it.'

'We? You and Rimmer? I can't believe Rimmer would transgress like this.'

'Not Rimmer, sir.'

'Aah. Your precious Chancellor.'

'It's nothing to do with her. It was my call.'

'Where the hell is this gun?'

'Chancellor touched it, sir. The e.gang have it.'

'They have the murder weapon and it has Chancellor's prints on it? Sweet Jesus, man.'

'We need a warrant, sir.'

'I'll be the bastard judge of that.' Pennington stands, turns his back on Staffe. His shoulders rise and fall and his hands hang by his sides in tight fists. 'You need to get out of here, Staffe. Take those papers and bring me Carmelo Trapani.'

'Something for the front pages?'

'Don't be so bloody facetious. We all want the same thing, including Pulford. I should never have brought you back.'

Staffe tries to stand, but the breath in his throat gushes away and nothing comes in its stead. He gasps, sucking at the air. He reaches for the desk and hears Pennington say something. He puts the other hand on the desk and bends double, gulping air.

For a moment, his lungs won't work and the blood in his body seems to stall. He makes an almighty effort, sucking at the air and finally, it comes. It rushes into him like the ocean and he stands double, feels his belly clench.

'What the hell's wrong, man?' says Pennington.

Staffe's heart batters at his skin now and in his gut he is sick. Sick at what might happen to Pulford.

'I heard you've not been so good. You'd better see someone.'

Staffe goes to the washroom, leans on the basin and splashes water onto his face. He tries to get his brain working but it stalls, keeps coming back to the mirror.

He calls Josie, but there is no reply.

Staffe puts a hand to his heart again. All alone, with just tiles and mirrors, he watches Josie's name fade from his phone and his fingers work away, of their own accord, until a voice comes to him. It is a voice he has loved. His last resort.

'What time is it?' Sylvie sounds drowsy and he pictures her smudged smile.

He says, 'I'm in trouble. Can we meet? Please.'

*

A line of inmates walk across from the wings to Gym and Workshop. There is something weird about the light today – a light mist in the air and the sun paints unlikely haloes around the hunched shapes of the cons.

Pulford has been watching the day since its first tweet of dawn. For hours, the place has chirruped, from window to window, dragging him down. This is not going to get any better. His first thought when he woke had been the trial.

Last night, his brief had told him the Crown is very confident of a conviction now. There is, apparently, a collective will to see this put to bed, and he pictured himself being led up – by a colleague, a look of disappointment in the officer's eyes.

He has been expecting it for weeks, but it was still a punch to the belly. He spent most of the night up and down to the toilet, squatting on its cold steel rim, coming up empty but his guts twisting.

Two raps at the door and he steps away from the window. He hears a low murmur of voices and the bolt is shot. The door opens, revealing Beef.

For a moment, Beef looks as if he really doesn't want to be there, and then his expression tightens and his eyes come to life – in a bad way. 'I'm like your copy of the *Daily* fuckin' *Mail*. Got some news for you.' He advances towards Pulford.

'I already heard. I've got a court date.'

'You've got a date with the grim reaper, is what you've got. You can't do life, Pulford. You're a pussy.' Beef is in his face now, standing toe to toe.

'I won't be doing life.'

'There's new evidence.'

'You're a lawyer now, are you?'

'Don't be fuckin' clever, you pussy.' When Beef says 'pussy', he showers a light spray of spittle in Pulford's face. His breath is rank and it makes Pulford want to heave. 'But they got new stuff on that gun, see? That gun with your prints on it? Well, that's in the fuckin' evidence now. They call it "discovery", you know – that whole scene of sharing what everybody knows. I know my law, and I can tell you, that gun – the one that's going to shoot you in the face—'

'I can explain how those prints got there.'

'Your prints are not the only ones on that gun, is what they just discovered.'

'Brandon's are on it.'

'Course they are. Everyone knows Jadus came running to Brandon when he shot your mate. But how did that pretty little copper get her dabs on my man's weapon?'

'What?'

'She's a fine piece of pig, that Chancellor. How d'you think she got her fingers on my man's heat?'

'She had nothing to do with Jadus Golding. It was me. Just me.'

'The two of you were in it together. Why else would she have her prints on the gun?'

'I was working alone.'

'You're going to have to convince the judge. Not me,' says Beef, who must see something he didn't bargain for in Pulford's eyes because he steps back and taps the door.

Crawshaw appears.

Beef backs out of the door, saying, 'You going to have to do what we say. You best listen up.'

Pulford rushes at Beef, but Crawshaw steps across, catches him across the jaw with an elbow. Pulford crashes to the deck and looks up, watches them retreat. He tries to get up, to have another go, but his legs have gone and Crawshaw closes the door, shoots the bolt for what sounds like a final time, but Pulford doesn't feel that lucky.

*

It might just be the last day of the long summer and Staffe sits in a deck chair by the open-air swimming pool at London Fields. He wants to get into Maurice Greene's place, but not until the SOCOs are all done; he also wants to have heard back from the *polizia* in Siracusa.

A bloke in a suit chats with another fellow in a Hawaiian shirt and combat shorts. They both have sunglasses on and they each call out to their children every now and again. Staffe wonders how a child might fit into a grown person's life. He never really understood how it did for his own father.

The two men seem to be making friends and each takes out a handset and taps in some data. Are they exchanging numbers? He pictures the two of them maybe doing a bit of spliff or going to a game, and the delight that would ensue when their partners also rub along quite nicely.

His phone beeps and he watches as the message comes up. First, the text. Then the picture, but the glare from the sun obscures the image so Staffe puts the handset up his shirt and peers down at the screen, inside his shirt.

It's clear enough, this photo they have sent at the click of a button from the south-eastern tip of Sicily. It will be less fuzzy when he sees it on his desktop, but even in this light, the truth is crystal clear.

'The fuck you up to?'

'Fuckin' pervert!'

Staffe pulls his head out of his shirt, looks up at the new friends in the suit and Hawaiian shirt bearing down on him, their children stood by the edge of the pool, shivering.

'I was looking at a picture,' says Staffe.

'Call the police, Marcus,' says the one in the suit. 'I'll keep holda the cunt.' His suit is eight hundred quid, the accent pure Canning Town.

Staffe knows they're not the enemy, but he stands up and shrugs the man off, holds out his warrant card like it's Mace. 'I'm police. Sorry.' He looks at the two children. One is afraid, the other is loving it. 'I'm so sorry.'

Twenty-six

On his way to Maurice's flat, Staffe replays how strangely pleased Sylvie was to hear from him. She said something about fate that didn't really make sense to him and how nice it was that they could chat like adults and it would be lovely to get together.

The SOCOs have dusted every inch of Maurice's flat and his writing desk has a stack of clear plastic evidence bags, numbered. The head of the team points to an indexed tabulation of finger-prints, says, 'Carmelo Trapani's prints are in the lounge, kitchen and bathroom. And so are Miles Hennigan's.'

'Hennigan? What the hell would he be doing here?' says Staffe, looking at Tatiana.

Tatiana shrugs.

Staffe looks at the summary of items: an old mobile phone with the SIM card bagged separately; an Oyster card; a pair of boots with mud dried to their soles; and an SLR digital camera, with its memory card separately bagged.

He says to Tatiana, 'We'll need to see your phone, and your Oyster card.'

'I need them!'

'I'll bring them back as soon as I can. I promise.'

Tatiana opens her handbag, disgruntled in a theatrical way. As she looks for her Oyster card, the head SOCO says, 'And you might want to see this.' He takes the photo memory card from its evidence bag, puts it into his laptop and a fast reel of images scrolls down the screen, eventually settling on a sequence of Staffe at Carmelo's house, and two of him coming out of Leadengate Station.

'These are Maurice Greene's?'

'Yes, sir.'

Staffe points to one image, says, 'This is the one Jacobo Sartori had.'

Josie appears from the kitchen, holding a clear plastic bag with a pair of boots in it. 'We've just got the match, sir. The mud is from Carmelo's place, and there's a matching imprint, too.'

Rimmer says, 'He wouldn't take Carmelo. He's too fond of the old boy.'

'Yet you think it was Attilio, his own son?' says Staffe.

'There's no love lost there. And Attilio knew he was being squeezed out.'

'But there's nothing for him in the will,' says Staffe.

'Aah.' Rimmer reaches into his pocket, pulls out a folded piece of paper. 'Your friend Martin Goldman sent this through. It's a petition from Attilio Trapani and Helena Ballantyne, to nullify the last will and testament of Carmelo Trapani.'

'He told me he would do the honourable thing and not go digging up the past. This isn't Attilio. This is Helena's doing. She needs to keep Ockingham Manor. She doesn't want Abie Myers getting his hands on it.'

'How would Myers get his hands on Ockingham?'

'He already has a stake in it through Blackfriars, Rimmer. Do your homework.' Staffe turns to Tatiana. 'Does Maurice have a passport?'

'Of course. We love to travel.'

Staffe says to the SOCO, 'But it's not here?'

'We've been through every pocket and every drawer.'

Staffe looks through Tatiana's bag, sees her passport and says to the SOCO, 'Make sure you bag this passport and the Oyster and her phone.' He ushers Tatiana out of the flat. 'You'll get your things back when we find Maurice.'

'What if you don't find him?'

'Then you should get a decent lawyer. In fact, get yourself one anyway.'

'Don't worry,' says Tatiana, staring hard at Staffe. She doesn't blink and he is first to look away. 'We have one.' She makes her way onto the street, turning towards Kingsland Road.

Staffe has to be at the St John in Spitalfield for twelve noon to meet Sylvie, and woe betide him if he is late.

Tatiana disappears round the corner, towards the Overground, and Staffe legs it to the corner in time to see Tatiana climbing the steps to the Overground platform. As he follows her, he thinks about Attilio, the digging up of the past and the image they sent from Siracusa.

*

Louis Consadine punches his own chest. His heart is burning from all that fried chicken and over-proof cider, and Leilah is still passed out on the mattress on the floor. No matter how hard he shakes her, Leilah won't wake up. Whilst he slept, she had finished off their crack. He loves her so much it's fucked up, but sometimes he wishes she wasn't so full on.

Sometimes, Louis wishes he could do what his brother Curtis says. Ditch the bitch. A couple of weeks ago, Curtis went round to see Leilah, told her to sling it, but the other day she texted Lou back, even though she's a year older and could have anyone she wanted.

Curtis doesn't get her and neither do the rest of his mates. Sometimes, Leilah isn't a bitch and he sees the bits of her that she can't reveal to the world, and it's this that makes him forgive all her sins.

He puts the sole of his Nike Shox on her shoulder and rocks her. She grunts, turns over, shows her backside because all she is wearing is a bra. Her hair is matted and she has drooled in her sleep.

When Brandon pays him off for getting that policewoman's dabs on the gun, he will take Leilah away; get clean. But first, he has to sort Curtis. They have a plan and it all relies on Curtis keeping his nut down, studying and getting that job.

Louis checks Leilah's purse and counts out her money. She's got seven quid, an E and a wrap of MDMA for when she comes round. Louis knows how much he's got. Fuck all. He looks down on the gasworks and all the way across the Isle of Dogs to the Naval College. He's so high he thinks he might see the sea. It's Leilah's sister's place. She's doing a bit of time in Holloway at the moment but she told him once she could see the sea from her place in the Balfron.

This isn't his manor and he's scared to go out, unsure where he stands round here, and he wonders when Brandon will come. They need food and Nurishment – some weed, maybe. No more crack, not yet. Maybe a bit of Valium or tam. Christ, now he hopes Leilah won't wake up because she'll be a nightmare, and then he looks at her peach. He lies next to her and feels her soft skin and, just now, that seems like it might be enough.

He'll be sixteen in two weeks. That's a game-changer and he

wishes he was young again. He holds Leilah tight, just wanting her to hold him. He puts his hand to her gynie. It's stubbled. She says she shaves it for him, but he doesn't care about that. He just wants her to say something right into his ear: soft and warm and not dirty.

*

Tatiana is in the next carriage and Staffe sits on the same side as her, so she won't clock him if she looks over. A group of loud young girls get onto Tatiana's carriage at Haggerston, which means he can steal glimpses of Tatiana, jaw set, as if she knows precisely what she is doing.

As they pull into Dalston, Tatiana beckons one of the girls over to her – an Asian with dyed-pink Mohican hair. She offers a twenty-pound note to the girl and a commotion seems to ensue. Eventually, the girl with the Mohican hands Tatiana her phone and the other girls form a semicircle around her, but Tatiana says something to make the girls back off.

The SOCOs kept Tatiana's mobile phone so she must be telephoning a number that is in her own memory. Tatiana finishes her call and the girls shift to block the doors, so she hands over another note – presumably for a second call.

The train slows into Canonbury and Tatiana moves to the doors, not giving the handset back, and when the girl reaches out for her phone, Tatiana – despite the fact that she is outnumbered five to one and these girls seem equipped to handle themselves – shows the back of her hand to the girl, as if she might slap her, and the girls move away, as one. Tatiana steps out, ending her call and tossing the phone into the carriage so it skids along the floor.

Staffe checks his watch. It is twenty to twelve and he has to be back in Shoreditch for noon.

Two of the five girls want to get off and slap Tatiana. The other three don't fancy it. Tatiana turns her back and walks quickly to the escalators.

The train beeps and the doors begin to slide. Staffe has to decide.

He could follow Tatiana and see where she is going. It might simply be to see a friend or it might be to meet Maurice or even Carmelo; but he knows that if he lets her go and throws in his lot with the group of girls, he can see who Tatiana has called. He wishes he had the data from her Oyster card, which would confirm if Canonbury is a regular haunt, but he has to decide.

The door slides.

The train jolts away and he watches Tatiana go, in her short fur jacket and her soft leather boots. He walks to the girls, says, 'I'm police and I need to see that phone.'

The girl with the phone says, 'I fuckin' done nothing.'

'I know, but I need to see that phone.'

'You can frisk me, if you want,' says another girl and the rest of them snigger.

Staffe checks his watch again, plucks the phone from the girl and jots down Leadengate's address, tells her she can pick it up tomorrow. Or they will send it round to her house, if she prefers.

'My dad'll fuckin' kill me if there's filth to the house.'

At Highbury and Islington, Staffe steps off as the train pulls away and the girls mimic fellatio and give him the finger.

The Overground skims Staffe back into the East End and as he comes into Haggerston, running late for his lunch appointment, he has a sense of looking at London through a different lens, directly into lives suspended above the streets. In new conversions that back onto the lines, he watches an old trendy at a stove, a young couple rising from their sheets, a middle-aged woman hunkering over an analogue typewriter.

He looks at the two numbers which Tatiana had called: a mobile and a Brighton landline. He texts the numbers to Jom and when it's sent, he looks at the image that Siracusa police had sent – a brutish youth, tall with a shock of black hair and a broken nose, from a bygone era.

When the doors open at Hoxton, a church somewhere near chimes noon. He paces up and down the carriage, already late, waiting for Shoreditch, and when they get there, Staffe runs to Spitalfields, starting off at what was his usual pace – before the shooting – but he is soon out of breath, bent double and wheezing before he can even see the market. Is his heart too weak to pump the blood? Is he simply out of condition?

He gets to the St John in Spitalfield at twenty past twelve and Sylvie is paying the waiter for her drink. When she sees Staffe, she packs her phone and magazine into her bag, stands and puts on her coat. It is a light, mustard-coloured mac he bought her three birthdays ago.

'Don't even say it, Will.'

He puts a hand on her forearm, says, 'Please.' The waiter returns with her change. 'Don't let me spoil it. The soft-shell crabs are the best in London. At least have those and then go.' He turns to the waiter. 'Am I right?'

The waiter gives Sylvie a lop-sided, apologetic look. 'He's right. They are the best. They're very good with Chablis.' He winks at her. 'I have a *premier cru*.'

They both laugh, and Staffe says, 'A bottle of that, then.'

A silence develops. Eventually, Sylvie says, 'Have you seen a doctor?'

'What do you mean?'

'I popped into the station. I had a client at Franckesbanck. It's only round the corner.'

'You went into the station and—?'

'I ran into that woman you work with. The pretty one. She said she was worried about you and said if I spoke to you, perhaps I could have a word.'

'She's no right.'

'Not unless she cares about you. Don't be a bloody idiot, Will. Now, have you seen a doctor?'

'There's no need.'

'Well, I'm not here to bang my head against your brick wall. God knows, I've enough brain damage from that already.' The waiter brings the Chablis. 'Tell me about David. He's going to be all right, isn't he?'

'I thought so. But lately, he's giving in, and I know what that can look like to a jury.'

'You don't think he did it, do you?'

Staffe shakes his head.

'But you haven't got another suspect?'

'Everyone's treading on eggshells. I can't say too much.'

'But you've got to do your best for him.'

Staffe hisses, 'Don't you think I know that?'

Sylvie raises both her hands, palms facing him, and for a while they each look around the light, high-ceilinged dining room: bleached wood and a lively young crowd.

He says, 'Have you been seeing anybody?'

Sylvie nods. She closes her eyes as she drinks the Chablis, says,

'This *is* divine. I forgot about your good points.'

'Who is he?'

'He was kind and he loved me. He asked me to marry him, in fact.'

'What?' It is only a couple of years since she wore Staffe's ring.

'So now I'm not seeing anybody,' she laughs, feebly. Sylvie replenishes her own glass, takes another sip. She drinks nervously, is out of character.

'Are you all right, Syl?'

'Not really.'

'What's wrong?'

'You fucked me up, Will. This man I was with, he was everything I should want. He's got his own business and he's young, honest and reliable.'

'What business does he have?'

'Why would it matter?' Sylvie drains her glass and pours herself another, looks past Staffe, watching people on the street. A couple of hip young mothers talk, with toddlers at their feet and babies in buggies. Beyond them, trendy Spitalfields spins round at a million miles an hour. She seems unfocused, says almost under her breath. 'He isn't you.'

'You don't want me,' he says.

Sylvie raises a napkin, covers her face. Her shoulders rise and fall and she sighs, heavily. The crabs arrive and she remains like that until the waiter is gone.

She removes the napkin from her face and her eyes are pink but she has a forced smile upon her face. 'No, I don't want you, and sometimes that means I can't have anything and that—' Her chin trembles. 'That's just not bloody fair. It's not fair, Will. I didn't do anything to deserve this. I didn't do anything but love you.'

'I loved you.'

'Not enough.'

'I thought I did.'

Sylvie looks out of the window again. She has parted her hair on the side and it makes her cheekbones seem wider, like a dark, young, Debbie Harry, he thinks.

'What about you?' she says, still looking into the street. 'What about the pretty policewoman. Josie?'

He shakes his head. 'Not since you. Not really.'

'Not really? What does "not really" mean?'

'You know.'

'I'll be thirty-four in a couple of weeks.'

'What do you want for your birthday?' He smiles at her.

'I'm getting old.'

'Maybe we could go for dinner.'

'I don't think so. But I know what I want.'

'Tell me.'

'I want a baby, Will.'

'My pleasure,' he laughs.

She looks him in the eye. She doesn't laugh and he soon stops.

They eat the crabs and Sylvie finishes the Chablis. She says, 'You're right, they are the best. Let's have some more.'

Staffe orders more crabs and asks for another glass of Chablis each and when the Chablis comes, he raises his glass and Sylvie touches his with hers. She is glassy eyed and he remembers a few of the things she has forgiven him. His heart aches at the thought of her being unhappy and he recalls the times they talked about one day having a family. He blew that.

He says, 'Let's do it.'

'Don't say that just because you don't want to see me sad.

Don't think you owe me, Will.'

'I don't.'

'You need to think about it.'

'I want to be a father.'

'We wouldn't be together.'

'I want to be a father.'

'We'd rely on you. For certain things.' Sylvie reaches across and puts her hand on his wrist. She is shaking. 'You really want to do this?' Her voice cracks. 'You can't let me down again.'

Twenty-seven

'I saw Sylvie,' says Josie.

'I know!' Staffe snatches the pile of papers from her. On top, the potted biography of Maurice Greene. 'You shouldn't have said anything.'

She looks hurt. 'I was trying to be a friend, sir. We care about you.'

'We?'

Josie busies herself at the coffee machine in the corridor outside his office.

'I'm sorry,' he says. 'But I'm OK.'

She turns round, says, 'No, you're not.' And she walks away without a drink, leaving Staffe to the dossier on Maurice Greene.

Greene was born in Palermo, March 1982. His parents were Nicoletta Cottanesta and Claudio Verdetti. Claudio Verdetti was born in City Royal hospital, 1937, and was therefore forty-five when Maurice was born. Maurice's mother, Nicoletta, was seventeen when Maurice was born and she died when he was seven. Thereafter, Maurice was in the care of his father, until Claudio drowned whilst swimming off Cefalù when Maurice was thirteen. Maurice tried and failed to save his father.

Claudio's own father, Maurizio, died in October 1936 in London and he is buried in the church of St George-in-the-East, Cable Street.

Staffe flicks through the facsimiles of the source documents.

Every now and again, he rubs his temples, trying to get things straight in his head.

After Claudio drowned, Maurice entered the guardianship of Carmelo Trapani and was schooled at Stonyhurst in Lancashire. He later graduated in English from York University.

Staffe goes through each document again, ends up with ruffled hair and a thick head. Amidst all the papers, one fact announces itself with a hazy familiarity. Staffe taps away at his keyboard and his suspicions are confirmed.

Maurizio Verdetti died on 4 October 1936, the very day of the Battle of Cable Street.

*

Abie Myers' thick eyebrows pinch together and his large lips slant into a snarl. His old face seems younger today and it seems that the rising bile is good for him, because when Staffe enters the drawing room to his house in Stepney Green, the old fellow is quick to his feet, saying, 'I don't know what the hell gives you the right to treat me like a criminal. Look at this!' He gestures at a scene of crime officer still sifting his way through Abie's life.

In the corner, Miles Hennigan stands with his arms crossed over his chest, looking at Staffe, unblinking.

'The judiciary seems to think we have sufficient grounds to look more deeply at you.' Staffe approaches Abie and says, so just the two of them can hear: 'Maybe you should take a walk, if you're finding this too traumatic.'

'What in God's name do you expect to find?' hisses Abie.

'Tell me about Maurizio.'

'You mean Maurice?'

'I mean what I say. Maurizio Verdetti.'

'If Carmelo is alive, you should be trying to find him – not wasting my time.'

Staffe turns his back on Abie. Inside this house, the way Abie has kept it, the years might not have roared by. Right here, you could be back where you wanted to be. He says, 'When did Darens go?'

'You don't know Darens,' says Abie.

'Bread shop and bakery,' says Staffe. 'I have this hunger for knowledge, history, so I know that Maurizio Verdetti would have known little of your beloved Cable Street. It killed him, after all – just a month or so after he came here from Carmelo's home town. They were cousins, you know, and Maurizio's grandson became Carmelo's ward. Maurice. I really do think you and I should take a walk.' Staffe says to the SOCO, 'Have you found Maurice Greene's prints here?'

'Yes, sir.'

'Carmelo's?'

'Yes, sir.'

Staffe takes out the phone which he had taken from the girl on the Overground. He scrolls down to the mobile number she last called and presses green. All eyes are on him and he holds up the phone, says, 'I don't even know who this belongs to, but . . .'

Miles Hennigan blinks. He reaches for his pocket, like a gun-slinger, but he's too late on the draw. First, everyone hears the low buzz of vibrate, then the ringtone. Miles looks at the phone, so small in his large hands.

'Hadn't you better answer that?'

'Later,' says Miles.

'Don't mind us,' says Staffe.

'What's going on?' says Abie, looking daggers at Miles Hennigan.

The phone rings and rings, then stops and Staffe presses green again and Miles's phone begins to ring once more. The SOCO laughs and Staffe says, 'Come on, Abie, let's take that walk.'

As he leaves, passing Miles Hennigan, he says under his breath, so only Miles can hear, 'I call the tunes from now on. You'd better be a bit quicker with your answering.'

Abie and Staffe walk past the Ashbury Youth Boys Club to the Green, from where London seems spread flat all the way to Canary Wharf. Abie twiddles his cane in the air on the off beats. The sun is out and the sky is cloudless. Up above, the white vapours from traffic in and out of City Airport trail the blue sky.

'There was none of that when you first came,' says Staffe, indicating the sky.

'Plenty's changed.' Abie jabs at Canary Wharf: an oblong of nothing but money and a triangle on top. It looks near and modest, but is actually far away and not. 'Progress? Bah!'

'What happened to Maurizio, Abie?'

'How would I know?'

'You employ his grandson.'

'Maurice is a numbers man. He's a genius is what he is, but I am not his family historian.'

'Is he with you or Carmelo?'

'Why should it be a case of "or"?'

'I can't make him out, you know. He seems to have a fine life, gambling and consuming the arts, and now Carmelo bequeaths him half his home.' Staffe stops in the shadow of the four-storey tenements on Cable Street. 'Where was Panners, Abie?'

'Panners? Darens? What is it with you and the past?'

'I have a feeling. I think you know what I mean.'

'I don't give a damn for your feelings. Shouldn't you be trying to find Carmelo?'

'Would you be happy if we were to find him?'

'I don't care one jot for that money he left me, if that's what you mean.'

'I know, Abie. This has nothing at all to do with money, except Carmelo knew we would follow the money to get to something higher than money.' He nods at Canary Wharf.

'Higher?'

'Your hold over Jacobo Sartori intrigues me.'

'You talk in riddles.'

'I had to put a man on his door because he is afraid of you.' A train rattles past, above them, rollicking west to the Tower.

'Well, you can take him off. That's an absurdity.'

They pause by the Crown and Dolphin pub, its Meaux Ales livery all spotted and faded to almost nothing. Each looks up at the mural of the riots: police horses rising up on their hind legs, Blackshirts with venom in their eyes, and the people standing steadfast. Leagues of Jews and Communists shoulder to shoulder.

Abie stabs his cane again, up the road, says, 'That's where Panners Dairy was. I would go every day.'

'What exactly were you and Carmelo doing in those days?'

'I didn't know him so well then.'

'I'd bet my bottom dollar you were into illegal gambling.'

Abie laughs. 'That might be a good bet, but I do believe there's a statute of limitations on misdemeanours like that.'

This makes Staffe consider the legality, after all these years, of prosecuting buried crimes. 'It's all a question of reasonable doubt. The passage of time makes that difficult, but we can put it in the hands of the Crown if the evidence is there.'

'We covered our tracks quite nicely.'

'Evidence can be durable.'

'As you will discover, I went into property. Completely respectable. Carmelo was the same.'

Staffe says, 'And now he rewards you in his will. He shines a light on you, doesn't he, Abie? He shines twenty million watts right down on you, to put you centre stage. And then there is Blackfriars Holdings – you helping out Attilio; getting a chunk of that blue-blooded Britain. That must feel good. But only a month ago, Carmelo sold his stake in Blackfriars, didn't he? It doesn't add up.'

They are outside St George's Town Hall now, with its plaque declaring '*No pasarán!*' in memory of the many who went on from Cable Street to defend democracy in the Spanish Civil War. Staffe leads them into the gardens at the back of St George-in-the-East. Through the great arching oaks they look past a row of enormous gravestones, leaning against a wall, like soldiers enjoying tobacco between exchanges.

The church of St George looks French with its octagonal nave, but it was bombed and in its place is a smaller church – like a Russian doll, which sets Staffe thinking and he studies the dates on the gravestones, says, 'You know, sometimes it feels as though Carmelo's disappearance is like a Russian doll.'

'Enough with your riddles.'

'A crime within a crime, is what I'm thinking. What if I have to discover something far beyond his disappearance, to solve his disappearance?'

Abie says, 'Let's get on our way. I have plenty to do. You know, the closer you get the more there is to do.'

'You're good for a few years yet, I'd say.'

'It's not the time that's left that . . .' Abie's words trail in the air and his eyes become milky. The old man opens his mouth to say something but bites his lip.

'It's what you leave behind,' says Staffe, pointing to a grave-stone.

MAURIZIO VERDETTI
1914–1936
HE DIED THAT OTHERS MIGHT THRIVE

Abie says, 'I heard something of this fellow. It seems so long ago. It was a different age, thank God. You might hear people remin-isce, but it was hard, then. A bad time, through and through. You know, people can say what they like about the modern age and the violence but I wouldn't have those times back. It was so – so *hard*.' He wipes his eyes and peers at Maurizio's grave.

Staffe says, 'He was a cousin of Carmelo's.'

'He'd have been asking for trouble, I dare say.'

'Trouble?'

'They didn't care about what happened to us, those Italian boys, they were having their day in the sun. A free hit, they say now – just like those awful kids the other summer – when they rioted.

'The kids in '36 threw pepper in the horses' eyes, and rolled marbles under the hooves. Everyone was packed so tight. We kept being told this and that about where the Fascists would be and where they were coming from. It turned out to be a grand day, but it could have been different. History plays its tricks, but you know that, don't you, inspector?'

'I know there were casualties in the crowds, and I read about what they did to the police horses.' Both men look at the head-stone again: 'That Others Might Thrive.'

'Maurizio was trampled underfoot, by the very horses he was goading?'

'That's what I heard.'

'You were here that day.'

Abie looks away. 'Where else would I be?' He turns his back on the church. 'These places give me the willies.'

Staffe watches him trundle off, back the way he came, through the past and out the other side onto Cable Street. A group of youths huddles beneath one of St George's oaks, passing round a bag, washing it down with super-strength cider.

As Abie passes them, they say something and he goes for them with his cane. They stand up and Staffe walks slowly across, but whatever Abie said makes them disperse. They look afraid.

Twenty-eight

Attilio opens the bathroom window and steam rushes out. The sky is pink, the day nearly done. Beyond the gallops, he sees the horse box being towed home from Goodwood. They had a winner today. As a result, there is a fat wad of twenties on the Federal dressing table in his bedroom, next door. Funny, he might have had to sell the Federal to pay the lads' wages – if the deal with Blackfriars hadn't gone through.

Earlier, he took five hundred down to Rodney, to put behind the bar for the lads and lasses. Rodney said, 'Thank you', but with 'Sorry' in his eyes. Then he had insisted they had a large one together. It seems everyone was on Gemstone.

He rubs a porthole in the steam on the mirror and dabs his face with cologne. He has shaved twice, the way he always has since Helena first put her hand to his face and said, 'You have a fine jaw. A jaw to die for, but you prickle me.' Dominic Ballantyne had been there, at Cowdray Park, and Helena dragged her fingers down his back whilst her husband looked him dead in the eye, saying, 'You must come to Ockingham.'

He always liked Dominic.

A week later, Dominic had a pair of ponies off him and before long Attilio was coming to Ockingham once a week, discussing with Dominic and Helena his grand plans to establish a yard, to begin training as well as breeding and trading horses. And not long after, he was visiting Ockingham three times a week, but when Dominic was not there.

He dips his fingers in the pomade and patters his hair, draws a comb through, slipping for a short while into a trance within which he realises that when a man has almost everything he wants, those last inches can kill you – and they will. Tonight.

Lately, Helena doesn't even tell him when she is going to be away. A month ago, she took a room in the oldest, Jacobean part of the house. She said his snoring was keeping her awake. He doesn't snore. Many men say this, he knows, but one night when she was away, he paid the gardener to sit in the corner whilst Attilio slept and now he knows he doesn't snore.

Earlier, when he had just got back from Goodwood and was booking entries in the office, Attilio's heart had slumped when he heard the tyres of her car in the gravel – leaving.

Without her, he is nothing more than an imposter here. Helena was born to rule and this seat will cushion her nicely long after he is gone. With Fahd, she will be able to stop Abie Myers taking the place, if that was his game. She has an imperious instinct for survival, even though it had faltered that day at Cowdray when she chose Attilio, but now she is back on form. Fahd Jahmood would have sent shock waves through the county a couple of decades ago, but times change.

He puts on his Bengal striped shirt and selects the silver links that Helena had bought for him when he had his first winner. One is a cap and the other a whip. He steps into his ox-blood moleskins, pulls on the hacking jacket and finally dons a riding helmet, clad in his father's silks. He hopes the casing of the helmet will keep everything in. The hand-painted wallpaper is from Milan, cost three hundred quid a roll. It's vintage, from when she loved him.

The gun cabinet was a wedding gift from Jacobo. He can't remember what his father got him. Perhaps nothing, but Jacobo was proud that Attilio had managed to marry so deep into the heart of everything English. The boy might have killed his mother but with the marriage to Helena Ballantyne, Attilio thought he was giving the old man the benediction he always craved. Instead, it was treated as betrayal.

Attilio has long arms, a good thing for the task in hand. He breaks the Mossberg and loads each barrel with its twelfth of a bore. Out of habit, he looks down the barrels, then locks it, holding it aloft and turning it on himself, placing the end of the barrels in his mouth.

The metal is bitter and cold on his teeth and tongue.

His heart beats fast and he takes the gun out of his mouth. He pulls Helena's pillows across to his side, and lays down again, head propped up.

*

Tatiana is lost without her phone. She has tried Maurice from a payphone, but he's not answering.

Looking up at the window, she is not sure whether to go ahead, or to come back another day, when the instructions are clearer.

Miles Hennigan said to go ahead, but she isn't entirely sure he is to be trusted. She knows his type, ex-military. He is cold behind the eyes, not like Maurice who is full of warmth and love and humanity.

She checks up and down the quiet road and lets herself in by pressing the code into the keypad by the door. It is what Maurice would want, she is sure.

The place smells of vanilla and this makes her smile. Maurice has the vanilla plug-ins at home and the perfumed oil, and also the reed diffuser. He's done the same here.

On the top flight of stairs, she hears him stir, within, and this freezes her to the tread she is on. She looks at the door, wary. After a second or two, she pushes off, taking a hold of the newel post and then reaching out, putting the key to the Yale lock she and Maurice fitted. The house belongs to an owner Maurice knows from Dubai and the lock isn't an issue. Tatiana had wondered what hold Maurice has over the man.

The room is dark. They screwed the Georgian shutters closed and she puts on a small lamp, goes to the chair he is in, smells that he has soiled himself. She puts her hand to his cheek, says, 'Sorry,' even though she knows that he is responsible for a terrible, terrible thing.

Tatiana removes the tape from his mouth as gently as she can. When it comes away, the tape has blood on it.

'Hello, my dear,' he says, his voice hoarse as hair.

Tatiana sinks to her knees, says 'Sorry.'

'Good will come of this.'

She unties him, trying not to gag from the smell, and when she has finished, Carmelo gets very slowly to his feet.

'I will clean myself, then we shall have some dinner.'

'It is lunchtime.'

'I could eat a horse.' He tries to laugh, but his mouth and throat are too dry. 'I can't face Saint Peter on an empty stomach.'

'It's been difficult. The police, you know.'

'You didn't bring them? Why didn't you—'

'Not yet,' she says, handing him a roll of kitchen paper and a tub of baby wipes. 'I'll get you some clothes.'

While Carmelo is busy in the bathroom, Tatiana cuts some bresaola and improvises some bruschetta by chopping olives from a jar and dicing the lone tomato from the fridge. The bread is stale but she toasts it anyway, and throughout her preparations, the sound of Carmelo's coughing gets louder, deeper.

She goes to the bathroom and calls, through the door, 'You need a doctor.'

'Then take me.'

She knows, until Maurice gives the word, she can't.

Carmelo opens the door, cleaned up and shaved, his old clothes in a pile in the bag. He dabs cologne on his pudgy jowls and smiles with the certitude of someone who thinks he is saved. 'When will Maurice come? I'm not sure how much time I have.'

As he speaks, Tatiana sees a line of blood, thin as thread, tracing the line between his teeth and his gums. Still, he smiles – like the mad. But she knows he isn't mad.

Twenty-nine

Mister Crawshaw leads Pulford into the visits area. He says, 'Ten minutes and not a fuckin' second over.'

Staffe wants to collar Crawshaw and pin him to the wall, remind him that Pulford is a good guy who shouldn't even be here and that they are – in this unwinnable battle between law and disorder – supposed to be on the same side.

Crawshaw takes up a position between the door and the alarm bell and puffs out his chest, chin up, lip sneering, holding his keys as if they are a weapon. Staffe couldn't wait to get out of his uniform when he was accepted into CID. He'd like to ask Crawshaw if he really wanted to be a copper but wasn't the right stuff. He says to Pulford, 'Are you all set for court?'

Pulford can't even meet Staffe's eye.

Staffe lowers his voice, hisses, 'It was Brandon Latymer, wasn't it? Brandon shot Jadus Golding.'

Pulford mumbles, 'They haven't got enough on me.' He looks up. 'Have they?'

'It's time to speak up, tell us everything you know. Don't let them get this wrong.'

'They want me to plea.'

'We need another suspect, David. Throw us a bone.'

'I don't have any bones. I don't know who did it. But it wasn't Brandon Latymer.'

'What!'

Crawshaw flinches; tightens up his stance and barks, 'Keep it down!' He takes a step closer.

'They've made me a good offer,' says Pulford.

'There's no such thing if you're innocent.'

'I'll be put into a soft jail within a couple of months. Out before I'm forty. People live to a hundred now, don't they, sir? That's a whole life waiting for me.'

'But you're a copper. That will be over.'

Pulford leans forward, says, 'What's in the bag?'

Staffe takes out the papers, gives Crawshaw an index of the contents, says, 'Governor number two approved them. Look, there's his signature.'

Crawshaw sneers, 'Plenty time for your studies now.'

Pulford leafs through the papers greedily. 'Wow! This is all about Sabini and the razor gangs. Illegal books were a licence to print money and all kinds of operations from different backgrounds carved up the action. They learned to coexist in peace and harmony.' Pulford smiles, looks more like himself, as if he can be content in this parallel life of papers and books.

'How's it going with Carmelo?'

'I came across one of his cousins today. A chap called Verdetti. Maurizio Verdetti.'

'Verdetti?' says Pulford.

Staffe turns over some of the papers in Pulford's pile, shows him the photograph of an angelic young man beaming into camera, wearing a *yarmulke* and an easy smile. 'Have you come across this fellow – Abie Myers?'

'Is this to do with Carmelo Trapani?'

'The Italians and the Jews worked together, didn't they?'

'That's time,' says Crawshaw.

'Five more minutes.'

'No way.' Crawshaw takes a step to his left, within reaching distance of the alarm.

Pulford taps the photo of Abie Myers. '*Abie* Myers? You're sure it's Abie?'

'Dead sure.'

'It rings a bell, the Myers name. They were gangsters, right?'

'Perfectly respectable now,' says Staffe. 'He's got holding companies all over the tax-free world.'

'There's another Myers. A David Myers. He had a run-in with Sabini.'

'Time!' shouts Crawshaw.

'Do you know about the new evidence?' Pulford looks sheepish, now, all the confidence draining away. He can't look at Staffe as he says, 'They've got the gun.'

Staffe feels sick with guilt, says, 'What do forensics say? Are there prints on it?'

'We all know my prints are on the gun it. And Josie's.'

'How did they find the gun? And where?'

'It was handed in by some dog-walker – directly to the Prosecution.'

'You've got five seconds,' says Crawshaw.

'Brandon Latymer got you to hold the gun, didn't he?' whispers Staffe.

Crawshaw says, 'I warned you.' He reaches across and with a broad smile spreading across his face, he points a single finger at the alarm and presses. The bell is piercing. It drills bright and deep in the evening gloom and the fast tramp of feet follows swiftly.

Pulford leans forward, trying to get beneath the noise, says,

'Brandon is clean. Clean as a whistle, you hear?' He says it as if someone's life is at stake.

*

Attilio Trapani lies on his bed, counting the beams on the ceiling. There are fifteen, and he has moved the bed a few inches so he can lie directly beneath the eighth where the chandelier hangs dead centre. He enjoys the sense of alignment.

Again, he puts the barrel to his mouth. It doesn't taste metallic any longer and curiously, the longer he has been lying here, deliberating, the more ridiculous it seems to even attempt to persevere with life. It is absurd, to continue when the odds are so heavily stacked against him, and death has been between him and his shadow since he ever took his first breath – in the same short moments his mother took her last.

He removes the barrel, rests the Mossberg on his chest.

In the absence of siblings (how could he have had siblings when he determined a life as an only child so irrevocably?), death has been like a brother to him all the years, which makes him think of Maurice, left to fend for himself in Sicily and up in Lancashire with the Jesuits, brought up on Claudio's tall tales of the mother country and the old East End.

He thinks he hears a car, purring to nothing.

Yes, once Maurice's mother died and he was left in mad old Claudio's charge, the boy began his own journey of running towards the past and a truth that reflects ill on everyone. This re-stiffens Attilio's resolve, so he picks the Mossberg off his chest a last time and holds it aloft, turning the stock away from him and opening his mouth, feeling for the barrel the way the young might blindly reach for the tit – not that he ever did that.

This time his heart knows it – beating in pitter-patters now. He puts his thumb to the trigger and pushes. The skin beneath his nail turns white from the pressure. He reaches further out and presses the trigger some more. Mary mother of God, this Mossberg pulls heavy.

He makes the final press to the trigger and he prepares for a light to blind him, for the pearls of lead to explode through the roof of his mouth, and to smell the shot and to taste smoke, and for the backs of his eyes to burn and his brain to be wrested from itself and blood and flesh to discharge into the riding helmet; the green and white and red of his father's colours, stolen from the Italian flag.

And somebody comes into the room, he thinks. A door opens.

A shaft of amber scrolls onto the bed and Attilio can't help himself. He wrests the gun quickly away from his mouth and the gun explodes. He feels a dull throb in his ear, hears nothing at all.

Helena is standing in the doorway. She looks like an angel. Her eyes are wide and her mouth is fast but he can't hear what she shouts. She stoops, then reappears, holding a piece of skin. It looks for all the world as if it might be the pendant lobe of an ear. Then he sees a darkness, fears it is temporary.

*

Josie is in the Hand and Shears with Conor, just like Jombaugh told Staffe she would be. They are leaning towards each other. She looks sad and neither of them notices Staffe come in.

He orders a pint of Adnams and mulls how he might break the news to her – that Pulford is being coerced into a plea bargain on account of her fingerprints on the gun, which has now miraculously appeared as part of the prosecution's evidence, but the words keep getting muddled. The conversation he just had with Sylvie in St John is getting in the way. Did he really volunteer to father her child? Looking at Josie now, he can't see how he might navigate his way to such a union.

Conor leans across and puts an arm around Josie, obscuring Staffe's view of her. She pushes him away, but he goes again and she snaps at him. Behind the bar, April raises her eyebrows and nods her head sideways, encouraging Staffe to go across and intervene, but he bides his time. Josie's eyes are red and Staffe thinks this is what the end of a relationship looks like, so he asks April to give Josie a note when she leaves. He writes: 'Research Maurizio Verdetti death on day of Cable Street (4 Oct '36) and look for other deaths – esp. a David Myers.'

Out on Cloth Fair, he gets a cab and within five minutes he is in a different world. The City has a ring of invisible portals, like so many railway arches to different dimensions. Perversely, you can pass easily from shiny to dark, like the bankers who slip down Shoreditch for a bit of the other, but try going the other way. It's nigh impossible. Just looking at the glimmering towers is enough to cast your life in shadow, which prompts an image of Curtis Consadine at the LSE, one million and four miles from the Limekiln Estate, but with a key to the vault, it would seem.

And this is why Staffe couldn't live without this job: living a life that constantly passes from one world to the other. This freedom of the City.

The Limekiln Tower looms high. There are other towers that are taller, but none with such gravity in Staffe's world. Looking up from the Limekiln courtyard, he picks out Jasmine's flat. A peachy glow within.

As he climbs the dark and echoing stairwell, he has the strongest feeling that he shouldn't be here. But what can he do? Regardless of Pennington's warnings, he needs to do whatever he can to find Louis Consadine before Pulford stands up in court.

He takes pause outside Jasmine's flat. It is eerie tonight on the Limekiln's deck. Nearby, someone hammers on a door shouting, 'Open up or I'll have you, you cunt!' They bang on the door some more, repeating the self-defeating pledge. On the first floor deck, a family of Asians kneel on little mats. They fall forwards, hands outstretched, in unison, showing the way East.

Staffe presses an ear to Jasmine's door, hears a man's voice but realises it is only Jamie Oliver. Staffe knocks on the door, takes a step back, prepares a smile. He needs to get in.

The door opens. 'You can fuck off,' says Jasmine.

'I have good news.'

A gust whips across the Limekiln and Jasmine shivers, says, 'Be quick.' She looks at her watch. 'You're letting the cold in.' She stands back and immediately picks up Millie. She hugs her tight, as if the child might somehow keep her mother safe. 'So, what's happened?'

'I know who killed Jadus. They've found a gun.'

'I heard. Got a copper's prints on.'

'And do you know how the prints got on there?'

'Shooting my J.'

'Why wouldn't they just rub the gun clean and get rid of it?'

"Cos coppers are fucking stupid, man. Think they're above the law. Well, not any more. This is time for justice and if you cover this up, we won't take it. You know it.'

Staffe smiles at Millie and says to her mother, 'There's a young man, a fellow called Louis Consadine. He lives on the Limekiln and I think he can help put away the person who did for your Jadus.'

'You've got the man who did for my Jadus.'

'If Sergeant Pulford is guilty, then Louis can help us prove it.'

'You're shitting me.'

'You know where he is, don't you, Jasmine?'

The door from the bedroom opens and Brandon Latymer takes a step into the lounge. He hasn't bothered to put a shirt on and is wearing just a pair of Sean Pauls, low as can be and showing almost all of the V of his loins. When she sees him, Millie chortles and reaches out. He takes her.

'Cosy,' says Staffe.

'You leave her alone.' Brandon has knife-wound scars above his heart and two on the opposite ribs. He has fresh stitches in a wound to his hip and two perfectly round hollows in his left shoulder, which are clearly old bullet wounds. He looks at Staffe as if he can't be damaged by him or his law. Staffe knows that Brandon has never done time. This is a man who knows his law.

Millie, in his arms, snarls at Staffe, as if she knows wrong from right.

Staffe says, 'Jadus lost his nerve and shot a policeman – he'd become a liability and you don't need someone like that. You certainly don't need to be cutting him in every month. How much was he costing you? Three, four grand a month?'

Brandon sneers at Staffe. 'You know shit.'

Staffe looks at Jasmine, but talks to Brandon. 'And here you are, Millie's father still warm in his grave. If he is the father.'

'Watch your mouth,' says Jasmine.

'A man's entitled to follow his heart. Jasmine and me were

always fond. We was together when we was neck high, anyone can tell you that.' He goes to Jasmine, hangs an arm over her shoulder. 'I had the decency to wait till her man passed before I came here.'

Staffe's phone vibrates and he sees it is Pennington, texting. 'You and Chancellor in my office, 9 a.m. Meeting with Commissioner. CSPD.'

CSPD. Clean, sober, properly dressed.

As he reads it, Brandon reaches into his pocket and Staffe flinches.

Brandon smiles, wiggles his phone. He dials a number and says, 'Police. Yes. We have an intruder.'

'I'm going,' says Staffe.

'Shame,' says Brandon.

'Shame on you for coming in the first place,' says Jasmine.

On the way back into the City, Staffe picks up a copy of *The News*. Under a street lamp, he scrutinises the article which Nick Absolom has run on Carmelo Trapani. Absolom seems to be questioning where the case lies in the priorities of City police.

WILL IT BE A GOOD DAY FOR BAD CRIME?

This case of the missing Carmelo Trapani occupies City Police at a time when their resources are stretched beyond breaking. They already have a sergeant from Leadengate CID absent from the team, but that shouldn't be for too long. DS Pulford's case comes up for trial the day after to-morrow. Let's hope City can keep their eye on the ball. Or do they already know something that might keep their man off the front page?'

'Bastard,' says Staffe, looking across the Old Street roundabout to that different world of drunken lunches and galloping dead-lines, where they make up the news.

His phone beeps and he checks another text message, this time from Josie. It says: 'Come leadengate now attilio trapani sui-cide. Failed.'

Thirty

Pulford puts down his reading, another day drawn almost to its close. He began studying the new Charles Sabini material after his lunch and turned dinner away. There is a pink and coral sky tonight and he allows himself to briefly wonder if his mother might see the same, from the kitchen window in Whitley Bay.

These days count. Every day on remand will be docked from the time he is given in whatever deal they cut with the Crown. The plan is to try to come to an agreement before the trial starts. His barrister said, 'They've got you by the ball-bag,' and this, apparently, is the best deal he's ever seen, in twenty-six years. 'Everybody really wants this,' he had said, reminding Pulford that the new evidence makes a big difference.

Pulford sits cross-legged on his bunk with the papers between his knees, piecing it together. All day, he had been immersed in the East End's history and, eventually, he came across what he was hoping for – a small-time criminal called Maurizio Verdetti came to London from Sicily in 1936. Rumour had it that the family back home wanted a piece of the bookmaking business, but before poor old Maurizio Verdetti could get close to sidling up alongside the likes of Charles Sabini, he was tragically trampled underfoot by horses during the Battle of Cable Street.

Sabini and his boys were in the frame for the briefest time, but it took them only a day to verify that they were miles away, up at a race meeting in Pontefract. But as Pulford read around the subject, looking into Sabini's biographies, it seems that it was only a matter of time before Sabini would have discouraged Maurizio in the most direct of fashions.

Pulford goes to his index cards and checks that Sabini was also briefly questioned regarding the murder of a David Myers, but acquitted on account of his alibi. Referring to the original article, he says to himself, 'Christ. Small world.' A small world, in which on that very same day Charles Sabini was racing in Pontefract, David Myers, another of his supposed competitors, was stabbed to death – this time on Brighton racecourse. With more hope than expectation, he bangs on his cell door, calls out.

*

Josie stares into the dark as they drive west along the A3. She wants tonight to be over and tomorrow, too; can't bear the thought of explaining herself to the commissioner. Word is Pulford is seriously considering the deal he has been offered.

Once they get signs for Guildford, Staffe bears left onto Ripley Lane and the darkness drops a notch, their headlights illuminating the hedgerows and ditches. She says, 'April gave me the note. You could have come over.'

'Could I?'

'Conor's all right, you know.' Josie looks across at Staffe. 'But he's not for me. I don't know who is. This bloody job scuppers everything, doesn't it?'

'You broke up with him?'

'What do you care? You made it quite plain you didn't like him.'

'We need to talk about tomorrow and what we're going to say to the commissioner.'

'I should be doing it on my own.'

Staffe puts his hand on hers, says, 'I'm not coming as your boss. We're friends, right? I'll sit there nice and quiet. Just give me the nod if you want me to chip in, otherwise I'll say nothing.'

'Yeah. Like that's going to happen.' She laughs.

'You're the one with the wagging tongue.'

'Me? How?'

'What you said to Sylvie.' He takes his hand away, changing gear and turning sharply down an even narrower lane, following the beam.

'So, what can we expect at Ockingham? Not a pretty sight, presumably.'

'It can't be so bad. They discharged him from hospital. A bit of plastic surgery and he'll be OK, is what they said.'

'Not exactly Van Gogh, then?'

'His eardrum is the problem.'

Josie says, 'We're not going to charge Attilio, are we?'

'He's saying it was an accident. No one else was in the house.'

'When Guildford rang up, they said it was a suicide attempt.'

'I'm inclined to accept their word.'

Josie says, 'If a man could do that to his own father, it's going to mess with his head. And it takes a messed-up head to turn a gun on yourself.'

Staffe slows the car right down as they pass the Crooked Billet. Out front, three men are huddled by the door, smoking. They stare into the car as it glides towards them and Staffe winds down the window, waves to the men, and the men wave back. He says, 'How did you get on with looking into Maurizio Verdetti?'

'Seems his death was an accident all right – caught under stampeding police horses and trampled to a pulp according to the hospital records. Not that they're much to go by.'

'No post-mortem?'

'One line about the circumstances. I guess it was a busy day.'

'And what about other deaths that day?'

'There were hundreds, sir. You'd have to know what you were looking for.'

'David Myers. Abie's brother.'

'There was no David Myers in any of the registers for all the London boroughs and I checked the following two days as well.'

Staffe pulls into Ockingham Manor. 'Maybe we need to look further afield.'

'Should I mention it to Rimmer?'

'Rimmer?' He looks up at Ockingham Manor. 'Maybe I got him wrong. Why not?' And with that, the front door of the manor opens, and out walks Frank Rimmer, waving.

*

Staffe puts on his rubber gloves and lifts up the Mossberg shot-gun, looking closely at the end of the barrel. He smells it, says to Helena, 'I bet there's traces of Attilio's saliva.'

Helena's forehead wrinkles. 'We've told you, it was an accident.'

Rimmer says, 'We've got the audio from emergency services.' He reads from a small notebook: 'You said, "My husband has shot himself. He's alive but we need help. It's his ear. My God, I don't know what made him." It sounds as if you thought it was a deliberate act by him.'

'I was distressed.'

Staffe says, 'There's a thumbprint on the trigger. You only leave a thumbprint if you turn the gun on yourself.'

Helena kneels in front of Attilio, strokes his face, tenderly. You can see that she has loved him, that it has not quite all turned to hatred, and Staffe thinks perhaps he might have misjudged her; that she is simply the victim of an irrepressible urge for pastures new – eager to secure her corner of England, too.

Attilio says to her, 'I love you.' He is unabashed, ignoring the fact that the room has three police officers in it.

Helena Ballantyne rests her head on Attilio's knee and curls both arms around his leg.

Staffe says, 'I'm afraid I need to know about Maurizio.'

'No!' shouts Attilio, surprising himself, his eyes wide as a Munch. 'I don't know anything. Not a thing!'

Staffe crouches beside Helena, says, 'Your father arrived in London two weeks before the Battle of Cable Street. Maurizio died on the day of the battle.'

Attilio shakes his head, mumbles, 'No.'

'Inspector! Leave him!' says Helena.

'We need the truth, if we are going to find Carmelo. If you are lying to me, Attilio, I can only assume it is because you don't want your father found.'

Rimmer says, 'I've heard enough.' He holds up a clutch of evidence bags with swabs and prints inside. 'Carmelo Trapani was here. We have the proof.'

'I don't know how those prints got there.'

Helena says, 'Carmelo was here a week before he disappeared, to discuss the future of the estate. I invited him.'

'You didn't tell me,' says Attilio.

Helena Ballantyne releases the hold she has on her husband. Her face becomes softer and she says, 'I'm sorry, darling.' She looks at Staffe, then Rimmer, and back to her husband as the uniformed officer goes towards him. The officer handcuffs Attilio.

She follows Attilio as he is led out of the room by Rimmer, who simply cannot stop a broad smile spreading across his face. He gives Staffe a look that says, 'I told you.' But Helena stops at the door, lets Attilio go, and Staffe says, 'You spoke to Carmelo but dealt with Abie.'

'What are you talking about?'

'Just thinking aloud. Trying to make it all add up.' He looks around the room, furnished by the books of her prior husband.

Thirty-one

As they drive past the Crooked Billet, Josie says, 'I don't mind if you want a drink. It's been a weird day and I know I won't sleep.'

'You're worried about the commissioner tomorrow? We'll be OK.' He pats her on the leg and turns hard into the car park, sees the butcher's bike leant up against the back wall. 'Just a quick one, then.'

Inside, a group of young lads and two girls sit in the back room, laughing and joking, playing darts. Most have mud-spattered breeches and Staffe guesses they'll be from the Ockingham estate. Rodney seems happy enough to see Staffe and has clearly had a few already. 'We heard the ambulance,' he says. 'All kinds of rumours flying around. And now you're here, so I suppose it's true.'

As Josie takes a seat by the fire, her phone beeps with text.

'You can tell me,' says Rodney in a stage whisper, laughing but not joking. 'Has Attilio had a pop at her?'

'No! Nothing of the sort.'

'I knew something was up. He came in at teatime and shoved me a few hundred, said to treat the lads and lasses.'

'Maybe he was just being generous.' Staffe joins Josie, who is reading her mobile. He wonders if it is Conor. Her eyes are soft and glassy in the fire-glow.

'Jom's texted me,' she says. 'Pulford's been kicking up a stink. Demanding to see the governor.'

'He's changing his mind? He's not going to do a deal?'

'No. It's not that. It's about some bloke called Sabini. Here.' She hands Staffe the phone: 'Pulford kickd a stink + gvnr #1 called. Says myers killed by razor in brighton. 1936. Supposed to be sabini but not. Make sense?'

'Myers,' says Staffe, reading the message. Josie's previous text is from 'Con'. Staffe can't help seeing the first line: 'Cant we giv it 1 more go . . .' He hands her the handset.

'David Myers?'

'This whole thing goes back to Cable Street.'

'Poor Pulford,' she says. 'What an idiot I was, holding that gun.'

'You've been a good friend and you tried too hard. That's no crime.'

They sit together whilst Staffe finishes his pint and Josie pulls a small package from her pocket, slides it across the table, saying, 'I worry about you.'

'What's this?' He removes the outer packaging, which is in brown vinegar paper, revealing a velvet jewellery box. He opens it, pulls the watch out. 'A watch?'

'A heart monitor. You wear it on your wrist. You used to run all the time.' She pats his tummy. 'Time you took more care of yourself. It tells the time, too.'

He laughs, putting the device on his wrist, going for a fresh pint.

She fusses the pub dog, who rolls on his back so she can tickle his tummy. When Staffe returns, she says, 'We should have someone to love, shouldn't we?'

Staffe hitches his stool a little closer.

'I can't keep a boyfriend. All I have is this damn job and now that's blowing up in my face. Every year I see less and less of my friends. God knows, I'll never have a child at this rate.'

'You will.' He puts his hand on her shoulder.

'What about you? How do you feel about that? The chance you might never have children?'

He rubs the nape of her neck, says, 'You'll be a wonderful mother.'

Their faces slowly come together.

He closes his eyes, feels her lips softly against his. She opens her mouth, ever so slightly, and says, 'You love her, still.'

Staffe opens his eyes.

Josie's eyes are large and green. She blinks.

'I don't,' he says.

'There's something there.' Josie presses her face against his and she kisses him on the mouth. He moves closer, but she leans away. 'We can't do this. There is something. I can tell.'

'Having a baby is what she wants. Not for us to be together, but to have a child.'

Josie stands, picking up the car keys. 'When were you going to tell me?'

'I just did.'

*

Maurice Greene walks past the bandstand as a lone skater boy clatters the boards above the shingle beach. The pier lights still twinkle as he turns up into Brunswick Square.

All yesterday the police were up and down the prom, from Marine Parade to the Brunswick Lawns. He kept an eye on them as they searched for him. Now they have gone and Brighton is the safest place to be, but he can't stay here. The city beckons and the end of the line is almost here. The evidence is all in, almost.

He checks his watch, and walks briskly towards the station,

dreading the prospect of the last train and its revellers. He feels the absence of Tatiana as if it is an illness. It makes him doubt the wisdom of what he has got himself into; what he must do tonight.

When he gets up to the top of the town, drunken groups spill onto the station concourse. Maurice pretends he is gazing down towards the pastel terraces of Hanover, but using the full periphery of his vision, he is checking whether he is being followed.

Once he is in the mêlée of the station and in line for the last train, Maurice glances at his phone, but Tatiana hasn't called and he can't help thinking that something has gone wrong. He can't call her. He absolutely cannot call her. He pauses in the queue for the gate, stops shuffling forward and pulls up 'Tatiana' from his recent calls and his finger hovers on green. His heart drums and Maurice checks around him again, turning off the phone, denying himself.

'Come on, fella. We want to catch this fucker.' The man behind him, oozing fumes of alcohol, slaps Maurice on the shoulder.

Maurice trousers his phone and turns round, tells the man to take his fucking hand off him. The man's eyes widen and he looks Maurice up and down, trying to reconcile the appearance of him with the words he has uttered. The drunken man is taller and broader than Maurice and he lifts an arm, but Maurice acts swiftly, flicking the man in the throat, watching him crumple to the ground. As the man's girlfriend kneels over him, Maurice shares a joke with the ticket collector about day-tripping drunkards, all the time looking into the crowd, picking out the faces. He does it all the way to London.

*

The train slows into London Bridge and Maurice peers up at block after apartment block, lit up and soaring all the way to the sky. Lives unseen.

The journey on the underground is swift and quiet and by the time he gets to Highbury, Maurice's carriage is empty, bar a medium-height, medium-built, slender white man. Maurice takes note of his lightweight gabardine, the collar of a Prince of Wales check suit jacket showing.

The man in the gabardine gets off and this is Maurice's stop. He watches the man pause at an exit, messing with his phone before going into the passage marked 'Way Out'. Maurice takes a different exit and goes a long way round. As he goes through the ticket barrier, putting the Oyster card to its pad, he has a feeling of being watched but the ticket hall is empty.

Outside, he gives a tramp his Oyster card, wondering if it is possible to trace a person's movements from such a thing. He must tell Tatiana to pay as she goes.

Maurice turns the wrong way, walking briskly, switchbacking all the way to Canonbury, assuring himself that he most definitely has not been followed. He uses a call box to phone Tatiana and he lets it ring four times. Then he hangs up and waits for two minutes before calling again.

When this happens, Tatiana is supposed to either pick up on the first ring – if everything is hunky-dory – or she is supposed to have turned off her phone altogether, but as it is, when Maurice calls a second time, the phone just rings and rings and rings all the way to message service. Something is wrong.

Maurice walks along the New River Walk, deep into a darkening hush. The trees are big and in this small lung of the city night animals scratch and scuttle. He looks up at the big house at the end of its cul-de-sac. All the lights are off and he waits for ten minutes and not a soul comes by.

He taps the code into the keypad and pushes the door open. He goes straight up and doubles back on himself, crouching down in a dark corner of the half-landing. From here, as his eyes adjust to the dark, he can discern the dimmest light coming from the Yale-locked door – a small glow in the gap at the bottom.

Maurice waits and waits, and waits some more. His stomach rumbles. He needs to eat something. Eventually, he stands, prepares himself to go in, but he hears something below.

Wood is splintering and he thinks it must be the front door, so he hunkers back down, coiled, every muscle in his body taut, expectant. Blood surges through his body as steps climb slowly through the building.

He sees the arm of the gabardine coat at the far end of the banister, by the newel post. Maurice wraps his hand around his keys, making a fist but placing the sharp Yale between his index and middle finger. He takes a run up and leaps at the man, screams, and his target turns, open-eyed. The man raises an arm and tries to take a step back, but Maurice is too fast, uncoiling every sinew and focusing solely on thrusting, jabbing his fist at the left eye of the man.

Maurice feels the resistance and hears the sharp end of his Yale key ripping the skin between the bridge of the man's nose and the corner of his eye.

The face is familiar now and the man is no threat.

Maurice withdraws a half-step and watches Miles Hennigan fall to his knees. Maurice crouches, checks the cut and says, 'Shit. I'm sorry, Miles. That's bad.'

'What the fuck are you doing?'

'You followed me.'

'I'm making sure they're not following you.'

'You're wearing gabardine.'

'What the fuck?' Blood seeps through Miles's fingers, his hand clasped to the eye. 'Abie's on your case. He doesn't know where you stand.'

'Why break the door?'

'You wouldn't give me the code, remember? And you were in here twenty minutes and no light came on.'

Maurice wipes the Yale key on Miles's gabardine and lets himself in, going straight to the temporary kitchenette, removing a plate of bresaola with cling film over the top of it.

He counts the slices, knows Tatiana has been, and he cuts two slices of bread from the stale loaf in the cupboard, takes it through with a bottle of Sangiovese.

Opening the door to the dimly lit room, the television gloams silently and Carmelo looks over the top of his pince-nez glasses. From the clean smell of him, Maurice knows Tatiana has definitely been. Looking at the blood that stains the perimeter of the dressing she has taped over his mouth, he has come just in time. Things are getting worse.

Gently, Maurice removes the tape and dressing and calls Miles Hennigan to bring some water. Hennigan calls back that he can't fucking see properly, but Maurice concentrates on Carmelo, who says, dry as sand with the last drop his mouth can utter, 'Is it tonight?'

'Not tonight, uncle.'

Carmelo groans. He tries to swallow and Maurice pours him a glass of Sangiovese which he sips, cautiously. Eventually, he musters. 'Pity me. Pity a dying man's soul.'

'Pity doesn't come into it, uncle. It never did.'

Thirty-two

Commissioner Beverley Strong is a tiny woman but even so, Staffe, Pennington and Josie visibly clench in her presence, each sitting forward in their seats. She hands out a document. 'It's code black,' she says, leaning back. 'Take a minute to digest.'

The report makes grim reading: outlining the latest intelligence regarding the simmering unrest surrounding the murder of Jadus Golding.

'Of course, we could be in there like that' – Beverley Strong clicks her fingers – 'if I gave the nod, but we are already distrusted in our community, even though we are straining every sinew to save it from itself. This is the status quo. We run to stand still, so you will understand my loathing of surprise. Especially surprises from within.' She gives Pennington a long, withering look and puckers her mouth.

Pennington addresses Staffe and Josie, says, 'I can't tell you how grave this matter has become and I want you to know, before I even get started, that neither of you will go within a country mile of Jasmine Cash or Brandon Latymer. If you see them in Tescos, I expect you to drop your bastard baskets and run for the door.'

Beverley Strong says, 'Part of the problem is you have allowed yourself to become so inextricably entwined with DS Pulford's fate.'

Pennington sips from his glass of water. 'Perhaps I was too optimistic, in thinking we could get to the bottom of this.'

Staffe and Pennington exchange a long look in which they each acknowledge that it was Pennington who brought Staffe back from Spain to help clear Pulford. Within the taut silence, Staffe nods and his chief inspector closes his eyes, slowly, respecting the fact that he is not going to be dropped in it by his subordinate.

Josie says, 'We can't sell DS Pulford down the river, sir.'

'If I may warn you, DC Chancellor,' says the commissioner. 'Your interventions so far have hardly helped Sergeant Pulford. We now have a murder weapon which the Crown will prove to have been in your possession.'

'I can explain, ma'am.'

'I hope you can, but the fact is, there is not a centimetre for error here. Do you understand? Not a twitch from either of you.'

Pennington says, almost mechanically, 'We fully accept your version, Chancellor, that Louis Consadine entrapped you. But Consadine cannot be found and we have to accept he won't be found. In fact, it might be better if he isn't found. You know what's saving your bacon, Chancellor?' says Pennington.

'No, sir.'

'The fact that Louis Consadine has done a runner. That will help Pulford when he cuts his deal.' He leans back, says, 'Unofficially, of course, we know you were trying your damnedest to help a colleague, and that is what's stopping me from suspending you.'

'I had to make a snap decision, sir. I saw Brandon Latymer with Jasmine Cash – Golding's partner.'

'Ex-partner, according to my intelligence,' says the commissioner, exhaling loudly, and leaning forward. 'You need to take your medicine, young lady. Do you understand?'

'It's Pulford's medicine that Chancellor is worried about, ma'am,' says Staffe. 'We encourage loyalty, don't we?'

The commissioner says, 'There is a greater good here, detective inspector. Somebody has to tend to that.'

Staffe seethes. His heart beats time and a half and he tries to swallow his words away, but he can't. 'It wouldn't do to have another Summer '11, ma'am.'

'Indeed.'

'Jadus Golding might be a black man and a dead man, but he is not a martyr,' says Staffe.

'Out!' says Pennington.

Staffe stands, says to the commissioner, 'I'm sorry, ma'am, if I'd known the truth was to be buried here, this morning, I would have stayed away.'

'Watch your tongue, Wagstaffe!' says Pennington.

'Oh, I'm watching my tongue, sir, and I'm sure you're watching it, too.'

The two men glare at each other.

'Sit down, Wagstaffe,' says the commissioner, setting her beady look on Staffe. 'You *will* hear your chief inspector out.'

Pennington says, 'We know there's going to be activity on the streets as soon as the trial starts. It will be precipitated by a group of anarchists, then sustained by the local gangs. We have to control this. We all know the full cost of Summer '11 as you call it.'

Commissioner Strong says, 'We won't be having any more nights where smoke fills our skies.'

Pennington continues, 'If this does get out of hand, DS Pulford's cause will be irreparably damaged.'

'You make it sound as though he is a pawn,' says Josie.

'This *is* chess, Chancellor. And we will win with our minds,' says Beverley Strong.

'But Pulford needs evidence,' says Staffe.

'The evidence is all in,' says Pennington. 'Your association with that investigation is absolutely over.'

'Have faith in the long game, inspector,' says Strong.

'It's not a game, for me, though I appreciate there is a bigger picture.' There's too much blood flowing to his head now and the words trip out. 'You go along Holborn, through the Inns of Court, up Fleet Street – past all the bloody lawyers and the journalists – you get to the biggest trough of them all. Bloody Parliament. Well, I haven't got my snout in that trough. My job remains the same. My *calling* remains the same.'

He breathes deep and Pennington glares at him. Commissioner Strong swivels on her seat, left and right in small arcs. She lets the silence gather. Eventually, the commissioner says, 'I have been following the Carmelo Trapani case, inspector. It's the sort of thing I would have loved to get my teeth into when I was a DI.'

'The son just blew his ear half away, ma'am,' says Josie. 'We were there until late last night, and we got a new lead.'

'You have a suspect?'

'We have more than one,' says Staffe. 'But DI Rimmer made an arrest.'

'The son,' says Pennington. 'You need to overcome your doubts and get a conviction here.'

Beverley Strong says, 'Don't let us stop you.' She stands, drawing the meeting to its end.

'I prefer not to jump the gun, in the pursuit of truth,' says Staffe.

As he leaves, he sees how upset Josie is, and once the door is closed and they make their way down the back stairs, he turns, holds her, whispering into her hair that everything is going to be all right. They stand there, by the window that looks down on Cloth Fair, until a footfall approaches. He says, 'I have to call on Curtis Consadine.'

'You can't go down that road.'

'No. *You* can't go down that road.'

The footfall comes close, passing them. She stands on tiptoes, whispers, 'Don't put yourself at risk,' and she kisses him on the cheek; longer than a friend.

*

Staffe jumps on the bus that would take him home. It carries him along, twelve feet above the madness on High Holborn and heading for Piccadilly, then Knightsbridge and Gloucester Road beyond, but as soon as he sees the ornate towers and spires of Lincoln's Inn, he hops off the bus and strolls across the green, which is pale black in the night. He looks up at Curtis Consadine's student digs. If Staffe had travelled this far in the other direction, east not west, he would be on the Limekiln by now. But far more than one world and half an hour separates the two Consadine brothers.

He shows his warrant card to the GA in an office in the lobby of Curtis's residence, and is told that Curtis Consadine and his girlfriend left the building a while ago. He tells the GA that he has to have a look around Curtis's room and the GA shrugs, watching football on the tiny TV on a shelf in his office. Staffe can smell skunk on the man and he thinks it must be the perfect job for someone. The GA reaches across his desk and pulls a key from a hook. He breathes heavily from the effort and hands the key to Staffe.

On the stairs, he passes a happy gang of boys and girls glowing with the carefree glaze of pre-drinks. This is a country mile from the land of guns.

The official version of the gun that killed Jadus, with Josie's and Pulford's prints on, is that it was found wedged in a hawthorn bush on the towpath about fifty yards from the cycle caff. A dog-walker handed it in to the nick in Dalston, said his setter had found it in the bush. 'That's shit, and you know it,' Staffe had said to Pennington. 'The e.gang planted it.'

He knows every inch of that towpath was scoured – from Kingsland Road to Shepherdess Walk. If Pulford shot Jadus Golding, there is no way that gun could have ended up being put in the hands of the CPS.

Staffe lets himself into Curtis's room.

He can't turn the place over or even be seen to be going through Curtis's things because he shouldn't even be here, so he has a surface rummage, sees that Curtis has the latest iPad and an old phone with no battery on his desk. Staffe makes himself comfortable in the only chair and reaches for the iPad, which opens to Curtis's Facebook.

With one eye on the door, Staffe navigates as best he can through the collage of Curtis's social network. This isn't what he came here to do. He wants an actual conversation. There seems nothing untoward and absolutely no sign of contact from Louis in recent messages. He browses Curtis's photos, reel after reel of drunken youths leering into camera, most often in bars and clubs. Some of them have names against the images.

Curtis has 1,746 photos in his gallery. Staffe isn't sure he has taken this many photos in his life. He scrolls though quickly, looking for anything different, and finds some photos of Curtis and the Japanese girl from the other day, Mako. There are some pictures of the two of them at a seaside. It looks like Whitstable. Another has them outside an old house, which Staffe thinks is Dickens's home. And there's one of them with Louis outside the Naval College at Greenwich.

Louis looks different, as if made for this better world, not the life he was given. He isn't wearing his baseball cap and he isn't trying to look hard. He is laughing and Mako and Curtis have their arms around him. Staffe rubs his eyes and he feels tired. Can you be made for one world and given a life that takes place in another? And who took the photograph?

He moves quickly onto the next picture and the next, where Mako is making horns with her fingers over Louis's head. In the next, they are more formal, just Louis and Curtis and Mako standing up straight, not smiling so much, with another girl, thinner and paper white. She looks vacant and, according to the tagging, she is Leilah F. Staffe recognises the name from the statements that were taken. Leilah Frankland gave Louis his alibi. He goes faster through the photos and after a few dozen he gets what he wants: an interior.

Curtis and Louis are in a nasty flat with no furniture and pizza boxes and their eyes are gone. Louis has his baseball cap on and there is no Mako. It's a different day. Different clothes. But through the window, Staffe can see they are way above the Isle of Dogs. He knows exactly where this must have been taken, so he calls Jom and as he waits, his tiredness percolates through the muscles in his legs, up through his sides and shoulders. He gives Jombaugh the name 'Frankland' and the place: Balfron Tower.

It has been forbidden, but he must take Curtis there with him.

Jombaugh hangs up and the tiredness washes back down his body and up again, in slow waves, tugging the last pockets of energy down and down into the undertow.

Thirty-three

Staffe's sleep fractures and though he tries to fight it, feeling so hopelessly tired and with his muscles turned to sap, the sound of the key in the door won't go away.

He hasn't a clue where he is. It could be the guest room in his flat, but the window is too small.

'What the fuck?' says a male. He is young and impossibly lithe. His hair is lustrous and pre-Raphaelite.

'It's him, the policeman,' says a female, passing her hand through the arm of the young male, taking refuge behind him.

Staffe blinks, sits up in the chair, says, 'Hello, Curtis. The GA let me in.' He takes out his phone, reads a new text from Jom. It determines his next move.

'You're not allowed to be anywhere near me.'

Staffe wonders how Curtis would know that. 'I'm here to make sure everything works out for Louis.'

'Louis is going to be fine. I'm looking after him.'

'You have a plan, don't you?' Curtis has two towers of reading material under the window – one stack of books on econometrics, probability and the history of stock markets, and another stack of published accounts of Footsie and Dow companies. 'You seem to be ahead of the syllabus,' says Staffe. 'Part of your plan?'

'You didn't tell me you have a plan, Curt,' says Mako.

'We spoke to your tutors. They say they've never seen the like in a freshman.'

Curtis puts an arm around Mako but she shrugs him away. He says, 'You'd better go.'

Jombaugh's text tells Staffe that they have been down to the Balfron Tower and removed Leilah Frankland from her sister's flat. They left Louis there, as per Staffe's instructions, and he is OK, medically, but he is out of it on a downer. There is an officer on the door. Staffe calls Jombaugh, says, 'Make sure they detain the girl.'

'Detain which girl?' says Curtis.

'I'll be right down to see Louis.'

'What's happened!' says Curtis.

'Rimmer's snooping, Will,' says Jombaugh.

'Make sure it's Josie who questions the girl.'

'You should concern yourself with Rimmer.'

'I want to see Louis,' says Curtis.

'Thanks, Jom,' says Staffe, hanging up. He turns to Curtis, says, 'Come on then. That's what I came for. See, we all want the same thing.'

*

Josie sits opposite scrawny Leilah Frankland whose hair is greasy and flat to her head. She smells of sweat and smoke but she has big, pretty eyes.

She introduces Leilah to the duty solicitor and tells her she can call her own brief if she wants.

Leilah holds herself by her own bony shoulders and says, 'Fuckin' get on with it, I ain't done nothin'.' She scratches her neck. 'I just need to speak to Curtis.'

'Consadine?'

She nods.

'You mean Louis?'

'No, I don't. I need a drink, man. I need some Coke. Full fat. I need some fuckin' sugar.'

The duty solicitor tells Josie that Leilah must be allowed fluids.

'Absolutely. We're doing this one by the book. No wriggling off the hook, Leilah.'

'I'm not on no fuckin' hook. I just need a little something.'

'That stuff will kill you and we have to protect you, so as long as you're in our care, you won't be poisoning your body.' Josie reaches out and touches her hand. 'You know what I'm saying?'

Leilah looks up. 'You bitch. You can't keep me in here and not let me have anything.'

'You don't get better without a little suffering. They're very good up in Holloway.'

'I told you, I ain't fuckin' done nothing.'

'We found plenty, Leilah. It's not just possession this time. And there were weapons on the premises.'

'They can't put me away,' says Leilah to her solicitor.

The solicitor refers to her file, says softly, 'I'm afraid you have eight months unspent on your suspended sentence. We need to remember that. I'll try for bail, don't you worry.'

'Bail!'

'You're here to stay, Leilah, unless you do yourself a favour,' says Josie.

'I want to see Curtis!'

'You mean Louis.'

She looks confused, rubs her temples with the fat pads of her wrists. 'This is fucked up.'

'That alibi you gave us for Louis was fucked up, wasn't it, Leilah?'

'Alibi?'

'You said he was with you when Jadus Golding was shot.'

'Curtis? Curtis was with me for sure. We was . . . we was . . .'

'Not Louis?'

'It was Curtis.'

'You weren't with Louis Consadine?'

Leilah shakes her head and her eyebrows pinch. 'We was drinkin' brandy at the seaside, I swear to God that's what we done. All day. All the time when Jadus was shot. I swear.'

'You weren't with Louis Consadine?'

She shakes her head.

Into the tape, Josie says, 'Leilah Frankland shakes her head. Will you swear to that, Leilah?'

'Will you let me go?'

'We should discuss this, Leilah,' says the duty solicitor.

'We will take into account Miss Frankland's co-operation,' says Josie. 'Full account, I promise you.'

'That's on tape, Leilah,' says the duty solicitor.

'I was with Curtis.'

Josie leans forward, presses the intercom and asks for a WPC to be brought in to take Leilah's new statement about the Jadus Golding shooting and to chase up that Coke and to get some Haribo.

She crosses paths with the WPC on her way out, says, 'She's going to erase Louis Consadine's alibi for the Golding murder. Make sure it stands up. Make sure he hasn't got a bastard leg to stand on.'

Josie stops by the tall window on the back stairwell, watches dawn coming up slow over Saint Paul's. She recalls the first time she ever met Louis, how she liked him straight off. She could see he was a good boy; so young. They sure can fit a lot of shit into fifteen years these days.

She makes the call, says, 'It's good news, Staffe. The best.'

'She's changed her statement?'

'Not everyone's going to see this as a good thing. They'll be looking at how you've gone about this.'

'Was she with Louis when Golding was shot?'

'Swears blind she was with the brother.'

'Curtis?' says Staffe.

*

Curtis hears his own name, looks as if the hand of something bad has come down hard as hell on his narrow shoulders.

They are outside the Balfron Tower where Leilah Frankland's sister has a flat. Leilah's sister is doing a little stretch in Holloway, was only too pleased to let Leilah have a key – in exchange for a little something.

Staffe says, 'Leilah Frankland was with you on the day of Jadus Golding's murder.'

'She's a fuck-up, that girl,' says Curtis.

Staffe hangs up, pushing open the broken main door to the block of flats, listening to Curtis dragging his feet behind. He wishes he didn't have to do this.

*

Frank Rimmer put a call into Staffe but got no response. He could have tried harder, but he knows what Staffe will be up to, out of his sense of loyalty. A shame he knows nothing about chain of command. If Pulford had stuck to what he learned at Hendon, they wouldn't be in that boat.

Had Staffe picked up, Frank would have told him where he was, he really would. But he didn't have to, so he waits for the nurse to bring Esther Myers, and reruns all the conversations he has had with Pennington in the last two weeks. He can read the signals. Cuts are being made and if it comes down to him or Staffe, he has to do what he can to get ahead. If he can just get the last bit of evidence against Attilio, that could make all the difference.

And he credits Staffe with the flair he can show. His idea – that the abduction of Carmelo Trapani has its roots in the past – is totally plausible now, especially with what he knows of Abie Myers' brother David, which completes Frank's theory as to how Attilio stacks up in that Russian doll.

The television blares its morning nonsense to three residents of the Nazareth House nursing home who stare blankly through the open french windows and onto the lawns where the early sun is drying the dew. Thin wafers of vapour rise from the ground – like truth coming up from beneath, muses Frank.

'This is Esther,' says the nurse as a woman in a wheelchair pushes her joystick and whizzes across the carpet, stopping abruptly just inches from the shiny toes of his perfectly polished shoes. 'Not inside, Esther!'

'Oh, go to hell,' says Esther. She is wearing a turquoise turban. Jade birds of paradise flutter in the print of her dress from the breeze through the french windows. She gives Rimmer the once over. 'You police?'

'Detective Inspector Frank Rimmer. A pleasure.'

'You look like police and you've never done me any good. No how.'

'Calm down, Esther,' says the nurse, leaving.

'I'm damn sure Abie doesn't know you're here. He'd stop you in your tracks and that's no mistake.' Esther looks away, across the lawn. She seems to doubt what she has just said. 'I don't mean that, of course. You have to be careful with what I say. I'm crazy, you know.'

'Tell me about Abie, Esther. You've been here a long time, haven't you? Does he know where you are?'

'I won't tell you a darned thing, so you can go to hell.'

'You don't mean that,' says Frank, taking a seat, looking her in the eyes and watching them flit: to the TV and back out across the lawn.

'Don't I? Some days I'm not sure what I mean.'

'You know Carmelo is missing, don't you?'

'Do I?'

'We're trying to find him and Abie has helped all he can, but we seem to have strayed off track.'

'Strayed off track?'

'Looking into Carmelo's past, that's all. Those days at the races and the trips abroad, and the Battle of Cable Street.' Frank smiles. 'You remember those days, with Abie and Carmelo, and David.'

'There's no David.'

'Abie's big brother. It was just before you and Abie got married, wasn't it?'

Esther is flustered. 'I don't know a David.'

'He was ever such a handsome fellow,' says Rimmer, sensing a sadness in Esther. 'Cut down with all his life ahead. They butchered him good and proper.'

'Be quiet!' Esther looks out to the lawn and keeps her eyes on the grass.

'You were fond of David?'

'Was I?' Esther Myers leans forward in her chair, peering into Rimmer's eyes with all the unbridled curiosity of the mad. 'I *am* crazy.'

'You know what they did to David Myers.' Rimmer leans forward and whispers into Esther's ear, smelling lily of the valley. His mother used to wear it. His father bought it for her every Christmas and if she missed a day, he asked why. 'You know. And I know you know.'

'You're mad, too, you fool. Don't you know that?'

'I know David Myers was cut to ribbons on Brighton racecourse and they never caught the man. They never really tried because it was one villain against another and everyone assumed it was Charles Sabini but they couldn't prove it. And the same day, Maurizio Verdetti copped it on Cable Street whilst the city raged at itself.'

'You got a turn of phrase, mister.'

'It's an amazing story, Esther. And it's got you at its centre. It's your story, Esther.'

'Maybe it's you should be in here.'

'For my own good?'

'Your own good?'

'Like you. Was that the deal?' Rimmer stands up. 'Come on, Esther, let's take a look at your room.'

'No!'

Rimmer leaves the room, hears Esther Myers whirring up behind him and she clatters into the backs of his legs. He falls and the nurse comes rushing up, but Frank says, 'It's all right.' He stands, putting his hands on the arms of Esther's vehicle, and unhitches the leads from the battery to the motor.

Esther has a suite of rooms overlooking the lawns with a wide-screen TV and a beautiful, walnut writing desk upon which sits an electronic typewriter with a ream of paper beside it. On the bookcase, two entire shelves are taken up by the novels of Esther Samuels. Rimmer counts thirty-eight volumes.

Esther appears in the doorway, pushed by the nurse.

Rimmer says, 'I see you have stayed with the same publisher. Loyalty counts for a lot.'

'I just like Esther Samuels. We share a name.'

'You've had a rich life, hey, Esther?' Frank taps his temple with his index finger. 'But all up here.' He goes to the coffee table, leafs through the copies of the *Spectator* and the *New Statesman*, all the broadsheets from the weekend. 'I suppose a writer can travel any-where, any time. Maurice Greene is a writer, so they say.'

'I don't know any Maurice Greene.'

'He's missing, too. He would have been born whilst you were in here. Didn't Abie ever tell you about Maurice? You'd get along like a house on fire, I'm sure.'

Esther looks sad. She says, 'That's a cliché. I wouldn't get along with anybody like a cliché.'

'Perhaps you knew his father. Claudio.'

'I don't know any Claudios. I don't care for the Italians.'

'And I'm sure you knew his grandfather, Maurizio. Maurizio Verdetti. Like I said, he died the same day as David Myers. We need to know what happened that day, Esther. I won't rest until you tell me, but I know you want to. How can you live with a secret like that? And when you tell me, I'll make sure you are safe. Safe and free.'

'Free?'

'You know what they did to David Myers, don't you, Esther?'

She pushes herself to the window and she stands, leans on her armchair and she sits herself down, looking at her small segment of world. Frank can understand that even if you can only see a little of the physical world, you can travel through other people's words and through your own memories and imagination. In Esther's case, that's a well-ploughed field. 'A well-ploughed field.' Is that a cliché?

'It's time to leave, Esther,' he says.

'He was the love of my life, you know.'

'David Myers? It's time to tell the world what happened, isn't it? He deserves his story to be told.'

Thirty-four

Louis Consadine sits cross-legged in a litter of greased Dicksy Chicken wrappers and bones and two-litre plastic bottles of Ice White, one of which has been fashioned into a bong. He nurses his head and Curtis Consadine kneels beside him.

'Can't we just have a minute together? He's my little brother, for God's sake.'

'I'm sorry, Curtis,' says Staffe. 'We need to talk about Leilah and Margate, the day Jadus was shot.' Staffe goes down on his haunches. 'Was Brandon behind it all, Louis? If you bear witness to that, we will keep you safe. I promise you.'

Curtis says, 'Don't say anything, Louis.'

'Brandon's not here?' Louis looks around, his eyes wild and red, black bags beneath them. His cheeks are sunken and his teeth yellow. He looks more like forty than fifteen.

'Some wires got crossed,' says Curtis.

'Where did Leilah go? I want her. It was like you said it'd be, Curt. She's so perfect, you know, man.'

'We've got her,' says Staffe.

Louis looks at Staffe then back to his brother. He seems unsure who the answers are coming from. 'She's *my* girlfriend, man. You know that.'

'Of course she is,' says Curtis.

Louis says to Staffe, 'Who are you? You that copper from Shawne's place?' He looks at his bright-eyed brother, wanting a miracle.

Curtis says, 'I'm on your side, right. We're brothers.'

'You need her alibi, Louis,' says Staffe. 'You're in trouble without it.'

'She was with me,' says Louis, staring at his brother.

'Now she's saying she was with Curtis when Jadus was shot. That puts you in the frame.'

Louis says to his brother, 'What's he mean?' He shivers, rubs his hands up and down his arms like he's being crawled over by spiders.

Staffe says, 'She's changed her statement – to say she was with Curtis.'

'No way.'

'Why would she lie about that?' says Staffe.

Curtis says, 'She lied before, right?'

Staffe says, 'They were on the beach with champagne and oysters.'

'Oysters?' says Louis. He is shaking now and beads of sweat pop on his brow.

'They're an aphrodisiac,' says Staffe.

'I know what you're trying,' says Curtis.

'What's he trying?' says Louis. 'Where's Leilah? I've got to see her.'

'She's securing her liberty,' says Staffe. 'You should do the same.'

'The fuck's that supposed to mean?'

Curtis kneels beside his brother. 'He's winding you up. Stay strong.'

'We caught Leilah in possession of ecstasy and MDMA, Louis,' says Staffe, standing up, backing away to the window, raising his voice. 'You do know she has an unspent suspended sentence. She will do time for this charge we are holding her on. She's desperate, Louis.'

'Desperate?' he says, to his brother.

'Where did she get the money for that gear?' says Staffe.

'Look at me, Louis,' says Curtis.

'Did your student loan come through, Curtis?' says Staffe. 'Is she dealing for you? Are you speculating, to accumulate? Is that part of the plan?'

'Say nothing,' says Curtis.

'Looks like the best laid plans can go awry.'

'What's a wry?' says Louis, looking at Staffe then back to his brother.

'It's in the shit,' says Curtis. 'Like his man in jail. That's all he's trying to do, get his man off the hook and he doesn't care how.'

'Come clean and maybe we can get Leilah out of this.'

'Say nothing, Lou.'

'We can bring Leilah back home. Just tell me and she'll be free.'

Louis scratches his arms, leaves long red tracks, almost to the blood. He leans back and sweat coats his head and face with a dull sheen in the morning light. Louis reaches out behind a cushion and pulls out a bottle of Courvoisier. He takes a long glug.

'Leave that alone, Lou.'

'Tell me, Louis.'

'She'll be free, you say. You promise?'

'I swear.'

'She says she was with Curt? I'm only fifteen. You know that, don't you?'

'Louis!' says Curtis. 'Don't do this, man.'

'It was me.'

'Louis!'

'I killed Jadus.' He looks at Curtis. 'It was me all right. Not Brandon. Not anyone else. I'm only fifteen. You got that?'

'He's high. He's high as the fuckin' moon.'

'We'll see,' says Staffe, kneeling in front of Louis, taking the boy's head between his open palms. He waits for Louis's swimming, bloodshot eyes to assume some kind of focus. 'Are you absolutely sure about this, Louis?'

'I knew it couldn't work. It's all right.' He puts two fingers together, imitating the barrel of a gun and press them to Staffe's heart. 'Brap! Brap! Two bullets, right to the heart.' He looks across to the window where his brother is standing, blocking the light, but Curtis has his back turned, looking out, past the gasometer all the way across the Isle of Dogs to the Naval College.

*

Pennington's phone goes off and he takes it, seeing it is Staffe. He listens to the good news about them tracking down Leilah Frankland and the younger Consadine confessing. He can imagine how keen his man is to rush to Pentonville and see his sergeant, tell him the good news. 'I told you not to get involved. I'll have to tell the commissioner that you ignored me. You ignored a direct order not just from me, but from her.'

Staffe tells him they got the truth, they found Jadus Golding's killer.

'We have a version of the truth, Will. You know that. It's as much as we can ever hope for.'

Staffe starts apologising for dropping Pennington in it. He says he will personally explain to the commissioner.

'Shut up, man! What I'm telling you is to come into the station and to deliver Louis Consadine into custody. He will be questioned and held on remand but this trial is going to happen. This is new evidence, is what it is, and we have to process it and

Pulford's prosecutors will need to be told. The CPS will evaluate the situation, but your work is done, you understand?'

Staffe says he wants to be there when Pulford is released.

'We're a long way from that. Not everybody is going to be as pleased as you. Some people don't want this.'

Staffe says he is going to Pentonville.

'You can try, but they won't let you in.' Pennington chooses his words very carefully. 'I need Carmelo Trapani, Staffe, and I need him today. I want it to be you delivering him. Hear me? Do you bastard well hear me! Make sure it's you delivers him to me.'

*

Two uniformed officers lead Louis Consadine away to the meat wagon, destined for Pentonville. Staffe sits in Leadengate's reception, watching the new shift come in. His limbs are heavy and his eyes ache, but he knows if he tried to sleep, the anger wouldn't allow him.

He can't believe they won't let him see Pulford, that Louis Consadine's confession is simply added to the pile of evidence. Right now, a team from Internal Investigations is corroborating Louis's confession. They are treating it with suspicion.

'You need to get it together, Will,' says Jombaugh, sitting beside him, slapping him on the thigh. 'You've heard the rumours, about cuts? Well, I say, bring it on, but they won't let me go. I'm too expensive to get rid of – this close to retirement. But watch out for yourself, Will.'

'What are you saying?' Staffe has a flash vision of what life would be like without his job. It makes him feel afraid, alone.

'Rimmer's been hard at it, you know. While you've been on

Pulford's case, he's brought in Attilio Trapani and now he's found Abie Myers' wife.'

'What?'

'Interviewed her and got some evidence that the whole thing goes way back, to Abie Myers' brother David and a fellow called Maurizio Verdetti.'

'The bastard!'

'Verdetti?'

'Rimmer. I got all that stuff. Is he passing that off as his own work?'

'He's uncovered the evidence. This Verdetti character was murdered on the day of the Cable Street riots.'

'And he knew Carmelo and Abie.'

'He was Maurice Greene's grandfather, so they say.'

'I discovered that, not Rimmer.'

'Seems to me, you've got to bring in Maurice Greene.' Jombaugh hands him an envelope, dressed with Italian stamps and stamped 'SICILIA'.

Staffe stands, looks down at his old friend. 'You know, they won't even let me see Pulford.'

'It stinks, Will, but you've got him the evidence he needed. You've just got to let it play out. Trust in justice.'

'They would let his mother in to see him. Can you get hold of her, Jom? Ask her to come down. Tell her there's good news.'

''Course I will. And we got a call from City Royal. The shared database flashed up a name you might want to hear. Miles Hennigan.'

'Thank God something's working. What did they do for him?'

'He's still there, I think, with a laceration to the face. Lucky not to have had his eye out.'

Thirty-five

Miles Hennigan curses as he twists into the jacket of his suit. He is in a private side ward in City Royal and the nurse tells him he is in no condition to leave.

'He has no choice,' says Staffe.

Hennigan and the nurse turn around, in concert.

'You need to make yourself scarce, don't you, Miles, before Abie Myers finds out where you are. Are you rumbled?'

'Would you mind if I had a couple of minutes with the inspector, nurse?'

When the nurse is gone, Staffe says, 'Tatiana called you the other day. Why would she do that when she is Maurice's fiancée and Maurice is harbouring Carmelo from Abie?'

'Is Maurice harbouring Carmelo?'

'He wants to be the one to reveal the secret. Or not.'

'I don't know what you're talking about. Secret?'

'And Abie desperately wants to keep it buried.'

'You've lost me completely.'

Staffe reaches out, puts his index finger to the patch on Hennigan's eye. 'Did Abie do this – when he discovered you are a turncoat?'

'I am a man of honour.'

'Where would a man of honour look if he wanted to find Maurice Greene?'

Miles Hennigan sits on the edge of the bed and sighs. 'It's not what you think.'

'What I think is that Maurice lives in the past. It's where he belongs. And Carmelo needs to face his past, to prepare his redemption, but I don't understand why Maurice would protect Carmelo, if he played a part in the murder of his grandfather. Surely Maurice wants revenge for Maurizio. Why not let Abie do his worst?'

'That's quite a theory.'

'Maurizio Verdetti died on the day of the Battle of Cable Street. He was crushed to death, but nobody saw it happen. He died just two weeks after Carmelo and Jacobo Sartori landed in Tilbury, from Sicily.'

'And Carmelo wants redemption? How poetic. But what you have is a thirteen-line sonnet, inspector.' Hennigan smiles, enjoying the look of surprise on Staffe's face.

'You mean something is missing? Do you know what it is?'

Hennigan shakes his head. 'Maurice discovered something that freaked him out. It made him rethink everything. That's why your precious secret's not already out. He's unhinged. He did this to me.'

Staffe takes out the photograph of Jacobo Sartori from the envelope stamped 'SICILIA': a mop of unruly curly hair and a broken, Roman nose – a rugged beast of a man. 'Seen this before?'

'Maurice had the same one,' says Miles, resigned.

Staffe turns the photograph over, shows Miles the reverse, where it says: 'CERTIFIED LIKENESS OF JACOBO SARTORI: MILENA SARTORI, DAUGHTER.' It is stamped 'POLIZIA SIRACUSA.' 'Not the Jacobo Sartori you and I have come to know. And if that's not Jacobo, then Maurizio isn't Maurizio.'

'I can't help you. You know how it is.'

'Maurice was going to save Carmelo. He wanted the truth to come out. Now, I'm not so sure. At least tell me what state Carmelo is in.'

'He's going to die. Soon.'

*

All the way from Luton, where she's staying with her sister, Maureen is up and down from her seat: to the loo and back; to the buffet car and back; constantly to the luggage rack and back. Much as Maureen keeps herself busy, she can't stop the ebbs and flows of her heart.

Just a couple of days ago Maureen had learned that David would plead guilty, take his punishment and, in a few years, he might get a generous parole. He always had his own way of doing things, especially after his father deserted them. It was her fault, of course. Then Sergeant Jombaugh had called her.

As the train rattles into the thick-skinned city, she prays to Saint Jude, to thank him for saving her lost cause.

After Sergeant Jombaugh had called she got Ray to make enquiries and he confirmed it is true – that another boy had confessed to killing that man who had shot David's boss. Slowly, very slowly, with her sister holding her tight for an hour and more, she came to believe what these police were telling her. She knows it's the hope that kills you, though.

The train begins to slow and the vast Kings Cross canopy makes the carriage go dark. She thinks what a fool she has been. If it is true, why isn't David released already? She had asked Ray and he said the Crown has to consider the evidence. What has the Crown got to do with it?

At this point, she tried not to believe, but something in her heart sang. She tried to resist, but the hope had already risen.

Everybody rushes to gather their things. They cram into each other, shuffling for the doors as if their lives depend on it. Maureen sits alone, until the man with the large bin bag comes to clear the newspapers and coffee cups. He tells her to move on, doing it with a kindly smile and a soft hand on her shoulder, as if he could possibly understand.

*

Jacobo Sartori moves away from the window of his fine Edwardian villa. The window is etched with long-stemmed flowers, stained emerald and rose.

Within sixty seconds, Jacobo is back, looking up and down the street. Before long, Appolina appears at his side. The two of them appear to be in some well-mannered disagreement and Jacobo points up the street, in the direction of Muswell Hill Road.

Five minutes later, the front door opens and Appolina leaves the house, pulling a shopping bag behind her, on wheels.

Jacobo waves from the window, looking quite mournful. She waves back and looks equally sad; Staffe lowers his field glasses as she comes towards his parked Peugeot 406, battered and inconspicuous. He turns down the music, which is Bartók. It makes him think of Curtis Consadine and Mako, two long lives ahead of them.

Staffe watches Appolina until she is completely out of sight, and considers his next move.

*

'You are in a strange mood today, my boy,' says Carmelo, sitting in the back of the car, which has blacked-out windows.

Maurice locks the doors from the switch on the driver's door.

Carmelo lights up a cigarette. 'Is this the day?' He takes a drag as best he can, coughs until his eyes water.

'Those will kill you, uncle, and you don't want that.'

'Are we finally done with all this prevaricating? The truth is what's killing me.'

'Which truth?' Maurice keeps an eye on Carmelo in the rear-view.

The old man is looking out of the window, watching his adopted city scroll by. 'The truth that it was Abie Myers who killed your grandfather; that I completed the pact and ran David Myers through on Brighton racetrack. It was straight after the third race. You can corroborate.'

'There is only one truth, uncle. You can't give one to me and the police, and keep another to yourself.'

'I'm coming clean, so why would I lie?'

Maurice drives steady.

Carmelo says, 'You drive slower than me – like an old man. You should be fast, at your age, eating life up.'

'They say it is better to travel—'

'Than to arrive. Hah! Just like an old man. But where are we travelling to. What is this fateful destination of mine? A police station?'

'Not yet. Perhaps not at all – unless you tell me the truth.'

'I've told you the truth!' Carmelo takes a deep drag on his cigarette and holds his side as he coughs up. 'Where are we going? These are the woods. Is this Muswell Hill?'

'It's where you stashed Jacobo.'

'Stashed?'

'You've been a good boss. He lives like a successful man, perhaps the manager of a bank, yet all he does is make you risotto and collect your laundry. It doesn't add up.'

'He's a friend.'

'But I've been adding up, uncle. I wonder how I'll fare, with my total?'

'You talk in riddles.' Carmelo sits back and remembers when he and Jacobo first came here, thinking they were champions of the world.

Maurice turns slowly without indicating into Cranley Gardens and a horn blares from the angry driver behind.

They paid cash for the house: four hundred and fifty pounds – a fortune. Carmelo catches Maurice looking at him in the rearview mirror. A smile creases across the young man's face.

'I never thanked you, uncle, for that share in your house. I appreciate it, and I think I understand it.'

'There's nothing to understand.'

'Me and Jacobo and Appolina sharing – not allowed to sell. We'd end up living there together, wouldn't we? It's big enough for an extended family.'

'Extended family? What's that?'

Maurice pulls up, outside Jacobo's house.

Carmelo says, 'This is too obvious a place for me to seek refuge.'

'Refuge? We're simply taking our chances with the truth, and by coming here, a swift resolution is assured. That's what you want, isn't it?'

'I want to confess, damn you! Is that too much for a dying man to ask? What harm—' Carmelo coughs. '—what harm

261

can come of that?'

Maurice turns off the engine, twists in his seat to face Carmelo. 'Attilio rests heavy on my conscience. They arrested him for your abduction. We can't allow that.'

'He doesn't care a jot for his own father. He can fuck himself. He would see me die in sin just so he can cling onto his life as gentry. That's a lie, not a life, and they say he tried to kill himself. That's the act of a coward; and a sinner. My God! He deserves the truth to come out.'

'Does anybody really want the truth?'

'You want it, surely? You want justice for Maurizio, your poor grandfather?'

'I want what is best for my grandfather, after the life he has lived. That's the only thing that matters to me. Absolutely the only thing.'

Carmelo tries to say something, but coughs again, holding his chest and leaning back.

*

Staffe keeps an eye on the black Golf with tinted windows outside Jacobo's house.

After a short while, Maurice Greene steps out. He glides around the car, leaning into the back, helping someone out.

For the first time in many long years, Staffe sees Carmelo Trapani. His eyes are bright but his face is grey. In his hand, a bloodied handkerchief. Still, everything about the man exudes grandeur. He would draw the eye, even if you weren't looking for him.

Carmelo walks up Jacobo's path with his head high, his draped overcoat hanging from his shoulders in long folds, like a Bernini, and Staffe suddenly feels less capable of negotiating the conclusion he had in mind. At the door, Carmelo pauses and turns. He looks across the road and fixes his eyes on Staffe's Peugeot. His long jowls crease almost into a smile. His chin comes up an inch or so, like a leader of men. He grimaces and holds his side, coughing, bringing the handkerchief to his mouth. The door opens and Carmelo steps inside.

Staffe thinks, 'Stick or twist?'

*

Jacobo brings Maurice and Carmelo a tray of tea, with glasses of water and a bottle of aquavit, three tulip-shaped glasses from Murano.

'Will Appolina be gone long?' says Carmelo.

'Until she hears from me,' says Jacobo.

'Did she know we were coming?'

'She knows me well enough, after everything I have denied her.'

'You gave her plenty, Jacobo,' says Carmelo.

'She was here when Maurice called. I have never been able to lie to her.'

'You just didn't tell her. That's the same as lying. Don't think you're better than me, Jacobo. And Maurice called you to say we were coming? To what end, I wonder?' says Carmelo, looking at Maurice with some hostility.

'My only concern is Maurizio, uncle. I'm still unsure of the circumstances surrounding his murder.'

'I told you, Abie Myers killed him and in return I did for David Myers – to my eternal shame and suffering.'

'I need to hear Jacobo's version of events.'

'He was *my* cousin,' says Carmelo, 'And the important thing is, two men died. I must atone for what was done. Justice must be done.'

'What would my grandfather think of what we are doing, Jacobo? What part did you play in the murder of that poor soul on Cable Street?'

'Jacobo had nothing to gain,' says Carmelo.

Maurice sits beside Jacobo on the sofa and taps him lightly on the knee with his open palm. His knee is all bone. Jacobo, a shadow of his master. 'Is that correct? Does my grandfather concur?'

'Your grandfather?' says Jacobo, his eyes big and wide in his kindly, wrinkled face.

Maurice produces the photograph of the burly man with the dark hair and the broken, Roman nose. He shows it to Jacobo, turning it over, showing the yellowed reverse, with his name on it.

'What the hell is that?' says Carmelo.

'Jacobo Sartori,' says Jacobo, reading the reverse of the photograph.

'He is watching over us; looking down,' says Maurice. 'But he is not Maurizio Verdetti, is he, *nonno*?'

'He's not your *nonno*,' says Carmelo.

Maurice turns to Jacobo, holds both his hands. 'What did he do to you, *nonno*? What did you do with your life, and poor Appolina, and my damned father? Claudio was damned, wasn't he, *nonno*, even before he was born.'

'That's why we had to send him away.'

'And what of me? Am I damned?' He turns to face Carmelo. 'What must I do, to be absolved? I'll tell you what, uncle – I must save my grandfather from a prosecution of this awful truth. That's what I must do even if that means sending you to hell.'

264

Thirty-six

Maureen Pulford doesn't know where she is. These streets are a raggedy mix of the posh and the down-at-heel. Eventually, they stop and the driver growls, 'Twenty-two,' over the chunter of the black cab.

She looks up at HMP Pentonville: grim and impenetrable. Twenty-two quid seems an inordinate amount considering it only looked a mile or so on the map, but Maureen picks five folded fivers from her purse and tells the driver to keep the change. He doesn't say 'thank you' and gives her an untrusting smirk.

'He isn't guilty. Didn't do it,' says Maureen.

'Sure he didn't,' says the driver. He has an unkind face and Maureen wonders if that is what his job did to him.

She steps out and when she sees the young mothers and girl-friends outside the visitor centre, her last whisper of hope loses itself in the noisy London air.

*

Maureen looks at her boy on the other side of the glass, reinforced with wire patterned like the exercise books he would bring home from school. He stands out from the crowd he is in now. He doesn't belong here. She realises that what she thinks is unchristian and surely nobody is born to a life like this, but looking across at the other inmates, she can just tell that some of them are equipped to survive in here. Not David.

'It's good of you to come, mother.'

His voice is frail and that makes her heart bump.

'It's wonderful news. They say they have a confession. Somebody else did it.'

'I told you somebody else did it.'

'But now they can prove it. You're getting out, David.'

'The Crown is considering the evidence.'

'You don't sound pleased. Am I a fool to get my hopes up?'

David tries to make the shape of a smile but there's barely any life in his eyes. 'Of course not. Just that it might not happen in a hurry.'

'Why not? If you didn't do it and someone else did and he says he did it, that means you didn't.'

Maureen watches her son's eyes as they settle into a gaze to the floor.

They sit like that a while, neither speaking. She wants to hold him, but she can't and she feels now, so surely in her heart, that if she did hold him it would be for a last time. How can that be? Her voice breaks when she eventually says, 'What is it, David? I can bear anything, but don't lie to me.'

'I was with him. I was with the boy who confessed, so I know he didn't do it. I was following him, hoping he would lead me somewhere.'

'But he confessed.'

'So we shouldn't get our hopes up. Not just yet.'

*

'Call the inspector, for pity's sake,' says Carmelo.

'I want to hear your confession first, uncle,' says Maurice. 'Tell me exactly what happened in '36.'

'You know what happened.'

'Some of the threads are loose. In real life, there isn't such a thing as a loose end. Everything happens for a perfect reason. Everybody acts according to their heads or their hearts; from strength or out of desperation. Life is perfect, in that respect. Everything is explicable.'

'Riddles, riddles. You have your damned story.'

'My grandfather—' Maurice looks at Jacobo. '—is Maurizio Verdetti, is he not?'

'Of course.'

'And he is here, with us.'

'Names mean nothing. What matters is what we do with the lives we are given; finding a way to survive in the circumstances we are dealt. Jacobo and I have changed. We are different people.'

'I was denied a family because of you.'

'Your father's death was accidental. Your mother deserted you.'

'You sent my father away as soon as he was born. You lied. The least you can do is tell me what happened that day on Cable Street.' Maurice turns to face his grandfather. 'Say it wasn't you who killed Jacobo Sartori, grandfather.'

Carmelo says, 'For God's sake let me tell my truth. What does it matter if we did for Jacobo Sartori? We saved your grandfather. Two men were killed. The names don't matter.'

'It matters that I am not alone in the world. I have lineage. And what about the family of this Jacobo Sartori? Don't they deserve the truth about what happened to their husband, their father, their grandfather?'

'Not everybody is like you,' says Carmelo.

'And there's the pity,' says Jacobo. He stands, goes to his grandson and embraces him. 'It was supposed to be me who they killed, *nipote.* I did a terrible thing. That's why I had to leave Sicily.'

'What did you do?'

'I killed a man. The wrong man, and your uncle Carmelo was sent from Sicily to do for me, but he couldn't. We played together as boys. I bullied him!' Jacobo laughs, wipes his eyes. 'Then he met Abie Myers and they had this great idea.'

'I ran David Myers through on the racecourse at Brighton. That's what I did!' says Carmelo, short of breath. He clutches his chest and collapses into a chair.

'We told Abie Myers exactly what this new Maurizio Verdetti looked like.' Maurice's grandfather taps the photograph of the tall beast of a man.

'And Abie did a job on him,' says Maurice. 'Who was he, this Jacobo Sartori?'

'A fellow your uncle sailed into Tilbury with.'

'Poor bastard,' says Carmelo, wheezing.

'And you became my uncle's servant?'

'Maurizio Verdetti had to disappear, one way or the other.'

'But you shipped my father back to Sicily. Why do that?' says Maurice.

Jacobo says, 'Your grandmother wasn't fit to raise a child. Not then. You wouldn't believe the upset.'

'I thought you met afterwards? She was a seamstress for Uncle Carmelo.'

'We rewrote our history. You can't imagine how afraid we were, of being caught out.'

'We should never have sent your father away, but your grandmother was convinced we would be found out. It was for his own safety. Believe me, there's not a day has passed . . . So when Carmelo heard you were orphaned . . . We were so proud of you. We still are.' Carmelo's manservant, Maurizio Verdetti, looks across, kindly, upon his old friend and saviour. He says to Maurice, 'Grant your Uncle Carmelo his peace. It is in your gift. Do that, after everything he did for you.'

'I have to think of you, *nonno*. You are my flesh and blood. You plotted and played a part in the murder of Jacobo Sartori. I can't allow that to come out.'

'It was so long ago.'

'There is no statute of limitations on murder here, *nonno*. If I don't protect you, who will?'

*

When Leilah Frankland has signed her statement and is released, it is Brandon Latymer who is waiting outside. It's true what he told her all those weeks ago – that he'd always be there for her, if she did the right thing. She feels herself smile, for the first time in a long one.

She gets into his big rig on the Farringdon Road and they take a high-wheeled ride through the shiny City and on the way he starts fixing her up, gently. He gives her a little GHB and smiles with her as it takes her down. He puts his hand on the top of her leg and gives her a soft and long squeeze.

'You got some benzos, Bran?' she says, her eyes all dreamy and a little girl's smile smudging in her face.

Brandon doesn't know how people can live like this, but thank the Lord they do. This is his client base. He's not deceiving himself. He's a businessman and this is the consequence of his sales and distribution. The overriding truth is this: if Brandon didn't sell, he'd use. Economics isn't fair, but he looks at Leilah and can see that he and she had an equality of opportunity, as Curtis calls it. He loves talking to Curtis. Together, they are above where they came from and that is going to continue. It's what Curtis calls social mobility. Oh, man.

He says, 'You got to be up for this little thing we need you to do, Lay. Then we can bring you all the way down. Hear what I'm saying, doll?' He leans across, kisses her on the side of the mouth. 'How's I give you half a Val?'

He sparks up a Dunhill International and holds the tar in the back of his throat. He'll have some Armagnac when the sun goes down. It's superior to brandy, he thinks. Maybe a line of coke if it's just him and Jasmine and everything is quiet. But it's not quiet, yet.

Leilah lies back, presses her head against the black tint and she shifts in her seat, so she is facing Brandon. Her little skirt rides up along her skinny white legs and from his perspective, her thong doesn't quite do its job. Something in Brandon shifts. His libido is a constant threat.

'Gonna fix you up proper. Take you shopping and then there's that something you can do for us all.'

Leilah lifts her right leg and drapes it over his left. Brandon drives an automatic. It comes in handy every now and again. 'Can I do a little something for you now, Bran?'

'This something is for Curtis, really. I have a bad feeling about Curtis, if you don't do this thing.'

'Curtis? He's all right, right?'

'For the moment. But they've got Louis in Pentonville.'

'You got something more for me first, Bran?'

'Sure. We need to get you up and runnin'. You want me to do that?' He runs his hand, flexes his fingers.

Leilah gives him the biggest smile and lifts her top.

'Then you're going to jail, to see Louis.'

'Louis? What's he to me?'

'That's the point. He needs to do a right thing. I need you to give him a thing and tell him what's what.'

'He can fuck himself. I got pulled in 'cos a him.'

'He's going to fuck himself, Lay.' Brandon reaches into his pocket, pulls out a pill and puts it in her mouth. He holds onto it. 'Half, says Doctor Bran,' he laughs and she bites his fingers so he has to let go of the pill. She swallows it and sucks on Brandon's fingers.

The valium takes her down some more – not enough to sleep any time soon, but she feels soft and she drops her arm from across her breasts. Her smile spreads and becomes soft, lazy.

Driving along Spitalfields, with all the shops open and the people cramming the pavements and the Jeep's tints keeping out the afternoon sun, Brandon checks his watch, goes with the flow.

Thirty-seven

Leilah feels a million dollars, turning the heads of the other WAGs as she passes through Pentonville's visitor centre. The guard on reception pokes his tongue into his cheek when he sees her, looking her up and down.

Back in his rig, and when they were done, Brandon had given Leilah a hundred quid of Topshop vouchers and dropped her with Simone to cut her hair and do her nails, at Cutz. Had he given Leilah cash, she would have blown it on booze and crack, of course.

Every now and again, Leilah catches a whiff of herself and it gladdens her all the way through – until she realises what she is here to do. That makes her sad, but she reminds herself what Brandon said, and what she knew for herself, too: Louis has brought this on himself, he really has. He's a casualty of war and everyone in the game knows that score. In fact, when she thinks too much about it, like she's doing now, she's really annoyed with Louis. Like Brandon says, Curtis will be a prince of the City some day soon and they will all benefit, but Louis could've ruined it for everyone – if it wasn't for Leilah being a true soldier. This way, only Louis suffers. That's how it works.

She feels pure, uncut, and she stops at the airlock doors, waits for the woman in front to go through. In the glass, Leilah sees a faint image of herself. It is how she could have been under a different sign and how she will be from now on. Sometimes, she doesn't quite follow what Brandon says, and Curtis, too. But she knows she likes the way she looks now. This is her new life.

Leilah puts her hand in her top, like she's doing her tits, but lifting the fat capsule and popping it under her tongue. Everyone knows Louis couldn't do his bird. He's too soft. It's best this way.

The door slides open and the woman officer pats Leilah down. Leilah thinks the officer might be copping a feel, that's how good she looks today, but she knows there can't be any kick-offs so she doesn't even tell the woman to go fuck herself, just touches the fat capsule with the tip of her tongue and keeps schtum.

The coating of the capsule is getting tacky. Brandon said it'd be good for ten minutes, but it doesn't seem that way and she looks for Louis, wanting it done. He's over against the wall and there's an officer right by him so she sucks in her tummy and works on her roll, which is easy in these new heels.

Louis looks right past her, though. He seems out of it already. His eyes are slow, like he's on something already. Taz, maybe – poor fucker. 'Lou!' she says, just a metre away and talking funny because of the capsule. Shit! What if she swallows it?

'What?' He looks at her tits. They're gathered up nice and plumped with fillets. He looks up at her face. 'Lay?' he says. His mouth drops open and he stares a while. 'You changed.'

Out the corner of her eye, she can see the perv officer eyeing her up. 'You like?'

'Don't know.'

'You should.' She sits down and leans across. 'I miss the taste a you, Lou.'

'You're talking funny, Lay. Why you talking that way?'

She leans across further, getting the capsule in the curl of her tongue. His face is big now and his pores are all clogged with muck. His eyes are all pupil. She puts her hand on the back of his neck.

'We can't touch.'

'I want you, Lou.' Leilah glances at the officer and she smiles at her, watching. She raises her eyebrows, almost encouraging it, and Leilah reaches under the table, puts her hand on Louis's crotch. He's wearing thin cotton jogging bottoms and he's half-way hard already. She whispers, kissing him, putting her tongue into his mouth. 'Swallow.' She says it like she has a speech impediment, but the pill is gone from her mouth now and she pulls away, watches him moving his tongue around his mouth. She knows him, can tell he's thinking twice. 'You're all hard, Lou. I wanna kiss you again. Wanna kiss you hard, man. It'll make you better.'

'What is it?'

'It'll stop the hurt.'

'You don't sound like you, Lay.'

'I'm being the best I can. For you. I came for you, Lou. Swallow, so I can kiss you proper.'

He puts his lips tight together so the blood goes from them and he closes his eyes. The lump in his throat goes up and then down. 'Done?' she says.

He nods.

'You trusted me?'

''Course,' he says, coming forward, for his kiss.

'Oh, Lou.' And she feels a lump in her own throat. Silly cow, she thinks, kissing him hard, but like he's someone else now.

Thirty-eight

Louis looks around, doesn't know where he is. It's like a living room, but with too many books; DVDs and newspapers, too. He was in jail and he doesn't remember getting out. He tries to stand up, but his legs aren't working and his head feels too heavy for the muscles in his neck. His eyes close again but someone says his name and he blinks and the man he sees is kind of familiar. The man touches him and it feels funny but that's because the man is wearing gloves, the thin rubber gloves that doctors wear.

'Come on, Lou, stand up. Stand up, man.'

'Who are you?'

The man is big and strong and Louis can feel himself standing up. He tries to push the man away, but his arms are too heavy, and now there is something touching his neck, something tight around his neck. The man is making big circles in the air, wrapping this thing around his neck and Louis tries to ask him who he is and what he is doing, but he can't get his mouth to move. He can't summon the air to send the words out. He tries to breathe through his nose, but it's too tight and now his throat hurts. His Adam's apple is being crushed and he feels as though his head will burst. His face is tight and the blood is pressing up at the surface of his skin. He blinks his eyes and they feel as though they are bulging and now they are wide open he can't close them again. It hurts behind his eyes and in his temples. The man's nose is snotty and he says something but Louis can't hear the words,

275

but he can feel the draught of the air that carries the words, can smell foul meat in the man's breath. Louis realises that the man is crying, like a baby. He tries to ask the man to help him, but the words turn to dust somewhere between his chest and his head, and then he feels himself fall and the pain in his throat is white hot.

It's dark now, and silent, apart from a distant sound of water, slowly rising within him. Soon, even this recedes, and Louis makes a final attempt to gasp in some air, but he feels his jaw lock, and then there is nothing.

*

The door to the house of the man formerly known as Jacobo Sartori opens. For a few long moments, nobody emerges. Staffe slides down in his car seat, keenly watching the house and looking in the wing mirrors and up ahead. The street is empty and Jacobo emerges, fair haired and frail with his turned-up nose sniffing for trouble. Of the triumvirate of survivors, he is the best on his feet and looks nothing like his age. Staffe has a glance at the photograph of the real, brutish Jacobo and mutters, 'Hello, Maurizio,' watching Maurizio Verdetti walk down the path. When Maurizio gets to the gate, he turns, waves up to the house and his grandson Maurice emerges, pushing a wheelchair.

Carmelo is all wrapped up, but as Maurice eases him down the step, his head lolls forward. He is unconscious, and Maurizio scuttles back up the path and tends his friend and cousin and saviour.

Together, Maurizio and Maurice push Carmelo down the path, and seeing them this way, side by side, Staffe can't believe that he didn't identify the likeness of grandfather and grandson earlier. The fair complexion, the small, turned-up nose, their angular, narrow-shouldered frames.

When they get to the car and begin laying Carmelo down on the back seat, Staffe sees his moment for intervention so he gently closes the car door behind him and crosses the street. Maurizio is the first to see him and he looks afraid. When Staffe gets within five yards, he says, 'Hello, Maurizio.'

'Jacobo,' says Maurizio.

'Let's not pretend,' says Staffe.

Maurice looks up, says, 'You should go inside, *nonno*. I'll deal with the inspector.'

'I'll call an ambulance,' says Staffe.

'There's no time,' says Maurice. 'We'll follow you.'

'No way,' says Staffe.

'We need to get him there now. He's dying.'

'Isn't that what you want? When Carmelo dies, his secret dies.'

'I don't care about his secret,' says Maurice.

'Even if it means your grandfather will be exposed as a fraud.'

Maurice gets in the car. 'You follow me. I'm taking him to City Royal. They know him there.'

'How can I trust you?'

'He's dying, inspector. All he wants is to survive long enough to give you his confession. After all these years, it's what we all want.'

In the back, Carmelo's eyes flicker open and he seems to be trying to say something. His eyes plead and he tries to talk, a thick thread of blood trickling out of the corner of his mouth.

Maurice Greene starts up the engine and Staffe runs back to his car, follows Maurice's black VW down the steep road,

London laid out like a blanket below.

Maurice drives fast, overtaking and undertaking and going through ambers. Staffe goes through on the reds and stays within one car or two, all the way down the Holloway Road. As they approach Highbury, Staffe's phone rings and he ignores it because Maurice seems to be taking it up a notch, driving on the wrong side of the road to get past a line of buses.

The phone goes again as Maurice goes through a red light and Staffe downshifts, sees both calls are from Jombaugh. Horns blare and he misses a drop-topped TR7 by less than a foot, swerving towards the oncoming traffic and just about making it back, two cars behind Maurice again and almost on the New North Road.

He clicks callback and talks hands-free, asking Jombaugh what he wants. Staffe can tell from the way Jombaugh pauses before answering that it's not good news. 'Come on, Jom. What is it?'

'Louis Consadine is dead, Will.'

'What!'

'Suicide.'

A white van pulls out and a bus comes the other way as the middle of the road disappears to nothing.

'Shit!' shouts Staffe, braking as hard as he can, the pads squealing and his back end flicks out as the ABS judders and he's in a skid, pressing the horn hard as he can, still sliding, slowing, coming to a halt just inches from the bus.

On the pavement, a young mother with a pram shakes a fist at him.

'You OK, Will?' says Jombaugh.

He's got nowhere to go and he can just see the black VW turning left up Essex Road, going east, not south towards City Royal.

Staffe gives Jombaugh the registration of Maurice Greene's

VW and tries to get his head around just how Louis Consadine's suicide will affect Pulford's situation. As he drives slowly on, he begins to feel dreadfully sad, that Louis thought he had no other way. And he also realises that he must find Carmelo Trapani, hear his confession for the murder of David Myers before he dies.

He knows that Maurice won't go to his flat or to Carmelo's house. He has an idea that they could use the room in the Kings Hotel in Brighton. Maurizio had the room key, after all; or, if the plan is to nurse Carmelo to his death so he cannot confess, Maurice might be in cahoots with Abie Myers. Certainly, there is a mutuality of interest there now, especially if Maurice is acting to ensure the liberty of his grandfather.

Staffe calls Jombaugh and asks him to contact Brighton CID, and to also check Abie Myers' two houses.

An ambulance tears past him, on its way to Pentonville prison, and Staffe pulls in, a hundred yards shy of the jail. He imagines what despair Louis Consadine must have felt, how lost his soul might be now, and that makes him think of Vanya Livorski and her faith and Carmelo's preoccupation with Saint Peter.

He gets out of the car, and looks up to the heavens, realising what he must do.

*

Maurice Greene pulls the blanket up to his uncle's chin. Carmelo sleeps again now, but he had recovered consciousness once since they came here and Maurice gave him some morphine. He told him that he wouldn't be confessing to the police and that those old crimes would remain unsolved, there being no evidence without his statement.

279

At this, the old man had wailed and begged.

Maurice had said he was going to get a priest and did he know this diocese.

Carmelo had pleaded with his nephew to bring him his own priest. As he pleaded, he spat blood and Maurice's heart relented.

Maurice looks back a final time before he leaves, to speak to Father Penetti.

*

Staffe waits for Vanya Livorski to return with the information. He has baby Gustav on his knee and the young boy runs his pudgy hand across Staffe's stubble, chortling to himself with bubbles of saliva popping in his mouth. The infant throws back his head and claps his hands together, so funny is this ticklishness on the man's face.

'He likes you,' says Vanya, coming back in. She kneels in front of her alabaster crucifix and figurine and lights another candle.

Staffe offers Gustav to her.

'In a moment. You hold him while we pray. Come on, join me. We shall pray for Carmelo's soul and then you can have your precious information.'

When they are done, Vanya takes baby Gustav from Staffe, in exchange for a piece of paper. He says, 'This is the only way I can think of to save him. It's the only way I can find him and if I don't, as I have told you before, he will die alone. They will let him die.'

He reads the name 'Father Penetti' and the address.

Vanya says, 'Are you a father, inspector?'

'No,' he says.

'You should be. You would make a good one and you are full

of love, I can see that. You shouldn't try to cover it up. Love is no use if you are alone. You must love God, of course, but he wants more for us than that.'

Staffe kisses Gustav on the top of his head and leaves, checking the address, knowing he doesn't have a moment to waste if he is to catch Father Penetti before he is called away.

*

Staffe watches the priest press the bell of the grand house in Canonbury – a three-storey affair at the end of a lane by the new river walk. Maurice Greene lets him in and Staffe calls for back-up, tells Jombaugh it is urgent and not to let Rimmer get wind of it.

Earlier, he had raced around to the church of Our Lady Bernadette in De Beauvoir just in time to see Father Penetti leave the chaplaincy, clearly in a hurry. Penetti had walked briskly up Northchurch Road and across Essex Road. He had paused briefly on the new river walk to make a call from his mobile and after that had prayed, crossing himself, before walking slowly up to the house.

From here, it seems you might be able to leave the house from the rear and when he looks at the map on his phone, Staffe sees the garden leads back round towards Essex Road. The fences are prohibitively high and he hopes the back-up will arrive in time.

*

In the dark room on the top floor, Father Penetti chastises Maurice Greene for not taking his uncle to hospital. He kneels beside Carmelo and traces the cross with his thumb on

281

Carmelo's forehead. Carmelo blinks and Maurice takes two steps backwards.

'Are you police?' says Carmelo, his voice brittle and thin.

'It is Father Penetti,' says the priest. 'And I am here to pave your way to Saint Peter. Like we talked about, *figlio*.'

'Can't you bring the police?' says Carmelo.

'Forget it, uncle,' says Maurice.

'You should take him to a hospital.'

'And you should administer what God pays you to do,' says Maurice. 'Know your place, father, and save my uncle's soul.'

'He can't,' says Carmelo. 'I must confess to the police. Have pity, Father.' Carmelo musters what life he can. He knows he can't take any more morphine. He's no fool.

'My hands are tied, *figlio*,' says Father Penetti.

'But mine aren't,' comes a voice from the dim entrance.

Maurice turns, sees Staffe and walks quickly towards him, pulling a flick knife from his waistband. The steel fizzes as the blade releases and Staffe stands to one side.

In the hall, two uniformed officers in body armour flex into defensive positions.

'Please!' says Father Penetti.

'Thank God,' says Carmelo, his voice cracking. He raises his arm, limply, and beckons Staffe to him.

Maurice takes a step towards his uncle.

Staffe shouts, 'Don't, Maurice.'

Maurice says to his uncle, 'Please, uncle. Think of Maurizio. Think of him and his life and what you owe to me. You sent my father away. You ruined him. Let Maurizio enjoy his last days in peace, without this shame. They could prosecute him, still.'

'I must tell the truth, *figlio*,' says Carmelo.

'Think of Maurizio in this life, not yourself in the next.'

'This is for us all, in the next. We must do the right thing, no matter how late.'

Staffe comes to Carmelo, holds out a dictaphone as Carmelo begins to relate the events of 4 October 1936, and as he does, in the background, in words from another land, Father Penetti speaks the sacraments. As Carmelo tells his story, so Father Penetti concludes and with the viaticum still warm on his lips, Carmelo's hand slips from his chest.

Thirty-nine

Rimmer and Pennington stand shoulder to shoulder, each regarding the front page of *The News*. A picture of Carmelo Trapani dominates. It was taken in the sixties and shows him sharp as a knife in a suit and fedora. Now, he is laid out in front of the two police, a pale and withered shadow of the man in the picture, all wired up to nutrients and antibiotics.

'It's very decent of you, Frank,' says Pennington. 'Letting Staffe interview Esther Myers.'

Rimmer nods, earnestly, trying not to smile, but inside, he is overwhelmingly happy. 'We're a team. And we should all be there when we get Abie Myers.'

'We have enough evidence to convict him for the murder of Jacobo Sartori?'

'We need to reverse Esther's sectioning. The Crown is keen, but only if we can absolutely prove beyond reasonable doubt.'

'So you need Maurizio Verdetti to testify?'

'If he doesn't, we'll prosecute him for accessory and deception. Once we get Esther Myers under oath, she will do the right thing. David Myers was the love of her life.'

'Abie's brother?'

'It was years later, when Esther discovered what happened to David that she supposedly went insane. Abie had plenty of influence so it was no problem to put her away.'

'And we have the recording of Carmelo's statement, too.

Nice work by Staffe.'

'I wonder how much quicker we might have solved this one, sir – had Staffe not been distracted.'

Pennington puts a hand on Rimmer's shoulder blade, squeezes until Rimmer grimaces. 'Your old man would be proud. Let's keep it that way.'

*

Staffe runs up the Farringdon Road, checking his heart rate on the wrist device that Josie bought for him. He's ticking over at more than 150, which should be his maximum. His T-shirt is drenched and his shins have started splinting but he's in range of Leadengate now. He stops and leans against the craggy flint wall of St Barts church, waiting for the reading to tick down to 139. When it does, he kicks on for a final interval.

He wonders how long it will be before they can secure Pulford's release, and how he will fare when he is back on Road. Will he even come back into the fold, given the way he has been treated? There's every chance he'll face a disciplinary, too, for his treatment of Jasmine Cash.

And what of Louis Consadine? He didn't have it in him to take his own life, surely.

Staffe puts on a final spurt, the sweat pouring down his forehead and into his eyes. The salt stings and his heart burns. He checks the monitor as it clicks from 159 to 160 and he slows, jogging into the Leadengate car park. He leans on the bonnet of his battered Peugeot, just a few yards away from the clutch of Internal Investigations Officers sucking on cigarettes and untroubled by the rigours of the real world.

Staffe bends double, gulping for air. He can hear them laughing about something, probably him, but his thoughts have snagged. He can't stop thinking about Louis Consadine.

The head of Internal Investigations comes across. 'It's us supposed to punish you, Staffe, not yourself.'

'Very funny. Just trying to extend my life.'

'So are we. But you don't seem to listen.'

'You should be pleased we got a confession from Jadus Golding's killer. Surely, you wouldn't want to see the wrong man convicted, for the sake of a little police work. You are aware the words can be used together? Police. Work.'

'Now who's being funny?'

'It's not fucking funny. You'd have seen Pulford sent down just because it suited the police to be seen to be addressing themselves. Can you imagine—' Staffe slumps onto his haunches and clasps his chest.

'You all right?'

'Imagine Pulford—' He struggles for air. '—shooting a man? Twice in his heart?' Staffe recalls what Louis Consadine had said and done when he confessed. Two fingers on Staffe's chest. 'Brap Brap.'

'It wasn't the heart,' says the man from Internal Investigations.

'It was the stomach,' says Staffe.

'We need to speak to you, about precisely how you came to get that confession out of Louis Consadine. If there's any hint of coercion—'

'You'd love that, wouldn't you?' says Staffe, standing, feeling light in the head.

'Come on, we need to talk.'

All he can think of is what Louis Consadine said: 'Brap! Brap!

Two bullets straight to the heart.' 'It *was* the stomach, wasn't it?' says Staffe, seeing Josie coming down Cloth Fair and before she clocks him, he discerns a look of quiet despair in her eyes and he feels a yearning to save her from that. In this moment, he wants to go to her and wrap his arms around her.

'Are you listening to me?' says the man from Internal Investigations.

He waves to Josie and her eyes brighten as he walks towards her. 'You're running again.'

He wiggles the device on his wrist. 'Within strict parameters.' He takes hold of her arm. It is warm and soft, nutty brown still, from the summer. 'If those guys from Internal ask where I've gone, say I'm going to see Nick Absolom at *The News*.'

Josie says softly, 'You scare me.'

'I have to go.' He moves off, his hand sliding along her arm. Briefly, they hold hands and he hears a shout. He breaks into a jog, looking at Josie now, seeing a new angle of her jaw, the flow of her hair and the sun catching.

The men from Internal Investigations call after him as he runs between the slow-moving cars and buses, then down the steps from the Viaduct and up to Ludgate.

He is in a good cadence now, running in the gutter, between the traffic and the pedestrians, his thoughts synchronising with the rhythm of his stride. His heart is smooth and the truth comes, in glimpses and phrases.

Forty

The whites of Mako's almond eyes are pink and a clump of tissue juts from the tight fist of her right hand. The computer screen shows *The News* front page. According to Nick Absolom's live feed, Louis Consadine committed suicide whilst on remand at Pentonville and as a result his confession is in aspic. Absolom speculates this might suit the police. Staffe knows otherwise.

'Where is Curtis?'

'I don't know.' Mako bows her head and the computer screen lapses to a screensaver, of Curtis and Mako at the seaside. They are drinking champagne and are poised to swallow oysters. But he can tell, from the aspect of the shore, that this is not Margate.

Staffe moves the mouse and goes into Settings, sees the machine is programmed to time out after five minutes. 'Curtis searched for this article. He's here.' He takes a deep breath, sniffs the air and leans back, raises his voice, 'I can stay all day, if I have to.'

Mako looks at the ground. She is afraid.

The door to the bathroom creaks and Curtis enters, closing the door behind him.

'It's a hell of a price to pay,' says Staffe, nodding at the computer's breaking news.

Curtis can barely speak. One by one, the syllables utter, like cracking toffee. 'That is my brother.'

He slumps onto a bean bag by the window, puts his head in

his hands and when Mako goes to him, he shrugs her away. Into his hands, he says, 'I want to be alone.'

Staffe leans on the window-sill, blocking the light. 'You have to explain what Louis said.'

'That's your job.'

Staffe feels his skin bristle. The device on his wrist shows 115. Far too high for a resting pulse. 'My job is to select the truth from what people tell me. He didn't know it, but Louis told me the truth when he said he shot Jadus.'

'He shouldn't have,' says Curtis.

'He said he pumped two bullets into his chest. That's a lie.'

'What?'

'But it led to the truth.' Staffe goes down on his haunches. 'You killed Jadus so Louis didn't have to. That's a brave thing to do, isn't it?'

'Fuck you!'

'But you let Louis admit it. When it came to it, the coward in you is just too big, isn't it?'

A phone sounds. It is dull, coming through the door to the bedroom. All three of them look around. The phone stops ringing.

'What's that?' says Staffe, standing. 'Is someone there?' He calls out, 'Come out!'

Mako scuttles to the door, hissing at Staffe, 'Leave him alone. He's done nothing.'

'I'll call you,' says Curtis, as she leaves, and as that door closes, so the bedroom door opens, its frame filled by Brandon Latymer.

In one hand, he holds a bottle of red wine, patting it against the open palm of his other. The tempo is steady and Brandon doesn't blink. He seems to have it all worked out, says, 'You been warned time enough, inspector. What makes you think you have the right? This is a step too far, intruding on my friend's grief like this.'

'I know who killed Jadus.'

'And so do I. They're saying poor Louis was driven to take his own life, but me and you know that's not so. That poor boy didn't have the strength to do that. He was helped along the way by your man inside.'

'You're the one with people on the inside, Brandon.'

'From what I hear, your man didn't cover his tracks so well.'

Staffe says, 'There's only one reason Louis would lie about killing Jadus.'

'You scared the livin' shit outa him.'

'That poor boy had no life without his big brother. That's how you raised him, am I right, Curtis?'

'You know shit,' says Curtis.

'You've no right being here,' says Brandon, taking a step towards Staffe. 'You didn't even announce yourself when you came in. Your man Pulford, and now you, have been harassing us for months now. We're all pent up.' Brandon grabs Curtis by the hair on his temple. 'Stand up, man.'

Curtis yelps and grimaces, but he stands up.

Brandon thrusts the bottle into Curtis's hand. 'I saw it. As God is my witness, I saw what happened, and so did Mako. I came in as it was happening.'

'The GA knows you were already here.'

'Don't you worry about the GA. The GA knows what's what.' Brandon whispers into Curtis's ear and the fear crashes down, into his eyes. He takes a tighter clench on the neck of the bottle.

'Don't do it, Curtis. I know it was a gangland execution and you were coerced. You did it so your little brother didn't have to.'

'What the fuck you talking about? Curtis here was by the beach with a friend,' says Brandon.

'Louis was only fifteen, that was the plan, right? Just in case you couldn't pin it on Pulford. But you just couldn't let him do it, am I right, Curtis? When it mattered, your heart prevailed over that amazing mind of yours.'

'Do it, Curt,' says Brandon.

Curtis Consadine's eyes glaze. He says, 'You should have left him alone. He did nothing wrong, but you kept coming for him.' Curtis takes a step towards Staffe, who raises his hands, anticipating the blow, but Curtis is young and strong and the bottle comes down hard and cracks the bone in his forearm and Staffe falls back into the window. The window smashes and he hears it tear his jacket and skin, jagging into his arm with a flash of pain. He is leaning out of the window. The breeze is warm.

Curtis steps forward again.

'Push him out!' shouts Brandon.

The pain from the cracked bone in his forearm shoots up one side of Staffe's body and the jagging cut sears through the other. His heart stops as Curtis comes towards him, reaching for his neck. He tries to defend himself, but his muscles are limp, his energy ebbing away. Curtis smashes the bottle against the frame of the window and wine sprays red.

Curtis grips him tight and is pushing him now. He sees the sky. Pigeons flap way up and the broken neck of the bottle comes at him and he raises a hand.

Staffe hears a crash and thinks it must be him going all the way through the window, and then he sees Curtis's eyes go even wider.

Brandon shouts, 'Fuck!' and there's another crashing sound and Curtis releases his grip and Staffe falls. He falls away from Curtis and he knows this is it. He waits to feel the air beneath him and to maybe twist and see the ground, then feel the impact, the crunch of bones, but something holds him, pulls him back and he feels flesh on his face and arms around him and someone familiar whispers his name. They say, 'Staffe,' soft and gentle and they press their lips to his face, and finally, he knows who it is.

'Josie,' he says, letting her hold him, surrendering as she lowers him gently to the floor, where he sits in the broken glass and the wine and his own blood, thicker, redder. He looks up at her.

She kneels beside him and puts her hand to his cheek and says, 'You fool.'

Over her shoulder, he sees six men in body armour wrestling Curtis Consadine and Brandon Latymer to the floor. Latymer is advising them of his version of his rights as Rimmer reads them aloud.

'How did you know?' he says, to Josie.

She holds his wrist, taps the device. 'Tracker. It was Rimmer's idea.' She leans close to him, whispers, 'He's not what he seems.'

Staffe breathes in her scent, feels his body go loose and he surrenders as she holds him tight, her cheek pressed into his.

Forty-one

The doctor peers over his pince-nez glasses and snips the thread to the last of the eighteen stitches he has just put in Staffe's arm. He takes hold of the wrist of the other arm and Staffe bites his lip. 'We need to get this in a pot.'

'Can it wait an hour?' says Staffe. He turns to Josie. 'We've got to get to Pentonville and make sure Pulford knows we've got Curtis Consadine all stitched up.'

'There's a car waiting outside, sir,' says Josie. 'I'll go and see Pulford. You stay here and get yourself sorted. You look a wreck.'

'I'm coming,' says Staffe. 'And somebody's going to have to get hold of that e.gang member in there. What's he called? Salmon?'

'They call him Beef. I'll call the governor.'

Staffe tries to pull on his shirt, but he can't bend his arm. Josie helps him and the sleeves flap, where the doctor had to cut them open, to dress the wound then stitch him up.

On the way out, Staffe sees Rimmer waiting by a coffee machine, talking to a nurse. He goes across, says, 'Thanks, Frank. It was good of you, I suppose – to keep track. Beyond the call.'

'My old man used to say nothing was beyond the call. He ever say that to you?'

Staffe nods. 'Well, it was a brave and decent thing to do.'

'You look like you need a few nights in here.'

'I've got to see Pulford.'

'They won't let you in, but I could come with you. I know the guys on reception up there. They're OK.'

'Thanks, Frank. I'd appreciate that.'

'Let me do the talking, hey? This once.'

Josie joins them, says, 'I can't get through to the governor and the phone on the wing won't pick up.'

Rimmer looks at his watch. 'It's Recreation.'

*

The smell of six hundred men is something you can't escape. You can isolate six hundred hard and desperate men from society; you can even separate them from each other, but even through concrete and steel, a collective will prevails. Never, in his long weeks here in Pentonville, has Pulford sensed such menace, so he tried to stay in his cell, but his psychologist said he had to socialise and Crawshaw told him he'd be on another Governor's if he didn't do as he was told. Going into a trial, that's something he can't afford.

In the corners of the unit, men gather in twos and threes and the talk of suicide spreads. Pulford waits to be let into his pad.

'Suicide,' says his next-door, an Asian lad called Asif. 'Your boy, they reckon.'

'I don't have a boy.'

'His confession's your ticket out, pussy,' says Asif.

Pulford looks down, sees Beef coming up the stairs. He is wired, looking around for something, his eyes burning and when he sees Pulford, he mouths the words, 'Fuck you.'

Pulford calls to Crawshaw, 'You letting me in my pad, or what?'

Asif says, 'He tops himself just after he confessed your crime? Fuck, man, that's good for you.'

'Mister Crawshaw!' shouts Pulford. 'Let me in!'

Now, Crawshaw comes along the landing, swinging his keys on a chain from his thick leather belt. He catches them expertly and in one sweep, puts the key to the lock, opens Pulford's door and ushers Pulford in, but Beef appears before Pulford can close the door and Pulford glimpses a new expression on Crawshaw's face. It is humane. He looks afraid and he wonders what hold Beef and his gang must have over the PO.

'You can't touch me,' says Pulford, looking Beef in the eye. Something smells. A new smell, of rubber. It smells like Durex and Pulford watches as Beef pulls out a pair of thin, flesh-coloured rubber gloves.

'Put these on,' says Beef, offering Pulford the gloves.

'Why?'

'You don't need to know why.'

Pulford shakes his head. 'Louis didn't kill Jadus.'

'You should fuckin' know. But he's dead now and he can't take his confession back, can he? That suits you, right? That's reason enough for you to shut him up proper.' Beef tosses the gloves onto Pulford's bed and takes out a small brown bottle with capsules in it. He puts it under the mattress on the top bunk.

'What are they?'

Beef reaches behind him, delves into his pants, brings out a paring knife and points at the gloves. 'Put the fucking gloves on.'

Pulford realises why Beef wants him to wear the gloves, why the pills are under his mattress. Pulling the gloves on, he keeps his eyes on the sharp blade of Beef's paring knife. He looks quickly up at Beef, sees his eyes are dead. He seems to be on the very edge. Pulford says, 'Louis was a good boy, you know. He never harmed anyone. It's a shame he didn't have his brother's brains.'

'The fuck you know about Curtis?'

'Curtis?' says Pulford, feeling something click. He has the second glove in his hand now, stretching it. 'We can be better than this.'

'Can't be better than what I'm dealt,' says Beef.

Pulford grips the middle finger of the glove and stretches the rubber, aiming it at Beef's eye. He lets go of the glove with his left hand and the ribbed elastic of the wristband pings into Beef's eye.

'Fuck!' he says, holding his eye, dropping the knife.

Pulford stoops, reaches for the knife but Beef lashes out with his foot, catching Pulford on the jaw. The bone cracks, but he clasps the knife tight, lunging out and thrusting the blade into Beef's thigh. The blade goes 'Phiss' as it cuts through flesh and tissue and squelches as he pulls it out. Beef raises his hands, half martial arts, half boxer, his grey sweat-bottoms turning instantly maroon as the blood flows. Pulford takes a step back.

'You better mean this, man.' Beef steps towards Pulford, who backs away. A key rattles in the door. 'You going to have to kill me, to stop me.'

The door opens and Crawshaw shouts, 'Drop the fucking knife, Pulford.'

Beef says, 'My man cut your fucking dog up with a knife just like that.' Beef steps forward, pulling back to punch Pulford, who raises his hands, jabbing out with his left, holding the knife back, and he takes a blow to the head and falls back against the wall, but he pushes himself off and Beef keeps coming and Crawshaw keeps shouting and Beef is all over Pulford now, with his throat in both hands, staring wide-eyed into Pulford, whispering with rank breath, 'Do it, pussy. Do it,' and as the air backs up into his lungs and his throat screams with pain, Pulford tries desperately to stop himself jabbing out with the knife. He can only hear the drumming of blood inside his own head now and his hands are wet, cloying.

He puts the knife to Beef's throat and watches as the point of the steel presses into the flesh.

'Enough!' Crawshaw is standing in the door.

Pulford looks at him, sees the same fear in the PO's face that he saw before.

'Do it,' hisses Beef.

Pulford looks down into Beef's eyes, sees no fear. It is almost as if Beef has seen into what lies on the other side and knows he can take it.

'Do it,' he whispers.

Pulford grips the handle of the knife even firmer and closes his eyes. He pictures what they must have done to his dog, his mother's sadness. He thinks of the sacrifices his mother made and what she would say to him if she was here now.

'Do it,' implores Beef.

Pulford thinks about what he still wants from life: everything that could lie ahead – in here and beyond. Slowly, he opens his eyes. Slowly, his grip on the knife relents and he rolls away, hears the knife fall to the floor and Crawshaw rushes across, twists him.

*

The traffic is slow, as ever, on City Road but up ahead, the thick three lanes begin to separate, making way for a flashing emergency vehicle coming up behind, siren blaring, and Staffe shouts to the cabbie, 'Get in its slipstream. Follow it, man!'

They chase the ambulance all the way up to the prison, and Staffe's heart sinks when it turns right, up to the prison gates. He, Josie and Rimmer watch as the driver barks into his radio, gesticulating at the POs on the gate to open up, let them in.

'Do you think it's anything to do with Pulford?' says Rimmer.

'I'll ask at the gate,' says Josie.

'I'll come with you,' says Rimmer.

Staffe watches them go, but his heart is so heavy already. He fears the worst for Pulford, so close to making it out.

Slowly, Rimmer and Josie make their way back from the gate. Her head is bowed, his face is grim.

'It's Pulford,' says Staffe. 'Isn't it?'

'I'm sorry, sir,' says Josie, not looking him in the face.

The gates glide open and the ambulance goes through, high-revving and clearly a matter of life and death.

'Is Pulford in there?'

'Levi Salmon has been assaulted. It was in Pulford's cell.'

Behind them, screaming up onto the prison forecourt, a police car screeches to a halt. The uniformed men run up to the prison gates and they are let through straight away.

'What the hell can we do now?' says Josie.

'We make the Curtis Consadine conviction stick,' says Rimmer.

'It's not looking good for Pulford, though. They won't let him back into the Force if he assaulted Levi Salmon,' says Staffe.

'Maybe that's not what he wants,' says Josie. 'You saved him. Remember that. You found Curtis Consadine. He'll be all right.'

'Let me take it from here, Will,' says Rimmer. 'It calls for a cold heart.'

Staffe smiles. 'A cool head, Frank.' Standing, he says to Josie,

'Keep me posted. Every step of the way.'

'You're going to stand back?'

'I know the score. Pulford needs all the help he can get and I'm probably bad news right now.'

On the corner, he pauses, looks back at Josie and their eyes lock. Rimmer has turned away, talking into his phone, and Staffe raises a finger to his lips, winks at her.

Rimmer seems to have found a couple of new gears during the course of this case and Staffe wonders if that will put his own future in jeopardy. He feels sick and empty, deep in the pit of his stomach, as he contemplates his future, but a part of that emptiness is wanting to be with her. Can it be so?

Forty-two

Josie keeps half an eye on Rimmer who is busy on the phone, talking to Margate CID, who are questioning the man with the cockle van down there, showing him scanned photos of Louis Consadine and Leilah Frankland. Rimmer spins slowly in his seat, and she gets to work on the interviews at the LSE and down on the Limekiln.

When she is done, Josie calls HMP Pentonville and is told that DS David Pulford is being held in isolation, on a zero-contact regime, for his own safety. The prison is, belatedly, arranging for all known members of the e.gang to be relocated. As for the trial, an application to defer has been made by the Crown and it is expected that charges against Pulford will be dropped.

She leans back, exhausted, and asks Rimmer if he wants to go out for a coffee.

He's not there.

She stands up, calls, 'Boss?' and asks around, receives only shrugs as to where DI Rimmer has gone. One of the WPCs says, 'I heard him being super licky. Must have been onto a nob.'

'Pennington?' says Josie.

'Maybe. My guess is higher.'

Josie scoots along the corridor and up the stairs, dialling Staffe's number as she goes. When she gets to Pennington's office, a uniformed minion sits on a chair in the corridor. 'Is DI Rimmer in there?' she asks.

'Can't say,' says the young graduate, looking her up and down, adjusting the fall of his hair.

'Just tell me, you prick.'

'Potty mouth.'

Staffe answers and she whispers, 'I think Rimmer's in with Pennington, sir. And Beverley Strong.'

'That can't be good.'

'It's best if you don't—' but the line is dead and her phone beeps, like a flatline.

*

Staffe knocks and goes in, ignoring the pleas of both Josie and the pink-cheeked graduate sitting erect outside DCI Pennington's office.

'I'm sorry to interrupt, sir,' says Staffe.

Pennington stares at the ground, seemingly defeated. He lets Beverley Strong speak on his behalf.

'You are a little premature, but—' She looks at Frank Rimmer, who smiles. '—we were nearly done.'

Rimmer and Strong seem thick as thieves, with Pennington somehow on the outside.

'I was congratulating Frank on the Trapani case,' says Beverley Strong. 'Bringing in Abie Myers' wife was terrific police work. Just terrific. Without her evidence, the Crown was loath to push ahead and convict Myers.'

Staffe recalls the conversations about budgets and cuts, glimpses a barren future. Long empty days.

'Tracing it all the way back to Cable Street,' says Strong. 'Your father would be so proud.'

Staffe tries to work out how to tell her that he, not Rimmer, made the connection to Cable Street; how to say it without coming across like an arrogant prick, but just as he is about to speak, Rimmer says, 'DI Wagstaffe's liaison with the Sicilian authorities was key, ma'am.'

Beverley Strong beams at Rimmer. 'It's a wonderful story and so timely.'

Staffe realises he has to fight his corner, says, 'And to think, you thought it was Attilio who abducted Carmelo.'

Beverley Strong looks disdainfully at Staffe, says, 'It doesn't completely distract from the events at Pentonville, but we shall see what we can do to mitigate.'

'Tell him,' says Pennington.

'Tell me what?' says Staffe.

'You will have read about the cuts,' says Beverley Strong. 'You know how tight things are and we have to justify every single position. The bar is rising higher and higher and now more than ever—'

'For pity's sake!' Pennington stands up and walks to his beloved window, looks out towards the Gherkin, with Docklands beyond, the estuary that the Thames cuts all the way to sea. Beverley Strong, Rimmer and Staffe all look at Pennington and he speaks softly, as if to himself, 'Every dog has his day.' He turns, looks at Staffe. 'I'm sorry, Will.'

'That's all right, sir. I know you have no choice.'

Pennington shakes his head. 'It's me.'

'What?' says Staffe.

Beverley Strong says, 'Congratulations are due. You have a new DCI.' Beverley Strong extends her arm, like a magician's assistant, but no frills, no curtsey. 'Detective Chief Inspector Rimmer. Like old times.'

Staffe looks at Pennington, who seems dead behind the eyes. He shakes Rimmer by the hand, with his good one, the wrong one, then he goes to Pennington, wraps his stitched and plastered arms around him as best he can.

Pennington whispers in his ear, 'You'd think after all these years, I'd know what a friend looks like, wouldn't you?' He grips Staffe hard and says, 'Promise me, you'll start making life easier for yourself, hey, Will?'

'And easier for him?' They both look at Rimmer, who doesn't know what the hell they are saying. 'No way.'

The two friends unclasp, and Staffe leaves the room without a backward glance, but thinking how he never thought of Pennington as a friend before. He left it too late.

Outside, Josie leans against the wall, next to the ruddy-cheeked minion, and Staffe remembers Pulford's first days. He says, 'If you're done with your cradle-snatching, Chancellor, maybe you'd help an old man across the road. I could murder a pint.'

She says to the young copper, 'Cradle? Now, there's something for you to aspire to,' and she hooks her arm through Staffe's, says, 'I guess you'll tell me what happened in there in your own time.'

'Maybe it's a bad dream. Let's see if a drink might break it.'

They walk down the back stairs and she says, 'They haven't got rid of you, have they, sir?'

'Worse than that.'

As they get to the bottom of the stairs, she pauses, says, 'This drink? Can it be us? You know, just "us". Not the job.'

'I'd like that.' He steps towards her, places one hand on her shoulder, the other on the side of her face. He leans towards her and each closes their eyes, losing themselves in a long, passionate kiss.

They unclasp and smile at each other, glassy eyed. He opens the door into reception, lets Josie go through and he breathes in the scent of her. As she unhooks her arm from his, their fingers touch and trail and he dreams how this might pan out. Watching her go ahead, he enjoys the shape she makes, the waft of her hair, the smile that just seeing her brings to Jombaugh's face. Then she turns, her eyes wide and something broken in the outline of her smile. Beside her, Sylvie.

*

'I had to see you, Will,' says Sylvie, flopping onto the sofa in his Queens Terrace living room. It seems strangely normal. 'If I don't see you, it's not going to happen, is it?'

He knows every blade of her, and she him. Yet here he is, in the drawing room they shared together so often, tiptoeing around the matter in hand.

The sun is low, just clipping the roofs in Launceston Square. It washes in through the twelve-pane windows and makes her golden. Her hair is in a long bob and her skin is still perfect. Soon, she will be thirty-four. He is unsure he is quite ready for this.

He tidies up a pile of broadsheets. The flat is untidy, smells musty. He has barely been here other than to sleep since before he went to Spain.

'Come here, Will.' Sylvie pats the sofa beside her. 'You *are* OK with this?' she says, hooking her feet under her bottom as he sits. Her arm presses against the pot of his broken arm. 'Put the papers down.'

He does a rough sum on how many times they have been here,

and beyond. It was usually his place, not hers. A few hotels and cottages, but seldom hers. Either way, it's a lot – laid out end to end. 'You want a drink?' he asks.

'No!'

'Aah, sorry. Stupid of me. Shall I put some music on?'

'You could do with a massage. We could start there.'

He is strangely alarmed by her use of the word 'start', and now it occurs to him that this might not work straight off.

'I've had tests, Will. My eggs are good.'

'No pressure then,' he laughs, tensing up.

She leans across, says, 'You're made of good stuff. He's a lucky chap.'

'He?'

'Or she. Does it matter?' Sylvie kneels up and twists him round, so he is facing away, looking out of the window. They face the same direction, looking up towards the square with its black, filigree balconies. Her fingers work on his buttons and she peels his shirt away, gets to work on his bare shoulders, getting her thumbs into the taut sinew of him. 'You're tight as a drum.'

He feels her breath on his back. She smells the way she ever smelled: of soap and citrus. She never did sweat, always tasted fresh; fine.

Sylvie places the palm of her left hand under his chin and works the knuckles of her right slowly up and down, along his spine, explaining that all humans zip from the skull to the bottom. A good spine is essential. He has a good spine, she says, making him tingle and he begins to loosen as her hands make wider and wider circles, and the gusts of her breath become more protracted, heavier. He feels himself unzipping, wishes he knew the rules.

Sylvie slides her hands up over his chest and she says, 'Hmmm,' turning him, her eyes closed and her mouth just a little open. 'You got me, Will. You always got me.'

He kisses her and she hitches her skirt, takes his good hand and puts it on her. There is no underwear and she takes him in hand, guiding him.

'I . . .' he says.

'Yes?' Her eyes open and she looks afraid. Her eyes are big and he is transported all the way back to the first time he saw her this way – him opening his eyes in their first kiss. When he misses her most, this is what he sees.

'I . . .'

'What is it, Will?' Her fingers press into his flesh, and he is on the very brink of her.

'I don't love you.'

She closes her eyes, opens them again slowly. 'Me too.' She smiles.

'So, that's all right?'

Also by Adam Creed

Suffer the Children

No one is Innocent

Introducing D. I. Staffe . . .

D. I. Will Wagstaffe – 'Staffe' to friends and enemies alike – is a burdened man. When a known paedophile is butchered in his own home, Staffe finds himself at the centre of a horrific case which threatens to spread violence throughout London.

Would you protect your loved ones at any cost?

The deeper Staffe digs into London's dirtiest seams, the more his past comes back to haunt him. And to mete out justice, Staffe must hurt the ones he loves. Can he track down the killers before the line between right and wrong becomes fatally blurred?

'It keeps you transfixed right up to the nail-biting climax.'
Simon Beckett, author of *The Chemistry of Death*

'Pungent, edgy, visceral.' Barry Forshaw, *Independent*

ff

Willing Flesh

The Streets Aren't Safe

A murdered woman is discovered in a City hotel room: Elena Danya, high-end prostitute. Another working girl, her best friend, is found dead. Then aristocratic bad-girl Arabella, another friend of Elena's, goes missing.

The Dark Side of the City

The evidence points to a voyeuristic predator, but D. I. Will Wagstaffe is not convinced. Instead, his investigation leads towards three ruthless and dangerous men: a City banker, a Russian oligarch and a Turkish playboy. But are even more powerful figures lurking in the shadows?

You Can't Kill the Truth

As Staffe's inquiry takes him deeper into deadly territory, suddenly the women in his own life are under threat . . .

'Creed writes with a gritty realism that doesn't let go.'
Simon Beckett

Pain of Death

Who will protect the innocents?

Beneath London's Streets

D. I. Staffe is called out to the tunnels beneath the City of
London after the discovery of a woman, barely alive. How
long has she been there and who left her to die?

An Abandoned Baby

A baby is found in a car park near the police station. Staffe
links the child to the woman from the tunnel and his
investigation leads him to a well-connected gangster and an
organisation determined to give the unborn a voice.

A Missing Woman

When a pregnant woman goes missing in Liverpool, Staffe
suspects it's only a matter of time before another tragedy
strikes. Can he save the mother and the unborn child before
it's too late?

'Creed is a distinctive presence in crime fiction, his unusual subject
matter rendered in lyrical prose and studded with incisive
character portraits . . .' Cathi Unsworth, *Guardian*

ﬀ

Death in the Sun

The Past can never be buried

After his last investigation nearly killed him, D. I. Staffe is
recuperating high in the mountains of Spain.

He is a man with a complicated past and Andalucia seems
to offer him the chance of a fresh start. But he soon
becomes embroiled in a savage murder case – a death
invoking a shocking method of torture last used
during Spain's brutal civil war.

Everyone Staffe encounters seems keen to bury the past,
and his new life is threatened as he refuses to abandon
the investigation. The closer the enemy gets, the closer
Staffe will come to finally finding the man who
murdered his parents.

'Creed has the smarts to make a mark in an overcrowded field.'
Independent

Follow Adam Creed on Twitter @DamCreed
www.adamcreed.co.uk